Enterprising Widows

*Three women taking the business world—
and the men who run it—by storm!*

The Champagne Magnate

When Emma finds herself at the head of the family's struggling wine business, she must partner with neighboring vineyard owner Julien Archambeau, the brooding, reclusive Comte de Rocroi.

The Retailer

To honor her late husband's legacy, Antonia is on a mission to turn the ramshackle London property she inherited into the ultimate shopping experience! But she must rely on the guidance of her handsome rival, Lord Cullen Allardyce!

The Publisher

Saddled with an ailing publishing house, Fleur needs an investor to revitalize the business. But sparks soon fly when that investor comes in the form of Jasper Bexley...

Find out what happens to the
Enterprising Widows in

Liaison with the Champagne Count

Available now

And look out for Antonia's and
Fleur's stories, coming soon!

Author Note

The Enterprising Widows series was inspired by the changes occurring in the mid-nineteenth century that allowed women more latitude in how they could live their lives. Emma's story follows the trajectory of many other real-life female champagne entrepreneurs. Up until the twentieth century, champagne was definitely a female-dominated industry, with powerful businesswomen like Barbe-Nicole Clicquot and Louise Pommery leading the way. Like my heroine, Emma, neither of these women inherited a ready-made business. They built their champagne dynasties from the ground up. For an interesting read on women in champagne, check out one of my favorite resources for this story: *The Widow Clicquot* by Tilar J. Mazzeo.

Emma's story is also inspired by the hope of second chances and the tenacity of starting over in the face of great loss and change. Emma and Julien are two sides of the dilemma we face after loss: giving up or going on. Julien has retreated from the world, deciding to give up, while Emma has chosen to go on. Together, they help one another make a beautiful future from the ashes of their pasts.

BRONWYN SCOTT

Liaison with the
Champagne Count

Recycling programs for this product may not exist in your area.

ISBN-13: 978-1-335-59589-8

Liaison with the Champagne Count

Harlequin Enterprises ULC
22 Adelaide St. West, 41st Floor
Toronto, Ontario M5H 4E3, Canada
www.Harlequin.com

Printed in U.S.A.

Bronwyn Scott is a communications instructor at Pierce College and the proud mother of three wonderful children—one boy and two girls. When she's not teaching or writing, she enjoys playing the piano, traveling—especially to Florence, Italy—and studying history and foreign languages. Readers can stay in touch via Facebook at Facebook.com/bronwynwrites, or on her blog, bronwynswriting.blogspot.com. She loves to hear from readers.

For Huckleberry, the sweetest doggy ever who never forgot his kindness even when his own early years were not kind to him. I hope the last six years with our family made up for that rough beginning. You helped me start this book. I will finish it without you. The space under my desk will always be yours.

Prologue

February 5th, 1852

Emma Greyville-Luce was acutely aware she'd survived the night due—quite literally—to the turn of a card. Thanks to whist and a whim, she was sitting in the comfort of Mrs Parnaby's parlour, clutching a warm teacup, a blanket draped about her shoulders, ushering in the chilly February morning *alive*, something several others, including her husband, could not lay claim to. Garrett was dead. Keir was dead. Adam was dead. All three lost to the flood. She should be dead, too.

Her mind whirred nonstop with those two realisations coupled with the horror of the last seven hours and the narrowness of her escape. By the slimmest of margins, she'd evaded the raging torrent that had been the River Holme sweeping down Water Street, angry and rapacious at one o'clock that morning.

One choice made differently and she, Antonia, and Fleur would have been swept away with their husbands, but Emma never could say no to a hand of whist. Thank goodness she hadn't started declining tonight. It would have been easy enough to turn down Mrs Parnaby's invitation to play after supper and take her leave with Garrett. She very nearly had. After all, in seven years of marriage, she'd spent very few nights without him and he'd been ready for bed, citing the need for an early evening because of a morning meeting with the clothiers to discuss a joint venture. That venture was what had brought Garrett and his two friends to Holmfirth. But tonight, Emma had not done as she ought. She'd stayed behind at Mrs Parnaby's and begged Antonia and Fleur to stay with her to make up the foursome needed for whist.

Lady Luck had smiled broadly on her. Emma had just claimed the last trick needed for the rubber when the warning had gone up the street: *'The embankment's breached! The river's in Water Street!'*

Fear had seared through her at the words. Water Street: where they'd rented cottages for the duration of their stay. Water Street: where Garrett, Adam, and Keir had returned to seek their beds hours ago.

The women had raced to Mrs Parnaby's lace-curtained windows and peered futilely into the night. Even at the advantage of their slight elevation, they could see nothing in the dark. But what they couldn't see, they could *hear*. One might have mistaken the water for the howling of wind. It was the most malevolent sound Emma had ever heard; a churning, rushing, swirling, crunching foe she could not see filled the night, everywhere and nowhere all at once.

'We'll be safe here,' Mrs Parnaby had said. 'We're

back far enough from the river and away from the centre of town.' Their hostess had meant to be consoling but, in those panic-filled moments, Emma had not wanted to be safe. She'd wanted to be with Garrett. She'd run for the door, determined to throw herself into the night, to make her way back to Water Street, to Garrett, the river of terror ravaging Holmfirth be damned. It had taken both Antonia and Fleur to pull her from her folly.

'It is too late to warn them,' Fleur had reasoned with characteristically blunt logic, her own face ashen.

'They are strong men, they can take care of themselves,' Antonia had offered with her unequivocal optimism.

'We'll go help once the water has settled and there's less chance of us being another set of people in need of rescue ourselves.' Mrs Parnaby had been all bustling practicality, and Emma had needed to settle for that.

It was the longest night of Emma's life, filled with an uncustomary sense of helplessness for a woman used to being in charge. The morning brought no joy, only a renewal of the fear that had dogged Emma in the hours until dawn. The four women were able to pick their way through the wreckage to the Rose and Crown inn in hopes of lending a hand and hearing news. Emma gasped at the sight of a dead cow mired in the muck and turned her head away, but there was no escape from the devastation.

Morning light hid nothing, disguised nothing. Daylight only served to emphasise how futile any effort to go out sooner would have been. Waters had receded, leaving sucking mud and mangled machinery behind, murderous clues as to just how malevolent the angry waters had been and how strong. The waters that had broken the Bilberry Reservoir and overpowered the embankment had been forceful enough to demolish the mills that lined the river, feeding its fury by devouring machinery and vast quantities of soil.

At the Rose and Crown, the women put themselves to work, serving hot drinks and porridge to those who'd been brought in, wet, exhausted, and as hungry for news of family and loved ones as they were for porridge after a long night of fear, even as new fears began to add to their worries. Many were homeless, many had escaped with only the clothes on their backs. The places they'd worked—the mills—were destroyed. There were no jobs to go back to, no income to collect.

She was lucky, Emma repeated to herself as she served porridge. Other than the things she'd brought with her for the visit, her belongings were safe and dry far south of here in her home in Surrey, Oakwood Manor. Her home was safe. Her belongings were safe. She could leave here. She and Garrett could go home, could leave all of this heartache and devastation as soon as he walked through the door of the Rose and Crown.

Her gaze darted to the door yet again, her mind willing him to walk in as if she could conjure him out of thin air; the dark beard threaded with silver, the broad, bluff build of him draped in his greatcoat, the dark eyes that could melt an honest woman with desire and manage a dishonest man with a stare. She caught Antonia's gaze on her and they exchanged encouraging smiles, trying to lift one another up. Emma told herself no news was good news, especially when the news they were hearing wasn't.

There'd been tales of neighbours watching whole families swept away in the violent current. Near Hollowgate, Aner Bailey had watched his wife and two children carried away while he clung to a timber, he himself pushed downstream to the Turnpike Road. Joseph Hellawell on Scarfold had been rescued from a beam on the top story of his home but his entire family had been trapped below in the bedroom and drowned.

As the morning wore on, hope receded with the waters. Eyewitness accounts were coming in and a clearer understanding of what had happened last night was taking shape. The whole Holme valley had suffered enormous loss. Bodies were being recovered in places miles from Holmfirth in the towns of Mirfield, Armitage Fold, and Honley. Fleur was exceedingly anxious, Emma noted. The colour had not returned to her face and her hand strayed repeatedly to the flat of her belly when she thought no one was looking. Was Fleur expecting? Her husband, Adam, was Garrett's age, in his upper fifties. For him, it would be a late-in-life child. Emma sent up a prayer, *God, let the men be all right.* She'd uttered those words already times beyond count. For a woman who counted everything, that was worrisome.

George Dyson, the coroner, arrived shortly after ten, asking for a word in private. The man looked tired, and she could only imagine the horror he'd seen. These were his neighbours, lifelong friends that were being pulled from the depths of mill races and ponds. Emma gestured nervously for Antonia and Fleur to join her in the Rose and Crown's small private parlour.

She was aware of Antonia gripping her hand as George Dyson cleared his throat, the sound a universal portent of impending bad news. She braced herself, her inner voice whispering, *Be strong, Fleur and Antonia will need you.*

But no amount of bracing could protect her against the devastation of the coroner's words. 'Lady Luce, Mrs Popplewell, Mrs Griffiths, I wish I had better news. I will be blunt. Water Street didn't stand a chance. The river hit it from the front and the side, absolutely obliterating the buildings.' He paused and swallowed hard. 'James Metterick's family, and the Earnshaws, are all gone, their homes destroyed.' Homes that had been next to theirs, Emma thought. The Mettericks and the Earnshaws were the clothiers Garrett was supposed to meet with. Lead began to settle in her stomach and yet there was still a sliver of hope.

'But I heard James Metterick survived,' Emma protested against the news. She'd clung to that piece of news all morning since the moment it had been reported. Metterick was bruised and battered but he was alive. He'd been at his Water Street residence, and he'd survived. Surely, it was possible Garrett had as well…

George Dyson shook his head, his tone gentle. 'We believe the bodies of your husband and his friends have been recovered, Lady Luce. Your husband was found in the Victoria Mill along with others. I *am* sorry.' Emma felt her knees buckle. Mrs Parnaby was there with a chair, helping her to sit and murmuring consolation. But her world was a discordant blur. Somewhere amid her own disbelief and grief she heard Antonia wail, saw her friend sink to her knees. There was a burst of outrage from Fleur followed by plate shattering against the wall. Emma managed to rise, managed to get to Antonia on the floor, and then the three of them were in each other's arms, supporting and comforting one another amid their own grief. How was this possible? Garrett, Keir and Adam, all three of them gone? It was impossible, a bad dream from which she'd awake any moment. Only she didn't.

The bad dream continued. The next hours were surreal. There'd been a need to have them officially identify the bodies and perhaps she'd needed to do it, to have the closure of seeing Garrett one last time, horrible as it was. The bloated, drowned body wasn't her vibrant husband; that man had long since departed the corpse she identified.

George Dyson stood beside her outside the makeshift morgue. 'If it is any consolation, Lady Luce, I don't believe there was much suffering. It would have been fast. The looks frozen on people's faces have been those of confusion and disbelief. They died before they understood what hit them.'

He was trying to be kind, but she was in no mood for it. Some of her usual fire, her usual determination seeped through the numbness that had sustained her since the news. 'Did my husband *look* confused?' Emma snapped. He'd looked fierce, as if he'd battled

the river with everything in him. 'My husband is—'
Is. She couldn't use that word any more.

She swallowed back the thickness that settled in her
throat, threatening to destroy whatever aplomb she had
left. 'My husband was a fighter, the most determined
man I've ever known.' Garrett had fought for every
success he'd had, climbed his way up an impossible
social ladder to earn a baronetcy, and he'd fought for
her: Emma Greyville, the gin heiress of England, when
his family of grown children from his first marriage
had argued vehemently that a newly minted baronet
with a fortune could do better than the daughter of a
gin magnate. He should aim higher; they'd said to her
face when Garrett had announced their engagement.
He'd stared down his sons and their wives with a laugh.
'Higher than love? Whatever would that be?'

She'd remember those words always. They were carefully tucked away beside her other memories; how he'd
looked upon her with that love on their wedding day,
how he'd taken her to France for their honeymoon and
shown her the vineyard in Champagne he'd bought her
as a wedding gift. The best weeks of her life had been
spent at that vineyard. It was their place, their retreat
from the world. What she wouldn't give to be there again
with Garrett beside her, walking the rows of grapes,
sampling vintages.

Tears threatened. She turned from George Dyson
and found Fleur and Antonia waiting for her, their own
ordeals etched on their faces. They embraced each other
once again, holding each other up. 'What do we do

now?' Antonia whispered, her face tear-streaked, her earlier optimism gone, replaced with pale despair.

'We go back to Mrs Parnaby's. She has clothes and rooms for us.' Emma could manage to think that far but no farther. Her mind kept running up against one inescapable fact: Garrett was dead. The life they'd built together was gone. The truth was, she didn't *know* what came next and for the moment, she could not rouse herself to care.

Four days later, she was still numb to the realisation. 'We're widows now. Widows before the age of thirty,' Fleur ground out as she paced before Mrs Parnaby's fireplace, anger fuelling her steps and her words as Emma did the math: they'd been widows for ninety-six hours, or five thousand, seven hundred and sixty minutes. Numbers gave her comfort the way anger kept Fleur upright. Fleur had gone out each day to assist in the recovery effort, working until dark, coming home exhausted. Emma had asked her not to go out today, citing that they needed to make plans for departure. The roads were passable now, the rains and the river subsided enough to make travel decent. Her plea had been a bit of subterfuge. They *did* need to talk, but more than that, Emma was worried about Fleur. She was driving herself too hard, not taking time for her grief, but burying it.

'I still can't believe it,' Antonia said softly from her chair by the window. 'I always knew Keir would go before me. With the difference in ages, it was bound to happen. But I thought it would be old age, not like this, not so sudden with no chance to say goodbye.'

Emma nodded, unable to form the words to respond. The three men had been lifelong friends, long before they'd met their wives, navigating London together as newcomers in their twenties and later as established, savvy businessmen: Garrett the canny investor, Adam the intrepid newspaperman, and Keir the emporium magnate. Adam and Keir had already been married when she and Garret wed. She had liked Garrett's friends immediately and she'd liked their wives, women her age, even better. What a group they'd all made—three men in their fifties with their young brides. Now that life was gone. Quite literally washed away. Emma had replayed her final moments with Garrett ceaselessly in her mind—the kiss on his cheek, the whispered 'I love you' as he'd said good-night.

'This is *exactly* what Adam feared would happen,' Fleur exclaimed abruptly from the fireplace. 'It's why Garrett brought him along, to ferret out the truth about the reservoir's engineering.' Emma nodded. Garrett had told her there'd been rumours the reservoir was damaged. Disaster wasn't an issue of if, but when. But nothing was certain and of course the engineers and those responsible weren't likely to confess to construction shortcuts without some manoeuvring. Garrett had not been keen about a joint venture on the mill without knowing for sure what the environmental circumstances were like. His instincts had been unfortunately right.

Emma split her gaze between Antonia and Fleur. 'I think it's time to go. There's nothing more we can do

here.' Amid the numbness there was growing awareness of all that demanded her attention in the wake of
Garrett's passing. There would be paperwork to settle,
numbers that would need tallying. Already, her mind
was hungering for the peace of the familiar columns.
There was Garrett's business affairs to oversee, and
there would be his family to deal with. She'd managed
to send a note to his sons regarding their father's de-
mise but there was a will to be read, and there would
be…upheaval. Dealing with his family would be dis-
tasteful but it had to be done. The sooner the better.
She had no illusions his sons would be kind to her or
offer her any more than whatever Garrett had set aside
for her. Just the chateau. That was all she wanted, in
truth. If they would just let her have that, she would be
content. She began to calculate the odds.

Antonia exhaled a long, shaky breath. 'I need to go
home as well and see how things stand. Keir was in
the midst of restoring an old building in London. He
had plans to turn it into a department store, like the
ones in France.' Antonia drew another shaky breath.
'I think I will finish it for him. I think it's what I must
do, although I'm not sure how. I'll figure it out as I go.'
She looked to Fleur. 'Shall we all travel together as far
as London? It's a long train ride from West Yorkshire
when one is on their own.'

Fleur didn't meet their eyes for a moment and Emma
felt her stomach drop. She knew before Fleur spoke
she'd refuse. 'No. I think I'll stay and finish the in-
vestigation Adam began. There are people to help and

justice to serve. People deserve to know if this tragedy was a natural disaster or a manmade one.'

Emma chose her words carefully. 'Do you think that's wise, Fleur? If it is manmade, there will be people who won't appreciate prying, particularly if it's a woman doing it. You should think twice before putting yourself in danger.' Especially if her friend might need to be thinking for two.

'I don't care,' Fleur snapped. 'If Adam died because of carelessness, someone *will* pay for that. I will see to it, and I will see to it that such recklessness isn't allowed to happen again.'

'And Adam's child?' Emma decided to brazen it out. 'Would you be reckless with his child?' She was admittedly a bit jealous that Fleur might have one last piece of Adam while she had nothing of Garrett's. After the will was read and his family had their say, she might have even less. Garrett had been her buffer.

Fleur shook her head, her voice softer when she spoke, the earlier anger absent. 'I do not know if there is a child. It is too soon.' But not too soon to hope, Emma thought privately. Fleur must suspect there was a chance.

'Just be careful, dear friend. I do not want anything to happen to you.' Emma rose and went to her. Antonia joined her and they encircled each other with their arms, their heads bent together.

'We're widows now.' Emma echoed Fleur's words softly.

Ninety-six hours and counting.

There would be enormous change for each of them over the next few months, the loss of their husbands was just the beginning. Widows lost more than husbands. Society did not make life pleasant for those without husbands even in this new, brave world where women were demanding their due. But amid the chaos of change she could depend on two things: the friendship of the women who stood with her now, and the realisation that from here on out nothing in her life would ever be the same again.

Chapter One

February 19th, 1852

Everything depended on the will. Emma literally sat on the edge of her chair in the drawing room of Oakwood, aware that this was her space no longer. She had minutes left as its mistress. She swallowed to dislodge the lump in her throat that formed at the thought. The comfortable room she'd carefully cultivated for herself and Garrett, where they'd spent relaxed evenings entertaining their friends, felt more like an enemy camp on this grey February afternoon than a familiar, comforting space. Her foes had already invaded. Garrett's sons, Robert and Steven, sat alert and watchful on the blue-and-cream-striped upholstery of the matched chairs by the fire, their wives perched nearby on the settee, their avaricious eyes pricing the room and its contents, waiting to strip it bare. The two women reminded her of cats stalking a mouse, bodies wound tight waiting to spring.

There would be little she could do to stop them. She'd

resigned herself to the carnage. The law required she stand by and watch them plunder her life. Robert was the oldest. He'd get the baronetcy and Oakwood. His wife, Estelle—the granddaughter of a viscount—had already made a comment about selling off the items and redecorating. Estelle had not even pretended to be discreet about it, the implication obvious that a gin heiress's tastes were not up to par for a baronet.

The butler appeared at the doorway to the drawing room and cleared his throat. 'Sir Robert.' Robert looked up immediately. He'd taken well to the honorific that now marked his title, a title he'd done nothing to earn except to be born to a man who'd earned it for him. Now Robert would benefit from those efforts. Garrett had never thought of the title as his, but as the family's, something he'd been able to add to the legacy he'd pass on. That was the difference between Garrett and his entitled sons. 'Mr Lake is here. Shall I show him in?'

Robert gave a curt, almost pompous nod. Emma curled her fingers into the depths of the handkerchief she clutched in her lap. So it began. The next few minutes would determine what the shape of her future would look like. Would she live that life of a daughter dependent on her family, once more supported by her father's gin fortune? As a woman of modest means required to live alone and quietly in order to maintain her independence? Or would she have the financial latitude to remake her life somewhere else? Her worry, which had kept her awake several nights in a row since her return from Holmfirth, surged anew, twisting her stomach, making her glad she'd not eaten lunch. Surely, Garrett would not leave her stranded. He'd loved her. One did not abandon those they loved, not even in death. Emma clung doggedly to that hope as assuredly as Aner Bailey had clung to his timber amid the raging waters of the River Holme.

Yet doubt flooded her. Garrett had never spoken to her of arrangements in case of his passing. He'd only been in his fifties and in robust good health. Perhaps he'd felt there was no need and she'd foolishly allowed it. Like Antonia, she'd known theoretically what the reality was in marrying a much older man. But that had been a decade or two away when they'd married. Twenty years had seemed like a lifetime to a twenty-one-year-old bride in the throes of new love. If she had never bargained on losing Garrett to anything other than very old age, perhaps he hadn't either. Perhaps he'd thought he had time—time to say goodbye, time to plan for her.

Stop it, she scolded herself. *You are strong. There is nothing Robert can say or do that can truly hurt you. He is a spoiled boy, pampered by his mother who has grown into a selfish adult.*

Her eyes met Robert's gaze evenly, firmly, as she squared her shoulders while introductions were made and condolences murmured. She'd prefer that Garrett had seen to her protection but she could protect herself. A gin heiress was no sheltered debutante. She'd grown up learning her father's business and staring down women who thought she was less than they for being able to add ledgers and manage accounts, for navigating a man's world.

You faced down a ballroom of catty debutantes when Amelia St James told anyone who would listen the Earl of Redmond was only dancing with you for a peek at your father's fortune.

Whatever happened here, she would be fine on a functional level. Her heart was a different matter, but today was not for emotions, it was for practicalities. She had to survive this before she could start to put herself back together.

Mr Lake took a seat at the centre of the room with Robert on his left and she on his right. He was a spare man with a mop of messy grey hair that had probably started the morning combed back in preparation for the occasion but was already tousled. He wore the decent black suit of the country solicitor, and his eyes were tired as he put on his eyeglasses. Tired but kind perhaps? Sympathetic? Emma tried to read him as he glanced in her direction. She was usually a good judge of character. Her father had relied on that sense over several business dinners with new clients. The question was, what did Mr Lake already know? Had there been no provision for her? Was that why he looked at her with sympathy? The knot in her stomach tied itself tighter. Or perhaps it was empathy because she had to deal with the pompous asses that were Robert and Steven Luce?

Mr Lake efficiently got business under way, perhaps reading the room aright. This was the last task to complete the process of dying and Garrett's sons were eager to get on with living. Their father had been buried yesterday in a ceremony far larger than what Garrett would have preferred but what his sons had demanded. Where Garrett had been a behind the scenes man, his sons were showmen with a flair for the dramatic, something else they'd inherited from their mother, and right now those sons were keen on the world knowing how bereft they were over the loss of their father.

The will was unmistakably Garrett's, skirting the temptations of a flowery introduction and reflections of the lived life. Of course, he hadn't known he was going to die. Still, she didn't think it would have changed. She'd recognise that writing style anywhere; direct, straightforward like the man himself. Even his marriage proposal had been direct, honest if not romantic.

'I've never met anyone like you, Emma. I know it's only been a few weeks, but I want to marry you. I cannot imagine a life without you.'

Like the man himself, his will went straight to the details, bequests and the division of assets. There were no surprises but hearing the words made it no less sad. Robert would have Oakwood and most of its contents, which were both entailed with the baronetcy. The stripping had begun. It wasn't the things she minded losing. It was the memories they represented. That's what she was being deprived of: the right to live among those remembrances. Mr Lake looked up from his reading, eyeing Robert over the top of the documents. 'Lady Luce is to be allowed to claim whatever items she desires from the house.'

'*Dowager* Lady Luce,' Robert corrected, staring at Mr Lake, refusing to look at her. '*My* wife is Lady Luce.' Robert was plundering mercilessly today. She should have expected such callousness. Robert had been jealous when his father had remarried, fearful of sharing his father's love and perhaps more fearful of sharing his father's money and status. After all, his father had given her, a woman of no real standing, a title he himself could not have until his father died. She supposed it stood to reason Robert would take even her name from her—her married name—the name that said she was Garrett's partner.

Mr Lake was not intimidated. He gave Robert a stern look. 'Those are your father's words, Sir Robert.'

'Of course.' Robert's glance flicked in her direction with more disdain than consideration in his dark eyes. 'I am sure we'll come to an agreement. After all, several of Oakwood's unentailed contents are *my* mother's.' Emma met his eyes with the full steel of her own. She was not fooled. His polite words were the barely veiled throwing of a gauntlet. He, who'd not been interested in Oakwood's contents for years, would now use the shield of his mother's memory to argue every unentailed knick-knack, every piece of china, every chair and every picture. He wanted her to beg. But Emma Greyville-Luce begged no one, especially not a man who wanted her on her knees. She'd learned that lesson early at her father's knee. There was money, and then there was gin money, and no number of attempts to do clean gin business could wash away the stain. Society had wanted James Greyville to beg for their acceptance, but her father had refused. A Greyville had nothing to be ashamed of. Now it was Society begging him. She would not beg Robert for a single thing. Instead, she would flank him with Mr Lake in the room as witness.

She gave Robert a hard look, her terms ready. 'I want only the Baccarat glassware, and the chandelier we purchased on our honeymoon in France.' The collection was extensive but it would not beggar the estate of drinking glasses.

'I think that is reasonable,' Mr Lake put in swiftly, using Robert's own argument against him before he could interject. 'Surely, Sir Robert, you have no attachment to that? I can make a note of it today so it's on record.'

Estelle tossed her blond head. 'Let her have it, Robert. It's not even Bohemian crystal. We'll want something with a little more...*lineage* to it.' Emma let the snub go. Baccarat was not old but Garrett, always future-focused, had seen great potential in the French glassblower.

Mr Lake turned to her. 'Is there anything else, Lady Luce?'

'No, nothing other than my personal affects, jewellery and clothes.' She'd resigned herself to leaving much behind in exchange for her pride. She would not haggle with Robert like a fishwife, even if there was artwork and china she could rightly claim beyond the Baccarat. She did not expect Robert and Steven to be grateful though. And they weren't.

'We have an inventory of the family jewels,' Robert began as if they were a ducal family with a vault instead of a family in possession of a baronetcy for a mere ten years.

'I *know* what's on the list.' She cut him off sharply. 'Rest assured, I have no intentions of cheating you out of a single pearl.' It felt good to fight, to feel something, anything, even if it was anger, in her veins again. No wonder Fleur had relied on anger to get her through the early days of their loss. The last of the numbness that had enveloped her since the flood was losing its hold. Estelle gasped at her rudeness as if her own husband hadn't been insulting his father's widow since he'd arrived two days prior and taken up residence with an astonishing sense of entitled permanency.

'Well, so do I,' Robert retorted.

Mr Lake cleared his throat. 'Shall we move on? There are stocks and other assets to go through.' He dangled the carrot of funds and both Steven and Robert bit. The business investments were split between the brothers with the option to share ownership. She'd not expected it to be otherwise, although she'd be lying to herself that she didn't feel a sense of loss at watching her hard work being handed off. She'd helped build those companies as much as the Luce men had, spending her days with the ledgers. She'd been the one to tell Garrett he was being overcharged for his oak wine barrels at the chateau. She was the one who'd set up the dinner that resulted in Garrett winning the shipping contract for a large tea importer. She'd been an active and successful part of Garrett's business life as much as she'd been part of his private life. Still, one could hardly expect a woman to run a shipping empire even in this modern age. A woman at the helm of such a business would likely sink it and such an outcome did not honour Garrett's hard work. Hope whispered: there was one industry a woman might participate in—wine, champagne. If his sons had the British businesses, surely they were satisfied? Surely, Garrett would have saved her something, would have known what she wanted, where she could be success-ful on her own…?

'Lastly, there is the issue of the chateau in France.' Mr Lake's words had her sitting up stiff and ramrod straight, her body wound with tension. A glance passed between Robert and Steven that made her nervous. Everyone was bracing themselves. For her, this was the moment that decided everything. *Please, please, please…* The word became a litany in her mind.

Mr Lake's gaze was on the papers, inscrutable as he read. '"The chateau near Cumières in France is not part of the entailment and as such it and its lands are left to the care of my beloved wife, Emma Greyville-Luce, in the hopes that it will be a place of remembrance and renewal for her as long as she desires."' The knot in her stomach eased and her eyes smarted with tears. So many words. At last, a little poetry, a little flowery language Garrett-style. This was her husband's idea of a love letter and her heart squeezed. He'd not forgot-ten her. He'd known how much the chateau had meant to her. He'd not just lavished her generically with his wealth, but he'd given her something that held mean-ing for her, something she could build with her own efforts. He believed in her.

Mr Lake looked up and Emma did not imagine the satisfaction on his face. '"All accounts and papers associated with the chateau should be placed directly into her possession.'''

'No.' Robert's voice cut through the peace that had settled on her.

'Excuse me, Sir Robert?' It was Mr Lake who spoke, his brows arched in perplexity. 'No, what?'

Robert's face was thunderous. 'No, *she* does not get the chateau in France. I will contest this.'

Whatever numbness remained dissolved at this new threat. Fire began to burn slow and sure in her veins. 'Why do you care, Sir Robert?' she said with deliberate challenge in her voice, not waiting for Mr Lake. 'You've never even been there. You know nothing of the wine business.' And she did, or at least she knew the libations business through her father. Selling wine was not much different than selling gin, although producing it was. Like Antonia, she would figure it out as she went.

Mr Lake quietly came to her defence. 'There is nothing to contest, Sir Robert. The chateau is hers.'

'Fine, it's not as if it's a huge money-maker. It barely breaks even. It's an expensive hobby just so my father can import his own wines to his dinner table. I've been telling him to sell it for ages.' Faced with a twin front, Robert settled into his chair, fuming. His gaze landed on her, and Emma braced. Robert had been bested. He needed to save face. Whatever came out of his mouth next would be cruel, designed to hurt. 'Pack up your things, then. If you want that chateau so badly, be gone in the morning. I don't want your fortune-hunting shadow darkening the halls of Oakwood longer than necessary. This is not your home any longer.'

Mr Lake slid Robert a disapproving look and took out a packet of documents. 'These are yours, Lady Luce. You'll find the deed and other papers for the chateau. I will send for my wife to help with your packing. It would be my pleasure to make travel arrangements for you and a pleasure to give you a farewell supper at my home tonight once you've completed packing. You can leave from our place in the morning. There's a coach that departs from the inn for Dover in the morning if that's sufficient. My wife and I can send the Baccarat on later if need be.'

'Mrs Lake's company would be welcome, as would your kind offer.' Emma smiled her gratitude. This was an unexpected kindness. She would not be left here alone to endure Robert's and Steven's glares and the indignities of having every item she packed questioned.

Upstairs in her room, Emma shut the door behind her and allowed herself a deep breath—a breath to steady herself against the emotions of the afternoon, and another breath of relief. It was settled. The chateau was hers. Life was starting again—*her* life was starting again. After fourteen days, five hours, and thirty-six minutes, there was something to look forward to. Although, this was not quite the leave-taking Emma had imagined when she'd pictured departing Oakwood.

In her mind, she'd thought of it as a slow, gradual process, a chance to walk the house, to take out her memories one last time and savour her life here as if it were a fine wine. Instead, Robert's hatred of her had tried to turn 'seeing her off' into 'running her off.'

Perhaps it was better this way. After two weeks of

time standing still, of being trapped in a nightmare comprised of tragedy and the unknown, everything was happening at lightning speed. Within days, barring difficulty with travel and tides, she'd be in Paris. Within the week, she'd be in Cumières. She closed her eyes and leaned back against the door, doing the travel timetables. She whispered to the room she'd once shared with Garrett, 'Thank you, my love.'

Chapter Two

Julien Archambeau had been born to love the land. *La femme la plus difficile qu'un homme puisse aimer.* The most difficult woman a man could love—his *grandpère* would say. And yet Julien knew he'd choose no other, especially on a sharp, clear March morning with rare blue sky above him and the promise of spring lurking in the veins of his beloved vines.

On a morning like this, there was no better place to be but in the vineyards. He squatted between the rows of grape vines and pulled off his thick workman's gloves. He scooped the soil into the palm of his hand, weighing it, then sifting the silt through his fingers, his fingertips recognising the feel of Cumières earth, the sand, the marl, the clay and lignite, the undertones of chalk and limestone, all of it combining to create a soil, Julien was convinced, which existed in only one place on earth, a soil he'd been raised on. Julien didn't think he'd ever had much choice about it. The *terroire* of Cumières, of the Vallee de Marne, of the Montagne de Reims ran through his blood, the product and practice of generations that went back to the days of the Sun King. He stood up and brushed his hands against his work trousers.

Seven generations of Archambeaux had cared for the land, nurtured its crops, loved for it, lived for it, and died for it. When revolution had come, his great-*grandpère* had declared he'd rather lose his head than his land. In the end, he'd lost both, leaving Julien's grandfather and father the task of retrieving the family lands, a task that had only been partially successful. The remainder of that task had fallen to Julien and his Oncle Etienne.

Julien ran a bare hand over the vines bound horizontally across the trellises, looking for signs of 'bleeding'—the leakage of sap that signalled the vines waking up and that budbreak was imminent, that spring was officially here, and the growing season was under way.

There was nothing yet but March had only begun. It was too soon. The grape, like a woman, had its own mysterious time. Grapes and women could be wooed but not rushed. An indefinable instinct told him it would take a few more weeks of sun to see it done. He'd walk the rows again in the early evening before supper, after the vines had spent an afternoon beneath the sun and see if that was still the case. *That* was another Archambeau family ritual. A man must walk his land to know it; every lush curve and plain, every idiosyncrasy— where did water pool? Where was there excessive shade or sun? Any variation would affect the grapes.

He'd been walking the land since he was a boy and the family had been allowed to return to France. At first, he'd walked with Grandpère and Papa, then with just Papa, and now he walked alone. Oncle Etienne seldom walked the land. Grandpère would not approve of Oncle Etienne forsaking the old ways, nor would he approve of Julien's aloneness. Grandpère would say a man his age should have a son to walk the land with him and a wife to walk with him through life. It wasn't that Julien hadn't tried. Clarisse had been all a young man dreamed of and for a brief time the dream had been his. But dreams didn't last.

Julien reached the end of the final row and looked back over the field. *Famille et terre.* Family and land were the only things that mattered if one was an Archambeau. Grandpère would be disappointed to see how little of either the Archambeaux possessed at present. From a great house that had lasted centuries, there were only he and Oncle Etienne now and since Julien's father's death, they'd not won back any more of the old Archambeau lands. Grandpère would turn in his grave to know his grandson was walking another man's land, worrying over another man's grapes when the land had once been Archambeau land. It was not enough for Grandpère to have reclaimed half of what had been lost to the Revolution.

His *grandpère* was not a man for half-measures. Grandpère had counted on Julien's marriage to Clarisse Anouilh, the daughter of the owner, to gain the remainder of the lands, the Archambeau vineyards complete once more. When the betrothal had failed, Grandpère had tried to buy the lands outright but there'd not been enough money. Clarisse's father had sold to an Englishman who fancied the place for his young wife and was prepared to pay any price, besotted fool that he was. The Archambeaux could not compete with a man who had unlimited funds. A reminder, Monsieur Anouilh said, that while the Archambeau name was old, their aristocratic fortune was gone, their funds coming from the trades of shipping and wine these days and their once-esteemed title precarious. The Archambeaux were not what they once were. It had been an absolute snub. Grandpère had been furious.

Julien began the long trek up to the chateau where he'd spend the day checking the cellars and looking over ledgers. By rights and out of loyalty to his *grandpère*, he ought to dislike Sir Garrett Luce, the besotted English baronet. But Sir Garrett Luce had proved astute, interesting, and likeable. Sir Garrett Luce's only flaw was in being an absentee landlord. To his *grandpère*, such a flaw was tantamount to being the eighth deadly sin. A vineyard could not thrive without daily attention.

Grapes didn't grow on their own. Well, they did, but wild grapes did not make for consistent or even good vintages. Grapes had to be tamed and trained for that, curated like fine art, carefully coaxed like a woman to reveal themselves in all their glory. A grape might take three years to come to fruition well enough to harvest it. Grapes took and tried a man's patience. In this case, the patience was his, not Sir Garrett Luce's. Luce's business empire kept him in England most of the year.

As a result, Luce had entrusted the vineyard and the daily oversight of the business to him, his friend and neighbour, unaware of the history that lay between Julien and the land. Luce knew only that Julien and his Oncle Etienne held the property that abutted his. Etienne had felt it was unnecessary to disabuse Luce of the notion, citing the old adage that one could never have too many friends. This friendship might be the way back to possessing the land.

Oncle Etienne believed that Luce would soon tire of the vineyard, especially if it didn't produce a profit, and would want to sell. Who better to take the vineyard off his hands than his neighbour and friend? Until then, they had time to acquire the money needed to purchase the place. It was a delicate dance, his *oncle* said, of keeping Luce interested in the property long enough for them to raise the funds. They didn't want Luce tiring of it too soon before they could purchase it. The land had already slipped away from them once. This time, his *oncle* counselled, they just needed to play a long game. There would be no woman to mess the arrangement up. It would be a straight business transaction between men. And because his heart had been bleeding, and his soul battered over Clarisse, Julien had allowed his *oncle* to have his way.

That had been seven years ago. In the interim, Garrett Luce had named him as proxy, enabling him to live in the chateau in order to be on hand to oversee daily operations and conduct business in his name without much oversight. Oncle Etienne had crowed over the achievement. What an enormous step forward to regaining the land this could be, he'd said. Luce was all but in their pockets, as long as Luce didn't sell until they were financially ready to meet his price. Even then, if they had a good relationship with Luce, his price might be more forgiving. Meanwhile Julien appeased his conscience over the subterfuge with the fact that he genuinely liked Sir Garrett Luce. Luce was not the sort of man who was easily coerced. The odds were shifting in their favour but nothing was guaranteed. All they could do now was wait for him to tire of an overseas property, hope the timing was right and the price was affordable. Grapes took time. Reacquiring the Archambeau lands took time. Meanwhile, at least he got to keep vigil and walk the land. *Le tout en temps utile.* All things in good time.

She'd made good time from Paris. The roads had been dry, a great surprise given the time of year. The north-eastern landscape of France with its rivers and valleys had sped by outside the window of the rented post-chaise. Speed could be bought and she'd happily bought it. Emma wanted nothing more than to be at the chateau, to breathe the fresh country air, and to immerse herself in this new life. Maybe then, the ache within her would subside. That ache had been her constant companion in her month of loss. Who ever thought February could be so long? A month with only twenty-eight days? Usually, it was January that dragged and February flew. But this had been the longest February of her life. Now it was over. As of this morning, it was officially March. Time to begin again.

Yet as much as she wanted the ache to subside, she didn't want it to leave her entirely. To not feel that ache was somehow akin to forgetting Garrett. Mourning was remembering. Hurting was remembering. If she didn't do those things, how would she keep him close? And yet, she had to be stronger than her grief; she could not let that grief weigh her down, make her intransigent. She was not made for inertia. *'Une mille, madame,'* the coachman called down. She looked out the window. One mile until she was…home. Such as it was.

She'd not sent a letter of warning ahead to alert the various stewards Garrett kept on the property to see to its upkeep. There'd been no point. She'd travel as fast as the letter. But she was not expected. There'd be some upheaval upon her arrival and she was sorry for it. She didn't want to make extra work for anyone. Perhaps in this case, she could be excused for her abrupt appearance.

The post-chaise turned a final corner and the groomed parklands of Les Deux Coeurs came into view with their perfectly squared box hedges and the tall oaks that covered the drive to the house. She released a breath she'd been unaware she was holding, relief flooding her. The place looked very much as it had seven years ago when she'd come here as a new bride. Since then, the place had existed for her only on paper in the form of the quarterly reports, and in her mind in the form of memory. Garrett made occasional visits but she'd not returned, staying behind in England to oversee his other interests in his absence. They'd planned to come together this summer, though, to celebrate their seven-year anniversary. There was a vintage he'd put down that would be ready for the occasion. 'I'll celebrate for us, my love,' she whispered.

The chaise halted in the circle before the front door and the coachman helped her down. Emma lifted her veil and tipped her face to the house, to the fading blue sky above it. It had been sunny today. Now blue was bleeding to purple, day and night mixing their colours to produce a gentle violet sky. The dusky light bathed the limestone walls and the green-shuttered windows of the chateau in soft mauve. Lights filtered through the windows from the inside, giving the impression that someone was at home. The scene filled her with a sense of peace. She was glad of the haste if it meant arriving at this magical hour.

The butler, or rather the *maître d'hôtel*...she was in France now...came to the top of the front steps, not quite able to hide the surprise and consternation on his face. Richet was his name. 'Madame Luce.' It was part greeting, part question as he struggled to recognise a woman he hadn't seen in years. His gaze swept past her to the post-chaise, his eyes waiting for Garrett to emerge. Then came the registering of her blacks and veil.

Emma swept up the steps, feeling enormous empathy for the man. He was about to be dealt the double blow of an unexpected guest and the loss of the master of the house. She'd rehearsed the conversation in her head in the hopes that practice would help her get through the announcement without tears. But she wasn't sure she could. It still hurt to say the words out loud. Best to keep it abrupt and direct. 'Richet, Monsieur Luce has died.' She felt her throat tighten. 'I've come to stay. If you could send a few footmen to bring

up my trunks.' She managed a smile that was both com-
miserative and authoritative. She'd learned that it was
easier to cope with the loss if she stayed busy. Others
felt that way, too. When faced with loss, people wanted
to do something, as if that task could ease the pain. She
could see the relief in Richet's eyes at the instruction.

'I will have them brought up right away. Mrs Dormand will have your room readied. Perhaps you'd like
to wait in the drawing room while all is prepared.' He
was already leading the way, already remembering her
French was passable at best. He'd switched into English
that was far better than her French. It had been one of
the reasons Garrett had hired him when he'd bought
the chateau. Garrett had not wanted his bride to feel
the outsider because of a language barrier.

'Thank you, Richet,' Emma said softly. 'I am sorry
to be the bearer of bad news and to descend on you with
no notice. I had little choice in the matter.'

'Bien sur, madame. Ce n'est pas une probleme.' He
fell into his French, flustered for a moment by her kindness and explanation. She'd not meant to discompose
him. She never had got the knack of treating servants
with distance and disdain. She'd grown up with servants, but as a daughter of a businessman the distance
between servants and master was far smaller than in
a noble house.

In the drawing room, she took a seat on a daffodil-
yellow upholstered settee and let her gaze reacquaint
itself with the room. Richet cleared his throat. 'I will
send for tea for you, *madame*, and I will tell Monsieur

Archambeau that you're here. He's just come in from his evening tour of the vineyards.'

Monsieur Archambeau. They would meet at last and she could put a face to the name. Garrett's steward was the only one of the staff she hadn't met in person, although in some ways she'd felt she'd met him on paper over the years in the correspondence he exchanged with Garrett. She had formed an image of him in her head from the thorough reports and meticulously neat, crisp handwriting. In her mind, Monsieur Archambeau was a slender, elegant intellectual, as neatly kept in appearance as his handwriting was on paper; a rational, reliable fellow who perhaps tended towards more reserved behaviours; a man who was respectable and respectful. With luck, they'd have an amicable working relationship.

Richet bowed himself out. A footman came to stir up the fire and Emma made a slow tour of the room, taking in the artwork on the walls, the figurines on tabletops, and the tall empty vases flanking the mantel. All of this was hers. She was safe in a way she'd not been in England. There was comfort in knowing that no one, not Robert or Steven, could take *this* home from her.

She ran a hand over the smooth wood-carved figurine of a dog posed in full trot. This had been one of Garrett's favourite pieces. He'd kept hounds at Oakwood and had loved visiting the kennels. In a world that had been nothing but change in the past weeks, it was a relief to see that this place hadn't changed in seven years. Garrett had bought the place lock, stock, and barrel from a Monsieur Anouilh. The rooms would likely need refreshing to make the place truly hers. But all in good time. For now, there was comfort in the constant and the familiar. She rested her hand on the carving and closed her eyes. For the first time since the flood, she felt as if everything would be all right. At last, she could breathe.

'Madame Luce?' the low tones of a cultured, accented male voice intruded. Somehow, she knew Monsieur Archambeau would sound like that—calm, in control, like his reports. She turned and opened her eyes, prepared to greet the intellectual steward of Les Deux Coeurs, prepared to take the next step into her new life, but that metaphoric next step halted in midstride at the sight of the man who stood before her: tall, broad-shouldered, with a labourer's muscled build, and dressed to match in a homespun shirt open at the neck to reveal an indecent expanse of chest, heavy work breeches tucked into dusty boots and dark hair tousled from the elements. Monsieur Archambeau looked as if he *worked* the land he wrote to her husband about.

'Monsieur Archambeau?' She fumbled for words, the mental image in her mind and the reality standing before her scrambling to align themselves in a rare miscue for her. This could not be him and yet who else could it be? She was seldom wrong about people but she was wrong now. There was nothing of the slender intellectual in the rustic farmer who stood before her.

Chapter Three

No. Not even that assessment was right. She knew she was wrong even as she thought it. His eyes ruined it. A rustic farmer would have a humble gaze. There was nothing humble about the slate-blue stare fixed on her at present. This gaze was instead strong and assessing, making no secret that he was taking her measure, making her feel as if she was an intruder. Emma met his gaze with a strong stare of her own, one she hoped hid her own sudden turmoil as she struggled to realign her thoughts.

She extended her hand to him, trying to be friendly, a part of her mind clinging to her earlier hopes of an amicable business relationship with her husband's steward. But this man did not look amicable. He looked stubborn. 'I do not believe you were here when I first visited.' Every fibre of her being screamed a silent warning: If she'd been wrong about this, what else might she be wrong about when it came to Monsieur Archambeau and the chateau? 'You must be my husband's steward. I feel as if I know you from all the correspondence over the years,' which was fast becoming a polite lie. She clearly *didn't* know this man. Her images of him couldn't be further from the reality standing before her, a realisation that both intrigued the natural curiosity in her and unnerved her. What sort of man had her husband left in charge of the chateau?

He took her hand and bent over it, slate eyes holding hers with all the élan of a skilled courtier, at drastic odds with his appearance, a little joke flickering behind his gaze, a joke she suspected was on her. 'I am Monsieur Luce's man of business here, *madame*.' The correction was subtle and it contributed to a growing sense of unease, of being off balance.

Some of her newly acquired sense of peace evaporated. Her usually accurate perception of people had deserted her, leaving her feeling exposed, but she'd gathered her wits enough to be aware of his correction and what it might portend. Not steward, but the man of business. Had he corrected her out of manly pride, wanting to be seen as someone of importance? If so, she would take care to manage his pride in future interactions. It was easy enough to smooth feathers when one was aware they were ruffled. Or had he corrected her because his responsibilities extended beyond sending quarterly reports and overseeing harvests?

If so, had he been appointed to that responsibility by Garrett or had he assumed it for himself, something that was simple enough to do with an absentee landlord? She hoped for the former. Appointed power was easier to amend. The latter was not. It would be more difficult to…dislodge…if necessary. Power was a hard thing to give up and she was deeply curious to discover just how much power Monsieur Archambeau had been given or how much he'd assumed over the years here at the chateau. The potential of the latter was something she'd warned Garrett about when he'd first set up the arrangement. Instinct told her she might have a fight on her hands.

The same lead that had settled in her stomach at the reading of the will settled in her stomach once more. Monsieur Archambeau was an unlooked-for development. She told herself his position didn't matter, it changed nothing, and whatever the arrangement in the past may or may not have been, she would establish new ground rules. 'It seems we'll have much to discuss since I am here now and have every intention of overseeing the vineyards myself.' In other words, she did not need someone to act on her behalf when she was here to do it in person. She'd never been one for subtlety, neither had her father. This place was hers. She would defend it from those who would challenge that both inside its walls and out.

'Perhaps we might exchange news over supper, if you'd care to join me?' Archambeau was all cool smoothness, a veritable wolf in sheep's clothing, or was that worker's clothing? He was undaunted by her sudden appearance or the veiled warning of terminated employment. Did he not believe she would let him go? Did he think she was bluffing or merely meant to put him in his place? Whatever his beliefs, he obviously felt he had the upper hand. She would disabuse him of that soon enough. This was her home. Her vineyards. Her business.

'Are you inviting me to dinner in my own home?' She matched his coolness, his calm.

'Yes, I am.' He did not back down from the challenge. 'We dine at seven. I believe Mrs Dormand has your rooms ready. Shall I show you up?' He was treating her as a guest. She would not cede that ground to him.

'That will be unnecessary. I know the way.' It was the one thing she was certain of in a world that was suddenly filled with the unfamiliar. She smiled to match his politeness. 'I will see you at seven.' That would give her time to realign her thinking. Things were not as she'd anticipated at Les Deux Coeurs. By dinner, she'd be prepared to expect the unexpected.

Seven hells! Emma Luce was *exactly* what he'd expected, only he'd never expected to actually have to meet her. That she was here was a problem, a very large problem he'd have to deal with quickly and decisively. He'd start at dinner, which didn't give him much time. He called for Richet and ordered a bath for his quarters. A smug smile curled on his mouth as he took the stairs. What would Madame Luce think of *that*? Of him *living* in the house? If she were to contest it, he would relish informing her that it was something he and Monsieur Luce had agreed upon so there was always someone on hand. He had as much right as she to live here at present. That would, perhaps, surprise her. And if she thought the rustic farmer from the drawing room would show up at the dinner table, she'd be in for another surprise. If he hadn't been so wrapped up in his own shock at Richet's news, which had been two surprises dropped on him at once—Luce's death *and* his widow's arrival—he might have found some humour in the confusion that had lit her quicksilver eyes. While she'd been what he'd expected, *he* had not been what *she'd* expected, dressed as he was in his working clothes.

Upstairs, Julien divested himself of his dirty garments and slid into the hot water, letting it relax his body and his mind, his thoughts wandering through what he knew about Emma Luce and how best to deal with her. Sir Garrett Luce had once described his wife in glowing terms as a whirlwind, a woman of fortitude and presence. Those were all attributes Julien could appreciate when they belonged to a woman who was on the other side of the Channel, hundreds of miles from here. He appreciated them far less when they were in his drawing room—not that she would think it was *his* drawing room; that much was clear from their conversation.

Presence was a businessman's word for beauty and Emma Luce was certainly that: dark-haired, sharp silver eyes, a lithe figure shown to perfection even in an unadorned black travelling costume. On a woman like her, even mourning attire appeared fashionable. But all of that was a decoy, Julien suspected, for the intelligence housed within. Luce had mentioned his Emma had a 'rare head for business,' a woman full of ideas about how to get goods to the people who wanted them, and how to convince people that they wanted everything.

'Should have been born a man. She'd have made a fortune,' Luce had said once over brandies during one of his visits. Then, the man had winked at him. *'But fortunately for me she was not. I'm quite satisfied that she's a woman.'* He'd mentioned, too, that she came from a business background herself. *'We understand each other,'* Luce had said in the tones of a man well pleased with his marriage.

Julien sank lower in the hot water. He'd envied Luce that, a wife who was his partner *and* his love. Had the man understood such a combination was worth more than any holding in his business empire? It was what he himself had hoped to have with Clarisse. Together, they were going to turn the Archambeau lands into a great wine house known for its *vin mousseux*, its champagne. A house that would aspire to and rival the House of Clicquot, perhaps in time surpass it. The old widow of Clicquot wouldn't live for ever. She was already seventy-five, and everyone knew she was the genius and the mind behind the house. Her family hadn't the same fortitude for the business as they had for spending the profits.

He'd thought Clarisse had wanted those things, too. As the daughter of a self-made man who'd acquired his fortune in the post-Napoleonic world of the Bourbon Restoration, he'd assumed Clarisse would want what he wanted, valued what he valued, that nothing was more important than family and land. All else could be taken away in a moment.

A man had to make himself in this new world. Titles were fickle things. They meant little to Julien. The Archambeaux had lost their title in the Revolution. They'd regained it in 1815 only to lose it again in 1848. There were rumours the title would be restored again but that changed nothing for Julien. Things that could be taken away so easily were not worthy of his pursuit. Land was the only thing that lasted. Not even love could lay claim to that, as Clarisse had proven.

Now Emma Luce's unanticipated arrival threatened the plans he and Oncle Etienne had in place. She couldn't possibly know what she was walking into, nor could she find out, not yet. It was imperative that the running of the vineyards and control of the vineyard finances remained firmly in his hands for the time being. Not only for his plans but for the long-term viability of the vineyards. People trusted him; he had built a reputation for being both an excellent *vigneron* and winemaker. If anyone thought for a moment that he was not at the helm of Les Deux Coeurs or that the place was being run by an Englishwoman, all confidence—which manifested itself in wine orders and financial investment—would be undermined. What did an Englishwoman know of French vineyards? It was a question that must not be asked. And yet, it was a question he was forced to ask himself.

'I am here now and have every intention of overseeing the vineyards myself,' she'd announced, and he'd been glad no one else, not even the servants, had been around to hear her say that. He needed to be sure she never said such a thing to anyone.

Julien held his breath and slid beneath the water for a final dunking. Garrett Luce had picked a hell of a time to die. After seven years of an amicable arrangement that had allowed Julien to quietly assume a liberal free hand, all that was about to change. Whoever thought seven was a lucky number had never met Emma Luce.

Chapter Four

Emma entered the drawing room at the stroke of seven and not a moment earlier. To be early would require extra conversation with Monsieur Archambeau; polite small talk with the understanding that business talk would come later, perhaps at the table, or after. The French did not countenance the mixing of business with pleasure, and nothing was more pleasurable to the French than their food.

'Ah, Madame Luce, there you are, right on time.' Monsieur Archambeau came forward with a smile on his cleanly shaven face. Gone was the dark stubble of earlier, the dusty worker's clothes replaced with dark trousers, jacket, and a blue waistcoat that brought out the slate of his eyes. The dour worker had been replaced with a gallant gentleman. Perhaps he'd decided he'd catch more flies with honey than vinegar. Perhaps *she* ought to be wary of that. He offered her his arm. 'Richet has informed me Petit, our cook, is ready to serve the meal. Shall we go in? I've learned, to my hazard, not to keep Cook's meals waiting.'

So, he was not *all* honey yet. There was still *some* vinegar there. Beneath his smile and low chuckle, she detected a rebuke for having come down with no time to spare for the niceties of small talk. If there was one thing the French valued as much as their food and wine, it was conversation. Her late arrival had cheated him of the latter. He was taking care it did not cheat him of the former. Or perhaps he was reminding her that he'd been here first, been here longer, that he had a relationship with the staff she hadn't seen in seven years. Good Lord, was she going to spend the whole meal analysing everything he said? Turning his words and actions this way and that like a puzzle box? Probably. She'd not lie to herself. Her brain was excited by the possibility of doing *something*, of having new fodder to energise itself with.

'I packed so carefully that unpacking was something of a challenge,' Emma offered by way of polite apology. In truth, she'd lingered purposefully in her chambers, fussing over the unpacking of her trunks to wait out the clock. It had not taken long to change. When one was in mourning there were no decisions to dawdle over and debate: The black gown or the black gown? Mourning took away the feminine joy of selecting the right dress, the right cut and colour, a tool just as much as conversation and charm. In the past, she'd taken great care with her clothes, dressed with purpose. Now that Garrett was gone, she didn't mind the black. She had no one to dress for. The black suited her. It reflected the darkness, the emptiness she still felt. After nearly a month, perhaps those things would be a part of her for ever, going forward. She *did* feel fire; she *did* feel life. The haze of grief had lifted but in its wake the satisfaction, the completion she'd once felt, was missing. Her soul was empty, an intangible hunger gnawing at her, begging to be filled, to be fed. But with what? She hoped the vineyards could help, that being here in France would satisfy the hunger.

She smoothed her skirts, the gesture drawing Monsieur Archambeau's eye and, unexpectedly, his sympathy. 'I am truly sorry about your husband, *madame*. I considered Sir Garrett a friend as well as a business partner,' he offered solemnly, his hard eyes softening. 'You have my sincere condolences. I should have said so earlier.' An apology? That had all her senses on alert. Perhaps he was trying to reposition himself after a less than friendly start. Monsieur Archambeau was *definitely* on his mettle. A man never apologised for anything unless he felt himself entirely in the wrong. Or, unless there was something he wanted—*badly*. She'd wager the latter was the case if he was willing to apologise *and* put on quite the show in his dark evening clothes and excellently tied cravat.

The stern man she'd met upon arrival had been replaced by the most gallant of gentlemen, a transition that Emma thought had been rather seamless, quite natural for him, one that fit him as well as his clothes. That too was cause for caution. A worker with a gentleman's manners was an intriguing and unusual combination. Such a man had angles and facets, depths and agendas. He would not allow himself to be dismissed easily. Indeed, everything about him suggested he did not see himself as an employee to be commanded but as something more. That's what worried her. He saw himself not as a steward but as a partner, perhaps even as the superior business partner. She'd have to help him understand his role otherwise.

He ushered her into the dining room, playing the part of the gentleman to perfection. At the sight of the dining room, her breath caught loud enough to be noticed. She'd not been prepared for this. '*Madame?* Is everything all right?' Monsieur Archambeau solicited with a look of concern.

'I'm fine, it's just that my memories did not do this room justice.' Her memories had dimmed its magnificence and now, seen in person, the room laid overwhelming siege to those memories. It looked exactly as it had when she'd honeymooned as a bride; the beautiful turquoise damask on the walls, the creamy wainscoting that ran from floor to chair railing, the brass sconces set at intervals to illuminate the exquisite artwork, and the massive fireplace with its mantel of carved French oak from the chateau's own forests. The long table, capable of seating twenty, was set for two. A white cloth draped the far end closest to the fire. A heavy multiarmed silver candelabra stood in the centre of the cloth, its flame light glancing off the crystal goblets and elegant white china.

She was vaguely aware of Monsieur Archambeau's hand dropping to the small of her back as he guided her towards the table, of the effortless way he held out her chair and waited for her to arrange her skirts. In the back of her mind, it registered that these were routines he'd performed countless times, routines that came to him as naturally as breathing. They were not routines that came naturally to farmers.

Monsieur Archambeau took his own seat and Richet came forward to pour the wine, a pale gold white that sparked diamond-like in the crystal, while footmen served potato and leek soup in wide, shallow bowls. 'I hope the food is to your liking,' Monsieur Archambeau solicited. 'We'll just have three courses tonight. We were not expecting guests.'

It was a masterful snub, so implicitly done as a piece of self-deprecating apology, one might miss it. But not Emma. She'd weathered the implicit disdain of Society long enough to understand the messages wrapped within messages. *We. Guest.* These were divisive words that indicated who belonged and who was outside the inner circle. She matched his solicitude with a smile. 'The soup is delicious. I will send menus to Cook tomorrow.' Best to establish her authority immediately, starting with the running of the household. 'I'll meet with Mrs Dormand as well and renew our acquaintance.'

The last request seemed to perplex him. A small furrow formed in the space between his dark brows, as if she'd confused him at best, insulted him at worst. 'I assure you that is not necessary. We can certainly see to the care of one guest without her needing to oversee the housework.' He brought to bear all of his French solicitude. 'You should enjoy yourself while you're here; rest, recover. You have had a difficult month, Madame. You have much to think about.'

Truly, he was a splendid actor. If they hadn't got off to such a frigid start, she might have bought into it. A woman must constantly be on guard against such charm when wielded so expertly by a well-dressed and well-mannered man, she thought. Not that she and her broken heart needed such a warning. She was not in the market for such charm or winsomeness. She took a sip of the wine and let herself enjoy the performance before she destroyed it with another smile. 'This is my *home*, Monsieur Archambeau. I do not intend to be a burden, or a guest in my own house. I mean to see to the running of my household.' She did not add *and its lands* again as she had earlier in the drawing room. That would come in time. She hoped it would come by implicit coup instead of explicit, that he would get the message that his time here was coming to an end now that there was a landowner in residence daily. As such, his services were no longer needed. If she needed a steward, she could hire someone who was more amicable.

Another frown deepened the lines between his brows as he feigned perplexity. 'How long do you mean to stay?'

'Permanently, *monsieur*.' He did not like the word *permanently*. If the furrow between his brows deepened any further it would become a chasm. 'This is the property left to me by my husband. His eldest now holds the English estate, as is his right under British entailment law.' She did not begrudge Robert that, only the gloating way by which Robert had grabbed possession. She gave a soft smile designed to communicate graciousness and understanding on her part. 'The new baronet will not want his father's second wife under-foot as he establishes his household.' That was an understated way of putting it, but she'd not make herself vulnerable by telling *monsieur* she had nowhere else to go, that her husband's family had essentially turned her out the moment the will had been read and had been more than happy to see her 'exiled' to France. If they couldn't get their hands on the chateau, they could at least get rid of her.

'Of course, *madame*.' It was noncommittally said as they both smiled at each other over the rims of wine glasses and Emma was not fool enough to believe anything was settled, only tabled. Footmen came forward to take the soup bowls and replace them with steaming bowls of beef bourguignon. A loaf of bread was set between them, and fresh wine glasses were filled with a rich red, the table laid for the second round as much as for the second course. Round one had been about laying out her situation. It stood to reason that round two ought to be about laying out his. After all, she'd been the one to give out crucial information over soup. They now both knew her plans and expectations. It would be quid pro quo for him to reciprocate, and reciprocation was the foundation of good negotiation.

She speared a piece of the tender meat and waited. That was a tactical mistake. She ought to have guided the conversation more specifically even if it had required a blunt question. He took the opening she offered but he did not play by the rules, his voice gentle in the candlelit darkness. 'Sir Garrett and I exchanged

letters at the end of January regarding the spring growing season. He'd not mentioned being in poor health.'
Slate-blue eyes rested on her with empathy. 'I assume
his death was unexpected. If it is too indelicate to ask
or too difficult to discuss, you must tell me and I shall
cease, but I would like to know what happened.'

He was not play-acting now and his request took the
edge off the otherwise sharp evening. They were no
longer two potential foes circling one another, but two
people who shared a common loss, something she'd
not taken time to consider in her haste to protect her
position. But now, here in the intimacy of the dining
room, the belated realisation occurred that Garrett was
common ground between them, as was his loss. She'd
lost a husband. This man, this *stranger*, had lost someone he'd counted as a friend. Where she'd had weeks
to reconcile herself to the loss, he'd had a mere hand-
ful of hours and no details to help his understanding.
Richet would have told him only that Sir Garrett Luce
was dead, and his widow was here. Then they'd been
sprung on one another by mutual surprise, and both
had gone on the defensive.

'I am sorry,' she apologised hastily, 'of course, you'd
want to know.' Perhaps she should have offered the
information sooner. Perhaps she should have not gone
immediately on the defence. Instead, she should have
approached this stranger from a position of softness,
not strength. But in her experience, gentleness was
seldom rewarded and quite often taken advantage of.

'You guess right, it was unexpected.' She took a
sip of wine to steady herself. Even after a month, even

after recounting the horrible events at Holmfirth for Garrett's sons and for her father, it was still difficult to speak of. 'We were in Holmfirth,' which probably meant nothing to Monsieur Archambeau. 'It was business. Garrett was looking at a mill he was interested in investing in. But he'd heard rumours about the dam up-river being unstable. He wasn't going to buy a mill that was likely to be washed away.' She cleared her throat to dislodge the lump forming. 'But it was. There was considerable rain while we were there, and the dam burst. It swept through the street where our lodgings were.' She gave him a meaningful look, pleading with him to understand the implications without her having to say the words.

'Mon Dieu,' Archambeau breathed, automatically reaching for her hand where it lay on the table. 'I am sorry. But you were not there? At the lodgings?'

'No, my friends and I were playing whist.' It still pained her to say that. Perhaps she should have been there, perhaps she should have died with him or she could have saved him. Both were illogical thoughts as Fleur liked to point out, but Emma couldn't get over the feeling of having somehow abandoned Garrett to his fate in exchange for her own selfish survival.

'You were lucky, then.' Archambeau said gently. He gave her a sad smile, releasing her hand. 'We must toast his memory.' He reached for his wine glass and raised it. 'To Sir Garrett Luce, a true and generous friend who will be greatly missed.' The wine glasses chimed against one another, and they drank, the toast leaving her with a surprising sense of rightness. In all the mourning that had taken place, the initial loss in Holmfirth, the funeral in Surrey, there'd been tears and wailing but no toasting and wine. Garrett would have liked more toasts than tears, she thought.

The *plateau de fromage*, the end-of-meal cheese platter, was brought in, featuring a rich Roquefort, a complement of dried fruits and cranberries, and a small pot of honey to drizzle over it. Small glasses were filled with port. 'We farm the honey here on site in our own apiaries.' Archambeau raised the honey dipper over her selection of fruits and drizzled for her. There was no hidden message this time in the use of 'we' as he spoke of the home farm and it seemed to her that the moment to discuss business had long passed. But there was a quietly stunning unintended revelation in this 'we'.

He lives here. The chateau is his home.

It was why he'd been on hand when she'd arrived so late in the day, why there'd been lights in the windows despite no one knowing of her coming, why he'd had evening clothes to change into and a razor for his toilette, why he had such a close relationship with the staff. Perhaps even why he'd felt threatened by her arrival. Should she choose to do so, she would displace him from more than a job.

Should she choose?

Her mind stuttered on the idea. That was a very different thought than the one she'd entered the dining room with. She'd come downstairs determined to establish her position and to disabuse him of any belief that he had a toehold here. Now, one meal later, she was already recanting that position. She shot him a considering look beneath her lashes as she reached for her port. Well, damn him for being a master. For all of her confidence that she was immune to his persuasion, it seemed he'd got exactly what he wanted from supper, and he'd done it by using the oldest trick in the book: making her believe she'd been the one in charge.

She finished her port and rose. 'Please excuse me, Monsieur Archambeau. It's been a long day and I'm tired. I thank you for the meal. Even on short notice, it was the best I've eaten in a while. I will give Cook my compliments tomorrow when I submit the menus. Thank you also for your company. I hope it did not take you away from any plans.'

He set aside his napkin and rose with her. 'It was my pleasure, Madame Luce. I will show you up.'

'It is not necessary,' she began but he interrupted with a soft smile.

'I know, but I will do it anyway. My manners would never forgive me.' She recognised it was a détente of sorts as she took his arm. He accepted her presence, no longer acting as if she were a guest temporarily passing through his life. Perhaps in the sharing of Garrett's loss some of his barriers had come down, too. Or perhaps he could simply be magnanimous in victory because they both knew he'd won the night.

Chapter Five

He had won the night. Now he needed to make good on that reprieve. Garrett Luce was dead. His widow was *here* in Cumières, *in* the chateau, and intending to stay. Julien paced the faded Aubusson carpet that covered most of the floor of his *oncle*'s study at the farmhouse that bordered the chateau's property, his body as unable to still as his mind. After a sleepless night, he'd ridden over as soon as he'd completed his early morning walk of the vineyards.

Even his morning walk, usually a calm, meditative activity, had been disrupted with thoughts of last night. He was still reeling with the news. There was the veil of grief over the loss of Sir Garrett. The loss so sudden and unbelievable, given that he had a letter from Garrett dated just days before his death. He was also reeling from the practical impact of what Garrett's death meant to his plans and position regarding the chateau.

He stopped by a bookcase to finger a globe set on a gold-plated axis. He gave it a gentle spin with his finger. He tinkered with the decorative scales on another shelf, moving the little weights to redistribute the balance. Such fine shelf ornaments for a farmhouse. Oncle Etienne had still been abed when he arrived and was a stickler for his morning routine. He would not deign to receive anyone without being completely dressed and shaved for the day, not even his nephew. Julien would have preferred not to be kept waiting. He'd have been happy to have his *oncle* receive him in his boudoir while he shaved or even if his *oncle* had simply thrown on a dressing robe and come downstairs in *dishabille*. But that was not how Etienne Archambeau conducted himself. He might not live in the family chateau, but he never forgot he was the son of a *comte*, that centuries of nobility ran in his veins. Julien chuckled. As for himself, he was quite the opposite. He didn't stand on ceremony unless he had to. There was no one at the chateau to care how he dressed or when he dressed or even *if* he dressed. He could run around in *dishabille* all day if it suited him. And, honestly, sometimes it did. At least that had been true up until last night. That would have to change now with Madame Luce in residence.

Emma Luce had been something of a revelation; a beautiful woman with sable hair and a cynic's sea-grey eyes that said a man aspired to her at his own peril. It was the type of challenge that would have appealed to Luce, but the cynicism in her eyes surprised him. What did a woman married to Garrett Luce have to be cynical about? The marriage had been a love match. Luce had family from a previous marriage, sons, a fortune. Self-sufficient as he'd been, he had not been required to marry. He'd lavished every extravagance on his young bride. In return, his bride had loved *him*, not his money or the things he could provide. That had been evident last night when she'd talked of her husband. She'd taken the loss hard.

Proof of that had moved him. Moved him right off topic at dinner, in fact. He'd intended dinner to be a chance to stake his claim, to make it clear that he was in charge of the vineyards. He'd not nurtured these vines for years to have a newcomer interrupt and undo his hard work just when results were within his grasp. But instead of business, they'd ended up talking about Garrett and of her plans to stay, which had served his purposes nonetheless in the end. He'd emerged victorious on a technicality. Last night, he'd allowed her to establish that she was not a guest in *his* home but a resident in *hers*. He checked the mantel clock and wondered if she was up already, giving her menus to Petit and meeting with the housekeeper. By extension, if she was *the* resident, what did that make him? The outsider? His response last night had been alarming. He'd been too empathetic by far. From empathy grew attachment. The less he knew about her the more objective he could be. Had he in his empathy allowed her to usurp him, or was there room for two residents?

'Julien, you're up early.' His *oncle* entered the study, pressed and polished in perfectly creased dark blue trousers and jacket, paisley-blue waistcoat and white linen pristine beneath. His cravat was tied with sartorial excellence and his cheek was smooth. His abundant head of sleek silver hair was brushed back from his face, his Archambeau-blue eyes sharp, alert, and yet kind. His *oncle* carried with him an aura of confidence that immediately put one at ease and filled one with the sense that all would be well. It was what he'd come to admire about his *oncle* in the years he'd lived with him in England while he'd gone to school, and what he relied on now that his *grandpère* and papa were gone. Even this morning, the sight and sound of his *oncle* eased the night rumblings of his mind. He'd been right to come.

'I have news, Oncle, and I felt it could not wait.' Rather, *he* could not wait. He wanted his mind to still, he wanted to lay this latest development at his *oncle*'s feet so he could get back to his grapes and his solitude.

His *oncle* raised a silver brow in query, a smile at the ready. 'It must be quite the news indeed to make you leave the chateau.' Julien heard the rebuke. He seldom left the estate. Over the years, after the disaster with Clarisse, he felt more at home with the grapes than he did among people. Oh, he'd not forgotten his manners, but he had less call to use them and he was fine with that. Last night had been the first night in a year he'd had to dust those manners off. 'Come, have breakfast with me while we talk. If I know you, you've been too busy walking the vineyards to have eaten yet.'

Breakfast was a delicious temptation at his *oncle*'s. A man could feast at his breakfast table, really set himself up for the day. All of Oncle Etienne's years in England during the family's exile and then after—all total a sum of sixty-two years of his life—had resulted in a table that catered to his *oncle*'s love of hearty British breakfasts with their eggs and sausages joined with the traditional French preference for something simpler; croissants and tartines with a cup of coffee or tea. Today, though, Julien thought a croissant was all his stomach could handle.

'You're not eating,' his *oncle* commented with a pointed stare at his mostly empty plate. 'Is it bad news, then?'

'I'm not sure it's good or bad. At this point, it's only news, but I fear it does trend towards the bad.' They took their seats at one end of the table and Julien delivered his news. 'Sir Garrett Luce is dead. He was killed in a flash flood on a business trip a few weeks ago.' He watched his *oncle* for a reaction. Luce had been his friend, not his *oncle*'s. To his *oncle*, Luce was merely a means to an end. 'Luce's widow arrived last night at the chateau. She means to take up residence there.'

Oncle Etienne calmly sliced into his sausage and took a long bite before answering. 'And the vineyards? Does she mean to take an interest in them?'

'Yes. She declared quite specifically to me last night that she means to take them over.' She was looking for a project, something to assuage the loss he'd seen in her eyes. She was a woman at sea, looking for something to anchor herself to as she'd once anchored herself to her husband. It made him wonder what that life had been like. How had she spent her time? But these were questions he had to banish from his mind. To know her would be to invite disclosures, to bring emotions into the equation. That had not worked well for him in the past. He'd learned his lesson.

'No one can hear her say that. Her project *cannot* be

the vineyards,' Etienne said with firm finality, coming to the same conclusion Julien had last night. 'We've worked too hard. This a big year for us. The new grapes will be ready for harvest and the vintage we've been counting on goes to bottling. That *vin mousseux* will be the making of us.' They were counting on it. They had their extra funds invested in it. More than extra funds, really. There was his *oncle*'s loan against the farmhouse and the reclaimed vineyards, a loan granted on the collateral of the profits secured from pre-sales of the *vin mousseux*, and Garrett Luce's funds were invested, too, on the strength of Julien's reputation as a *vigneron*. To lose the confidence, financial or otherwise, of their backers at this point would be to court disaster. If they were unable to make payments on the loan they'd taken out last year to buy some additional acreage, they would lose the lands it had taken generations to claim in their play to raise funds to gather the rest. Neither of them had to say anything out loud about what a setback it would be. The expected profit was meant to go towards making Luce an offer for the vineyards, the last hectares of land to complete the restoration of the Archambeau holdings.

'I do not think she will sell any time soon.' Julien addressed the other concern. Even if they raised the money, even if they could continue to control the direction of the vineyards, it would all be for naught if the land could not be acquired.

Etienne nodded thoughtfully. 'That is the least of our concerns. We have choices there. We can convince her the land is not worth anything, that it is draining her coffers. She might part with the vineyards if not the house.' He gave a Gallic shrug. 'It would be a shame not to get the house back, but the land matters more.' The land could be turned to make more money. The house could not.

Julien frowned. 'That persuasion seems unlikely if we have the harvest we anticipate and the success we are looking for from the champagne. We can't sacrifice those things to promote a ruse of low productivity.' To say nothing of how uncomfortable Julien was with the idea of perpetuating a dishonest scheme designed to push someone towards a fabricated belief from which he'd benefit.

'There are other ways.' His *oncle* was undaunted. He spread his hands on the surface of the old oak table. 'Running a chateau and a vineyard is a large undertaking. Grapes are a year-round pursuit, they're a demanding mistress. She may tire of it. I think it's our responsibility to show her how time-consuming it is, especially if she has to make every little decision herself.'

Julien knew what his *oncle* meant: give Madame Luce everything she wanted and then ensure it became too overwhelming so that she'd beg for his intervention, beg for him to take on the responsibilities to the point of wanting to wash her hands of the vineyard completely. He was still sceptical. The strategy seemed mean-spirited.

'Telling people the truth, *showing* them the truth by letting them experience it, is not dishonest, *mon fils*,' Etienne soothed, reading his mind.

'But we haven't been quite truthful, have we? What

if she discovers how liberal we've been in Luce's absence?' Julien had never been entirely comfortable with a few of the decisions he'd made in Luce's absence over the years, like the decision to use Luce's grapes in the Archambeau vintages.

His *oncle* dismissed the concern with a wave of his hand. 'Luce hired you to act as his proxy, to make decisions that could not wait for letters to cross the Channel. You've done nothing but act in the best interest of the estate. You've cost him no money, you've not damaged the estate's reputation. There is nothing to worry about. You were simply doing your job to the best of your ability.' That was not quite true. If he had been doing his job to the *best* of his ability, the estate would have already been producing a profit. He'd merely been maintaining the status quo and making decisions that had been in the best interests of the Archambeaux. In most cases what had been good for the Archambeaux was good for the estate, but there were a few occasions when he'd had to choose and he'd chosen family. Nothing detrimental to the estate of course, just perhaps not a growth opportunity either. For example, he had not entertained offers for surplus grapes even though those offers paid more for them than the Archambeau vineyard did, knowing full well the Archambeau vineyard paid nothing for those grapes.

Oncle Etienne shook his head. 'She's a woman, and a grieving one. She'll have no head for business even if she does decide she's interested. You worry too much.' But his *oncle* hadn't seen her last night, those sharp eyes duelling with him over the rims of wine glasses.

Oncle Etienne always dismissed women, his own wife included, who'd been left behind in England with his son to run the British end of the Archambeau shipping business. Julien did not think Emma Luce would care to be dismissed.

'*Mon fils*, you are looking at these events all wrong. Instead of portending ill omens for us, it could be that this is the break we've been waiting for.' His *oncle* fixed him with the full force of his considering stare. 'Luce is dead, and that is regrettable. I know you liked him. But we could only have bought the vineyard and chateau from him at his whim. We might have waited years for that to happen. We'd already waited seven with no sign of him wanting to sell.' His *oncle* leaned forward, an idea brewing that made his eyes shine. 'But we don't need the widow to sell. You could marry her and claim the estate without us expending a single sou.' His *oncle* grinned. 'In one fell swoop, we'd have everything back.'

'She's in mourning, Oncle. Her husband has just passed. It would be, as the British say, bad form.'

'You don't have to marry her tomorrow. Marry her in the fall after the harvest. We've waited seven years; we can certainly wait seven more months.' His *oncle* scowled, no doubt thinking him a prude. Julien thought of the woman who'd sat across from him at the dinner table last night, whose loss was evident in the way she spoke of her husband, how difficult it had been for her to share the details of his death. He did not think seven months would change that for her. 'Marriage takes two willing partners. She's not emotionally available, not now, not in seven more months.' He knew from how she spoke of her husband last night that she was not envisioning a second marriage in her future.

'These obstacles are nothing, *mon fils*. You make too much of them.' Oncle Etienne gave a wry laugh. 'If she does not think she's *ouvert a l'amour*, then make her open to love, persuade her. You can be very charming when you choose.' Julien frowned and his *oncle* pressed. 'Or is it *you* who is not open to love?'

'I am not open to dishonesty,' Julien retorted sharply. 'Wooing a woman under the pretence of having feelings for her is cruel and devious.' He could not see Emma Luce tolerating such a betrayal. She did not strike him as a woman who forgave easily, or ever forgot. Such perfidious actions would drive a permanent wedge between them *if* she believed him. After last night's rather frosty start, he thought it unlikely she'd believe such a *volte face* on his part.

His *oncle* gave a negligible shrug. 'Fine then, you don't have to *court* her to wed her. This needn't be presented as a whirlwind romance or a love match. Tell her up front it's a marriage of convenience. She's a businesswoman. Convince her it's as convenient for her as it is for you.'

Julien's frown deepened. Usually, he admired his *oncle*'s strategic mind, his ability to look at problems from different angles. But not today. He fixed his *oncle* with a stern stare, a reminder that he was a man of thirty-seven, no longer a boy to be ordered about. 'I am to be bartered in marriage for the Archambeau restoration?'

His *oncle* let out a frustrated sigh. '*Mon Dieu*, Julien,

tu as besoin de te faire pousser un paire. I'd marry her myself, sight unseen, if I wasn't already married.' He gave an impatient wave of his hand. 'You were going to marry Clarisse for the estate. This is no different. It's not as if you're interested in anyone else at the moment.'

Julien bristled at that. What his *oncle* proposed went against his principles. Not even for the Archambeau restoration would he compromise his ethic, nor would he make such a decision that would take someone else at unawares, the full deception not revealed until it was too late to change course. He knew already what Emma Luce would think of such a strategy. 'It *was* different with Clarisse, Oncle. We were in love.'

'*You* were in love,' his *oncle* corrected without empathy. 'It's been seven years, *mon fils*. How much longer are you going to carry that carcass around with you? Clarisse certainly hasn't,' he added pointedly. No. She hadn't. Three months after the broken engagement, Clarisse had married a French politician whose star was rising in powerful circles. It had been an extravagant, very public summer affair at the chateau, her family making no apologies for the speed with which it happened after the dissolution of her engagement to the down-at-heel son of the Comte de Rocroi.

'She has two children now, lives in Paris in a *grande maison*,' his *oncle* persisted. 'She is touted as one of the city's premier hostesses.' His *oncle* raised a brow. 'And what do you have, hiding among your grapes?' He paused and then slapped a palm on the table, indicating that a decision had been made. 'You must come with me. I am meeting with the district growers today.'

Julien groaned. 'Those old men?' There were a thousand things to do at the chateau and any of them were more appealing than lunch with the district's growers, windbags that they were. They'd talk for hours trying to impress each other.

'Yes, *those* old men. They are our friends and our competition. We must keep an eye on them as they keep an eye on us. Charles Tremblay would like nothing better than to see us fail. He'd snatch up the land and we'd never get it back. And if you'd truly like a bit of revenge against Gabriel Anouilh, you need to show him you've moved on from his daughter and that you can acquire that land without him. To that end, it might not be best to mention that Garrett Luce is dead just yet. I don't want the consortium spooking and withdrawing their support.' His *oncle* gave him a stern look. 'The other thing you cannot continue to do, *mon fils*, is hide away and lick your wounds like a whipped cur. You're too young to be a recluse.' Oncle Etienne leaned forward. 'This is *our* year. We will throw a grand summer ball at the chateau in June, just as we've planned, to celebrate the new vintage. We will invite buyers and they will see your genius. It will be a success and I want you there beside me.'

'I am always beside you, Oncle.' Julien reminded him, trying not to take offence. He was the one who grew the grapes, who oversaw the harvests, who decided which vines to prune. Oncle Etienne might be the face of the Archambeau vineyards in their current state today, such as they were—a mid-sized, but high-quality winery—but Julien was the silent brilliance behind the scenes whose effort made those successes possible. It was something he had in common with Garrett Luce, both of them liking to build success backstage instead of on it.

'Publicly, *mon fils*. I know you've been with me, even when you were a schoolboy in England and living with your *tante* and I, you were beside me. But I want everyone to *see* us together. When we reclaim the land and the chateau, I want it to be *our* victory.' Oncle Etienne gave him a fond smile. 'That settles it. You can wash up and change into the spare things you keep here. We'll leave in an hour. The meeting is at Charles Tremblay's. He wants to show off his new carriage horses and his improvements on his stables. Pompous braggart.' His *oncle* rolled his eyes and then gave a sly smile. 'At least he sets a good table for luncheon, *non*? We'll get a taste of that red he's always talking about.'

Julien laughed. Sometimes it was hard to tell if his *oncle* thought the growers' consortium were friends or foes. The line was thin and often crossed and recrossed. Still, there was something comforting about knowing if there was trouble, *real* trouble like blight or drought or, heaven forbid, fire, the other growers would be there to support them. The consortium had celebrated with them when his *grandpère* had bought back the first of the acreage several years ago, some of them having been in the same situation not long before. They'd been there for them when his father had died, supplying them with enough workers to get the harvest in. If Charles Tremblay wanted to brag about his horses, he'd probably earned the right.

'I'll be ready, Oncle. I just need to send a note to Richet and let him know I'll be gone until tomorrow.' He had no illusions about 'lunch' at Tremblay's. The meeting would run well into the evening once they'd eaten and admired the man's stables, drank his wine, and then finally got down to business. They wouldn't be back to the farmhouse until evening, and he wouldn't risk his horse's legs on a pothole in the dark. Better to sleep over and ride home in the daylight. It would be safer, and it would give Madame Luce time to take stock. Perhaps his *oncle* was right. If she could see first-hand the enormity of running the chateau, it may go a long way toward her realising she was no match for it. This way, it would be her decision to step back.

Chapter Six

Richet took a step back from the breakfast table, his note delivered. 'Monsieur Archambeau will be away until tomorrow,' he informed her, making it unnecessary for her to read the note and making it clear that he'd read it before passing it on to her.

She fixed the *maître d'hôtel* with a strong stare. 'Do you make it a habit of reading your mistress's mail before she does?' Or reading it at all. Reading it after her probably wouldn't make things any better. It wasn't his business, regardless.

Richet had the good form to at least *look* scandalised. His brows went up and his long face gave a strong facsimile of shock. 'Absolutely *not, madame. Mon Dieu*, what sort of *maître d'hôtel* do you take me for?'

His disbelief was so creditably done she felt for a moment that she'd been the one in the wrong. 'I thought perhaps it was a French thing?'

Richet drew himself up to his full height, an impressive six feet, almost as tall as Monsieur Archambeau, she thought. 'I only read my mail, *madame*.' He nodded to the note in her hand. 'If you look at the outside, you'll see that it is addressed to me.'

Emma turned the note over, a slow horror dawning as she realised her *faux pas*, and something else, too. 'Monsieur Archambeau left word with you?' But not with her. He'd preferred to tell the *maître d'hôtel* his schedule but not to inform her? It was a most implicit snub. She scanned the note again, looking for a line that indicated Richet was expected to pass the information on to her, but there was nothing. Archambeau had written explicitly to Richet. It was only through Richet's kindness in *choosing* to share the message with her that she knew. Her cheeks flamed with her error. Emma squared her shoulders. 'I owe you an apology. I should not have assumed.' Should not have assumed she couldn't trust her staff's own loyalty. Should not have assumed she'd be treated as an outsider despite Monsieur Archambeau's attempts to do just that last night.

'It is no problem, *madame*.' Richet bowed and left her to finish her breakfast in penitent silence. She needed to do better. Monsieur Archambeau had put her on edge and in doing so, she'd not thought clearly, rationally. These were Garrett's people. People hired by him to see to the running of his home. Her home now. She may not know them the way Monsieur Archambeau did, but she did know Garrett. Garrett meant the chateau to be a place of refuge and recovery, a place to start her life anew. He would not leave her among enemies. Garrett had Richet's loyalty. That meant, she, as Garrett's wife, did, too. Yet Monsieur Archambeau respected Richet.

Of course. It was obvious. Monsieur Archambeau
had her so on edge, she'd forgotten one of her father's
most fundamental rules: if one wanted to fully understand a situation, one had to look at it from the view-
points of others, not just one's own. How difficult this
must be for Richet, to be torn between the two of them.
If she wanted to be upset with anyone, it should be Monsieur Archambeau for snubbing her. She finished her
breakfast and set aside her napkin. Well, lesson learned.
There was nothing to do but move forward. She would
allow this knowledge to inform her upcoming meet-
ings this morning with the housekeeper and with Cook.
She would also let it shape her choices. She had today
and tomorrow to herself without the risk of Monsieur
Archambeau's interference. It was the perfect time to
familiarise herself with the house. It occurred to her
that though she might have been here before, visiting
did not equate with knowledge. To be an effective mistress of her home, she needed to know it. She'd meet
with Mrs Dormand and Cook, then she'd change into
clothes that would allow her to get to know her home
more intimately, another lesson learned from her father.

One day and a whirlwind later, Emma was feeling much more at home. She'd spent the time clean-
ing, getting to know her new house, and most of all,
she'd spent it dreaming of the life she'd create here. It
would be a life of acceptance where the origins of her
family's fortune didn't matter. Where people would
come to her gracious home for tea and cards, garden
parties and picnics, and not look down their noses at

her. They would get to know her without her antecedents preceding her.

It was the type of acceptance she'd always dreamed of, of being part of the district. It was an acceptance she'd experienced in some small part as Garrett's wife. There'd been authentic acceptance within Garrett's circle of friends; Adam and Fleur, Antonia and Keir, people Garrett trusted with his life. Then there'd been the verisimilitude of acceptance among those in Society who'd recognised they could not entirely ignore Sir Garrett and Lady Luce. The Luces had piles of money *and* a title. But she and Garrett had been honest with each other about the foundations of that acceptance. They could laugh at Society, they could let Society have its foibles, because they'd had each other. She'd been alone no longer.

Here, in the middle of the French countryside, it *would* be different, and Emma could hardly wait. She polished silver, imagining the teas she would give, imagining walking through the gardens, her arm looped through that of a new friend's as they laughed together. She rubbed at a smudge on a teapot and laughed at herself. If she had an Achilles heel it would be sating her hunger for acceptance in the form of true friendships that weren't contingent on her money or where it came from. She would prove herself worthy of acceptance on her own merits. She would prove herself in the wine business. Here, there would be no spoiled debutantes like Amelia St James to look down at her, no lords like the Earl of Redmond who flirted with her money but shunned her behind her back. Yes, here it would be different. Garrett had given her a fresh start with his last gift.

Emma hummed to herself, tucking a loose curl underneath her kerchief as she stirred the pot of soup on the stove. She breathed in the herb-scented steam with satisfaction. There was nothing like creamy chicken corn chowder on a cold, damp night, especially when it was made with barley and garnished with sage and bacon. Best of all, she'd made it herself. She loved cooking, an activity her father had encouraged when she was growing up and one that Garrett had enjoyed the fruits of on the nights they'd chosen to stay in, just the two of them. She'd worked on this soup all afternoon, checking it between other sundry chores that had been self-assigned. Cook had been scandalised at the suggestion she make her own food, but when Emma had offered to give Cook the day off to visit her daughter's family and new grandbaby in the village, Cook had been far more accepting.

People had their pride. One must always be conscious of that. Mrs Dormand had been wary, too, when Emma had told her she wanted to do some chores. She'd had her own degree of scandal when Emma had shown up in a plain blue work dress and apron, a kerchief on her head, ready to sort linens and polish silver after a tour of the house from top to bottom. *'I will not be a tourist in my own home, Mrs Dormand,'* Emma had said strictly.

When put that way, Mrs Dormand seemed to understand. The best way to know a place was to be a part of its inner workings. It was also the best way to appreciate a place. Beautiful meals in a candlelit dining room didn't materialise out of thin air. There were laundresses that ensured the pristine quality of the white cloth, footmen who polished the silver and set the immaculate table, kitchen staff who saw to the cooking and plating of the meal. There were no happy accidents, as her father liked to say. That reminded her, she would need to write to her parents and let them know she'd arrived. They worried about her. In truth, they had not quite understood why she wanted to go to France instead of coming home to them and her family's business. Her father would always see her as his little girl even though she was twenty-seven. That was the main reason she couldn't go home again. She needed to be more. More than her father's bookkeeper, her parents' little girl. It would be her brothers who took over the business when her father retired. Her efforts would gain her naught. She knew her father simply wanted to protect her, but she didn't want to be protected.

Emma dipped a wooden spoon into the pot and tasted the soup. Delicious. She set the spoon aside and began to lay out her supper things on the worktable, a wooden bowl, a board for the bread, the crock of pale country butter. There was a half bottle of red wine left from the previous night and she thought, why not spoil herself in celebration of all she'd accomplished? She'd just set a goblet down beside her plate when she heard boots in the corridor, followed by a raised voice, its tone not unpleasant. 'Richet? Petit?' Monsieur Archambeau was back. Some of her hard-won calm satisfaction faded. But not all of it. She was *not* going to let him put her on edge in her own home.

The door to the kitchen swung open, 'Petit, where is—' His speech halted with his step when he saw her, surprise momentarily stymying him, some of his own casual ebullience evaporating. '*Bon soir*, Madame Luce. What are you doing here? Where is everyone?' The furrow that was all too commonplace on his brow returned as his gaze lingered on her clothes, her kerchief, and the idea that she was in the kitchen while Petit was nowhere to be found.

'I've given Petit the day off to visit her daughter and the others a half day. We've all been working very hard while you've been gone.' She still hadn't quite forgiven him for only informing Richet of his absence.

'You've been working?' He sauntered forward, taking an appreciative sniff. 'Did you make this? It smells good.' *He* smelled good, all cold spring wind and the fresh manly scent of neroli; citrus and bitter orange mixed with spices and honey. The scent gave her pause. The dusty-booted working man she'd met two days ago paid attention to such things? Certainly, the man in evening dress would, but who was the real Monsieur Archambeau? The man in evening dress or the man who'd come in from the land?

'Yes, I like to cook.' She wiped her hands on her apron, trying to remember her lessons; to see things from another's point of view. Where were her manners? 'Would you like to join me?' She couldn't learn about him if she avoided him. She reached for another bowl and glass.

'I wouldn't mind, thank you.' He pulled a stool up to the worktable with ease as if he'd eaten here before, the gesture more reminiscent of a worker than a gentleman. 'Is this what you're drinking?' He held up the bottle of red and shook his head. 'It's all wrong for this soup. It's too heavy. We need a *pinot noir* if we want red wine with chicken, a chardonnay if we want white.' He got off the stool. 'I'll be right back.' He disappeared and returned momentarily carrying a bottle in each hand. 'One white, one red,' he announced and set about un-corking them. 'If you mean to live in France, you'll have to learn your wines, although Richet has an im-peccable nose. You can rely on him.'

'He *is* reliable,' Emma said drily. 'He showed me your note. Thanks to him, I knew where you were.' She waited but he said nothing. 'You could have written to me,' she said bluntly. 'You *should* have written to me as well.'

'Why? You knew where I was. I was out conducting estate business with the district growers.' He flashed her a short smile, unbothered by her attempt at censure, and poured her a glass of white. 'Let me show you how to taste. It's all about the three S's: swirl, smell, and sip.' He walked her through the process. 'Now try the red.'

Audacity came naturally to this man. Emma fought the temptation to give vent to her annoyance. An em-ployee that came and went at will? Without so much as a by your leave? She drew a deep breath instead and searched for an alternative explanation for his be-haviour. Why would he think to ask permission? The answer was obvious: he'd never had to ask before. Gar-rett hadn't been here to oversee his activities. Garrett had in fact relied on this man to organise his day as he saw fit, building relationships for the chateau out in the community. She reached for the red and set aside her animosity.

He strode to the cupboard and retrieved another set of goblets. 'Now try the red you selected.' He poured her a small amount and she sipped with a grimace. Archambeau chuckled. 'See, it's too strong. If you want to serve a red wine with a chicken chowder, it's best to have a red with low tannins.'

'I think I prefer the white, after all,' Emma laughed and he poured her a full glass. She ladled the steaming soup into their bowls. He reached for the loaf of bread on the board and began to slice. A sense of calm domesticity permeated the kitchen as they worked, performing the simple tasks of dishing up dinner. It was a different atmosphere than the one that had imbued their supper in the dining room. This was a far friendlier setting. But she was aware that could change on a word, or a tone. *Play nice*, she reminded herself.

'This is good,' he complimented after a spoonful. 'It's very filling and the seasoning is well balanced.' His eyes twinkled. 'Which is unusual for English cooking. It's not known for its careful seasoning.'

He was teasing her, she thought, although there was some truth in it. 'How would you know about English cuisine?' She ventured a little teasing of her own as she tried to get to know this man her husband had hired to represent him.

He reached for a slice of bread and dipped it into the chowder. 'When I turned ten, my *grandpère* and my father agreed to send me to school in England. Trust me, English schoolboys have plenty of experience in unseasoned English cuisine,' he chuckled.

But Emma took the information thoughtfully, trying to imagine Julien Archambeau as a ten-year-old boy sent to England, so far from home. 'You must have been lonely.'

Julien shrugged. 'Not entirely. I had my *oncle*. He stayed on in England for several years after the Terror, after my *grandpère* and father came home. I lived with his family during the holidays, all except summer. There's no crossing the Channel in the winter.' He grinned. 'But summers, I came home.' She could tell from that grin how much coming home had pleased him.

She found the duality of his life intriguing. 'What did your *oncle* do in England?'

'My family has a small, regional, import-export business that is headquartered out of London.' He devoured the bread and took another slice.

There were a thousand questions to follow up that peek into his life but she had no chance. The next question was his. 'Why do you know how to cook? Surely Sir Garrett didn't expect you to do your own cooking?'

'My father was a great believer in a person understanding all the aspects of their lives, from finances to housekeeping and cooking. He taught me and my brothers how to manage money, and he insisted we all know how a big house ran.'

She paused here and sipped her wine as his dark brows went up.

'Yes.' She smiled at his unspoken query. 'Even my brothers learned how a household was run, even though they now have wives who handle that for them. As a result of my father's efforts, though, I am very good at accounting and my brothers understand how to plan a five-course dinner and seating chart for twenty.' She studied him for a moment, watching this register. He was having some difficulty grasping the idea. 'Is it too *bourgeoise* for you?' She was not teasing entirely. The French had strong ideas about classes crossing lines.

'You are a baronet's wife. These are not the skills of a noblewoman,' he said consideringly.

'I was not always.' She shrugged. 'My father was not a nobleman nor was he born to a fortune, although by the time I came along, he had acquired his wealth. But he believed it didn't matter how much money a man had. A man *or* woman still needed skills, still needed to understand all the pieces that made his or her lifestyle possible.' She nodded towards his empty bowl. 'More?'

'Yes, please.' The kitchen had darkened as the evening settled about them. He turned up the wick on the lamp as she refilled their bowls. 'Do you miss your family?'

'I do,' Emma confessed. 'But we write to one another and I would miss my freedom more. I don't think a married woman can ever comfortably return to her childhood home after having a house of her own to run. I would always be in my parents' shadow, always their baby. My mother doesn't need my help and my father especially is very protective of me, probably because I'm the youngest and a girl.' And because gin was a rough industry, socially, politically. Her father had valued her input even as he'd thought to shield her from the rougher aspects of his work.

She could see him think about that for a moment as he poured them another glass, white for her and red for him, each bottle more than half-empty. Goodness, had they drunk so much already? Or had they been at the meal that long? The candles were burning low. 'May I ask what line of work your father is in? I don't think Sir Garrett ever mentioned it.'

'Gin,' she offered smugly, waiting for his reaction. Would he cover his shock with a polite nod and a smile? Would he be outwardly horrified like the ladies and lords of the ton? For a moment she felt as if all her hopes of a new life untainted by her antecedents were held in the balance of his response. Perhaps she'd been wrong to think it could be different here, and yet she *did* hope. Gin wasn't a large French commodity but perhaps he'd lived in England long enough to know about gin and its dubious qualities.

'I know very little of gin.' He smiled over his glass. 'You said it like it's a bad thing, though.' His brow knitted. 'Is it, um, controversial?'

She gave a wry half smile. 'It's political. Gin is something of a social contradiction. It's risen in popularity as a drink among the upper classes and attained a certain level of distinction even as it remains the ruin of the lower classes, although it's nowhere near what it was a hundred years ago. Gin can be cheap, so all classes can afford it. Some employers even use it as part of paying wages, but again, not as often as before. There was a period of time when gin was effectively banned because it was so damaging to the public.' She shook her head, 'But not now. It's better controlled. England isn't selling gin in grocery stalls. Now there are gin palaces.'

He raised an eyebrow in speculation. 'Does *your* father own a gin palace?'

Perhaps this was where he'd become squeamish, and yet the French were notoriously more liberal about such things than the English. She offered her confession meeting him straight in the eye. 'Yes, several of them. Many distilleries do, it's a way to have a guaranteed outlet for the product. My father's are very high-end, though, almost exclusive, with crystal chandeliers and plush red velvet sofas, and polished walnut bars. They are frequented by the same gentlemen who refuse to acknowledge him in public.'

'And his family?' Julien put in.

'Yes, *and* his family. It made my debut tricky to say the least.'

He cocked his head to one side. 'I am trying to imagine you as a debutante, white gown, blue sash and all. Somehow, you seem too smart for that.'

'I was. But it made my disappointment sting no less.' She smiled. 'I shall take your words as a compliment. And now, I must confess, earlier I was trying to imagine *you* as a ten-year-old boy.'

He gave her a mischievous smile. 'Were you successful?'

'Somewhat.' She stared at her wine glass, twirling the stem a bit in her hand. This was nice, talking with him without tension, without wariness. But she needed to be careful. What was she doing, telling a stranger her story? She did not know him well enough, although in this moment she felt that she did. For all of his gruffness, he did have the talent of making someone feel as if they'd known each other far longer. It was the same talent he'd exercised at dinner last night. And they both knew how *that* had turned out.

That ought to be cautionary tale enough to curb her tongue. Who knew what he might do with tonight's information? He might ambush her with it later, or tell others and ruin her chances at a fresh start before she'd even begun. She chose caution and redirected the conversation. 'You know little about gin and I know very little about wine. I don't have your nose for it.' She nodded to the still half-full bottle of red she'd meant to drink with her soup.

'I just drink what someone else puts before me, *but*,' she gave a long pause to emphasise the *but*, 'I do know quite a bit about the marketing and selling of beverages, thanks to my father's business. I watched him take gin and elevate it. I think it would be quite similar to wine. And…' again, she gave another long pause for emphasis, giving him a chance to brace himself '… I want to learn. I want to know what you know. Not just which wines pair well with which foods, but why, and how to make a good wine, how to grow good grapes.' There was so much to know, she was nearly breathless with it.

'Whoa, slow down.' Archambeau held up a hand. 'I've worked with wine all my life. These are things not learned overnight or even in a few weeks, *madame*.'

'I have time,' she insisted. She would not give him a

chance to turn her down or ignore her. 'While you were gone, I got to know the house. Now that you're back, I want to know the vineyards.' She paused. 'That's why my husband hired you, isn't it? Because of your knowledge. Now it's your turn to teach me, to show me what you showed Garrett.'

Speculation moved in his eyes and the evening lost a bit of its pleasure. She almost regretted bringing the subject up. The moment to make her request had seemed perfect with the lamplight and their bellies filled with the comfort of warm food and good wine. But now she wondered if she'd rushed it. What was he thinking behind those blue eyes?

'All right,' he said at last. 'You may have your first lesson tomorrow. I walk the vineyards at six in the morning rain or shine. Dress warmly.' If that was a challenge, she was up for it.

Chapter Seven

She was waiting for him. That was a rarity in itself. Few people ever rose before him. But there she was, looking like a figure from a gothic novel, the dawn-grey vineyards a shadowy backdrop against her dark silhouette swathed in a black cloak, hood up to shield her hair from the morning mist. It leant her an air of intrigue, as if she needed any more of that. She already dominated too much of his thoughts as it was. She'd upended his world when she'd walked into the chateau.

He'd spent the last days trying to mitigate the effects of her presence on his carefully ordered plans only to come home and find her cooking corn chicken chowder and playing the housekeeper in her kerchief and serge. To a rather compelling effect, he admitted. Their meal together had been a striking departure from the tension-filled dinner. Last night's meal had almost been friendly right up until the part where she mentioned her desire to see the vineyards. It had been a reminder that she was closing in, like a relentless tide that crept up on the shore hour by hour, its arrival inevitable.

'*Bon matin*, Madame Luce,' he greeted. 'I am glad to see the early hour did not trouble you and that you've dressed accordingly.' She'd taken his advice in that at least. Beneath her cloak peeped the skirt of the blue serge she'd worn yesterday and sturdy half-boots that would hold up to the dirt of the vineyards. 'We will start here. This section closest to the chateau is where we grow the *pinot meunoir*.' He gestured to the nearest row of grapes and ushered her down the aisle lined with bare vines. 'There's not much to see but soon, though, these vines will sport tight buds, they'll flower in late April and May.' He launched into a treatise on the pruning process as he walked her up and down the rows, then explained the life cycle of the grape. To her credit, she offered no complaint or interruption. Julien stopped at one vine and took out his penknife, making a small nick.

'What are you looking for? Is everything all right?' They were the first words she'd uttered since he'd begun his monologue. Perhaps he *had* succeeded in overwhelming her. Perhaps his *oncle* was right—if she understood the enormity of the task she was undertaking she might rethink her goals. But even as he thought it, part of him rebelled at the idea—the part of him that didn't want her overwhelmed, the part of him that was remembering what it had been like to talk with her across the kitchen worktable while they ate soup and traded stories. In those moments they'd not been enemies.

She leaned forward towards the vine, towards him, the hood of her cloak falling back far enough to reveal the sable sheen of her hair. He caught a brief trace of her scent, the jasmine sambac and orange blossom he'd smelled on her the first night.

He folded the penknife and put it back in his pocket. 'I was looking for sap. It tells us when the grape will enter budburst.'

'And thus, alerting growers the season begins.' She flashed him a smile. 'See, I *was* listening. To *every* word you said, and there were a lot of them.' Her smile turned thoughtful. 'Is it bad there's no sap?'

Julien shook his head, wondering if he should be impressed or distressed by her attention. 'The vines cannot be rushed.' He looked up into the lightening sky. Perhaps there would be sun today. 'If the buds come too early, tricked by a false spring, a frost can kill or stunt them. A grower wants the buds to come when the weather is safe. They have no protection from the frost or the cold.'

'But they do from heat,' she said. 'The leaves offer shade in the summer.'

'Very good,' he complimented. What would Oncle Etienne make of that? Nothing good, he supposed. They wanted her uninterested, not lapping up everything he said. He'd have to try harder to bore her. A carriage pulled into view as they neared the end of the row. 'We'll drive the distance to the next section of vineyard where the chardonnay grapes are grown.' He helped her up and took the seat across from her, stretching out his legs. 'We grow three types of grapes here, the *pinot meunoir* you just saw, the chardonnay, and the *pinot noir*. They are the three grapes that can be used for the *vin mousseux*.' It was a perfect opportunity to launch into a dissertation on the quality of grapes.

She tossed him a smug smile and interrupted his train of thought. The sun *had* come out and she'd pushed her hood back, her face on full display to him, a sharp combination of beauty and intelligence. 'I cannot decide, Monsieur Archambeau, if you are trying to overwhelm me, bore me, or impress me with your extraordinary array of knowledge about vineyards.' Her smile turned smug. 'If your intention is the first or second, it won't work.'

'Most women would have been bored an hour ago.' Most women would not have got out of bed and dressed like a servant in order to tramp through the dirt to look at bare vines.

'I'm not most women, *monsieur*,' she said with all seriousness. Was that a warning? A reminder?

In hindsight, he should have seen it from the beginning. A traditional widow did not travel across the Channel mere weeks after the death of her spouse. A traditional widow did not attempt to take over a business she knew nothing about in a foreign country where her command of the language was no more than adequate. Neither did a woman of title and wealth dabble about in the kitchens making soup and eating at worktables. Yet she had done all these things. His usual attempts at warning off women by boring them to death would not work with her because she was *not* the usual woman. He'd have to try harder. Oncle Etienne would not approve of lacklustre efforts.

Julien crossed his booted legs at the ankles and

opted for a different tack. If one could not fight Madame Luce, one could always join her. 'And the latter? How is that going? Impressed yet?' Some part of him, the manly ego of him, wanted her to be impressed, wanted her to know what she was up against. He was good at what he did. He'd learned his craft well. In the Vallee de Marne, there was no one better when it came to growing and blending the wines.

'Fishing for a compliment, are we, Monsieur Archambeau?' She laughed and the carriage suddenly felt more like last night's dinner table than the sharp edge that had pierced the morning. Perhaps that was their pattern, to start each interaction wary, cautiously relearning one another before relaxing. 'At my peril, I will admit to being dazzled.'

'At your peril? Whatever can be dangerous about that admission?' He should not encourage this line of conversation. It was at his peril, too. An impressed Emma Luce would not be a disinterested party and that was the last thing he and his *oncle* needed.

'All that knowledge piques my curiosity. About you.'

That was *not* where he'd thought the conversation was going. He'd expected her to ask a question about the grapes, to lead him into another dissertation on viniculture. *That* he could handle. He could talk for hours about grapes and wine. Hadn't he proven that already? But he was not accustomed to talking about himself nor did he prefer it. Living alone had its perks in that regard. 'What about me?'

'A person does not come by such a vast compendium of knowledge without some effort. How is it that you

know so much about winemaking and vine-growing?'
She cocked her head and gave him a studious look. 'I
cannot make the pieces fit on my own. Last night you
told me you were schooled in England, a land not known
for its vineyards, I might add.'

'But I was born here, remember? I was raised in
Cumières until I was ten. My *grandpère* lived with us,
or maybe it was us who lived with him.' He offered
a small smile at his joke. 'Grandpère and my father
took me everywhere with them. Even as a small child,
I could not escape learning about the land, the vines.
I rode on my *grandpère*'s shoulders, listening to him
talk to my father. The grapes, the growing cycles, they
were as much a part of me as…' He couldn't quite sum-
mon an apt comparison. He couldn't ever remember
not knowing about budburst, or the rhythm of the year.

'As breathing?' she put in quietly. Up front in the
traces, the horse snuffled and whickered in the still-
ness that followed.

'As breathing,' Julien affirmed thoughtfully. It
sounded…right. It also sounded as if she understood
what that meant. 'You say that as if you know what it
means to be attached to something so deeply that it is
part of you.' If she was going to probe, he could probe,
too. He told himself he was asking because it would
help him understand her better, appeal to her better
when the time came, that his question had nothing to
do with him simply wanting to know, or because he
felt drawn to her in a way that had nothing to do with
her possession of his family's land.

She thought for a moment, her gaze dropping to her

hands, for once not piercing him, seeing through him, challenging him. Then she looked up. 'Numbers. I understand them intrinsically the way I understand how to breathe, how to walk. They make sense. They are constant and yet a source of creativity. They can tell me things. Numbers don't lie, they don't hide. They are always themselves.' He should have known then just how much danger he was in. She didn't just understand numbers. She *loved* them. Not unlike himself. He didn't simply understand the land—even Oncle Etienne, who'd spent his adult life in a shipping office, could lay claim knowing the land. No son of Matthieu Archambeau could escape such knowledge. But Oncle Etienne did not love it. To know something and to have a passion for it were not synonymous things. He should have asked her more about her numbers and redirected the conversation but he was not fast enough.

'The pieces still don't fit. Your family has a shipping business. That doesn't seem a place where one would come by agricultural knowledge.'

He needed to tread carefully here. He didn't want her putting too many pieces together. Neither did he want to offer a lie. 'I forget what short memories the English have,' he chuckled. 'During the Terror, my great-*grandpère*, Jean-Pierre, thought it best to protect the family interests. He sent his son's family to London to get them out of harm's way. His son, Matthieu, was an entrepreneurial sort.'

'*Your* grandfather,' she clarified, her grey eyes intent on him, giving the impression of hanging on his every word.

'Yes, my *grandpère*.' He smiled, part of him pleased she was so attentive, part of him worried about what other connections she might make and questions she might ask as a result. 'He knew we needed to find a way to support ourselves in England and he saw a need for shipping, particularly between France and Britain.'

Her eyes narrowed at this. 'While the two countries were at war?' He could see the realisation dawn. She was sharp, he'd give her that. 'By chance, was this "shipping" legal?'

'Well, not at first,' he admitted with a wry grin.

'Your *grandpère*...' she emphasised the French word '...came to England and became a smuggler. Do I have it right?'

He laughed because she was laughing. 'In Grandpère's defence, it was a mutually satisfying community service for all parties. The English had an insatiable desire for French wine despite their politics, and my great-*grandpère* knew several people with wine to sell lying idle in France. With the large legitimate British market gone, wine was languishing in cellars and warehouses thanks to the war. This arrangement satiated British need and kept food on the tables of many Frenchmen.'

'To say nothing of lining your grandfather's pockets.'

'*Bien sur*, it was lucrative enough to turn the Archambeaux legal once the Treaty of Amiens was signed. Now we are a small, respectable, legitimate shipping line, specialising in bringing French wines to British connoisseurs. Most of our shipping these days is done

through privately arranged contracts with rich men.'
The shipping line had been lucrative enough to even-
tually allow the Archambeaux, *sans* Oncle Etienne's
family, to return to France and start buying back land
slowly but surely, when that land became available.
'When it was safe to come back to France, my *grandpère* returned with my father, my mother, and baby me
in tow, leaving my *oncle* in Britain to handle the English end of things.'

That was all true as far as it went. There were pieces
he was leaving out; that the title of Comte du Rocroi
had been restored to the family—something that didn't
mean much given the title had been revoked again by
law four years ago. He'd left out, too, that his great-
grandpère had died, losing the chateau and all the lands
years before his *grandpère* had been allowed to safely
return with other nobles. His *grandpère* had never seen
his father again.

'Grandpère taught me about wine. He figured if I
was going to help with the shipping business, I ought
to know about the product we were exporting.' He gave
her a nod. 'Not unlike your father's rationale in teaching his sons and his daughter financial and household
management.' Still, not entirely false. Although Grandpère had imagined his grandson would be a *vigneron*
of his own grapes by the time he came of age.

The carriage halted at their next destination, fore-
stalling any more of her questions. He came around and
helped her down. 'Let me dazzle you some more, *madame*, with these chardonnay grapes. They're used to
make a *blanc de blanc*. It's a somewhat new blending

and a somewhat new grape for us, but I think the result is divine, it's light and it sparkles. There's a feminine *elan* to it that I think would appeal to women. Rich women, obviously. This could be a wealthy woman's equivalent to her husband's brandy.'

She slanted him a look, her silvery gaze interested. 'Why, Monsieur Archambeau, now you *have* impressed me.' This was followed by a genuine smile that stopped him in his tracks. 'This is the first time I've heard you talk like a businessman and not only a farmer. You have depth, *monsieur.*'

'Does that surprise you?' He slid her a brief, wry smile, feeling quite satisfied with himself because he had pleased her. It was a dangerous feeling.

'It does, most pleasingly,' she answered with a smile of her own, and Julien thought how pleasant it was to be with her like this, without sparring, without competing, without each of them trying to prove themselves. Of course, the sparring and competition *were* necessary. It was how he remembered they were indeed at odds with one another, their wants mutually exclusive. She wanted to run a vineyard he could absolutely not let her get her hands on.

And yet taking a break from being *en garde* was refreshing, enjoyable. It led to interesting thoughts—all purely hypothetical—like, what if they didn't have to be set against one another? What if they didn't have to compete? An idea began to root in his mind. What if there was a way to bring her alongside, to make her feel that she was taking control without really allowing her to do so in a way that undermined his own position?

What if they could be a team? It would be a chance to show her how much she needed him, how indispensable he was to her.

'Are you hungry? I'm famished. I've taken the liberty of packing a picnic breakfast for us.' Perhaps there was a better strategy than any of those posited by his *oncle*. If he and Madame Luce were allies instead of enemies, co-operators instead of competitors, perhaps she would relinquish the lands easily and with the understanding that it was in the land's best interest, because it made *sense*. Because he was born to this life and she wasn't.

Wasn't she? His conscience was an unwelcome intrusion on this sunny morning. *She's been a willing pupil while you prosed on trying to purposely bore her. She is trying to learn.*

And what was he trying to do? For all of his thoughts about bringing her alongside, guilt poked hard at him as he led her back to the carriage. Was he doing this for her benefit or his? What was his motive? Was he trying to steal her inheritance or secure his?

Chapter Eight

Emma stole a look at Archambeau setting out the plates of raspberry jam–filled tartines, her mouth starting to water at the sight of food. Breakfast picnics were something she could get used to, as were the feelings they engendered in her. This morning had turned out to be quite enjoyable. The realisation took her by not entirely pleasant surprise.

Guilt tugged at her. She *was* a having a good time. But should she be? Her husband had been dead a month and here she was laughing, enjoying an outing in the company of another man and thinking she could get used to breakfast picnics. It felt like a betrayal.

Emma settled on the old quilt spread on the ground and cupped her hands around a mug of hot coffee, willing the warmth to ward off the guilt as effectively as it warded off the chill of the morning, but the guilt stayed. What did it mean about her love for Garrett if she found enjoyment so easily, so quickly in the company of another? And yet, to not enjoy the company of another meant to remain alone. Surely Garrett would not want that for her.

'It's not very elegant.' Archambeau gave a self-deprecating shrug as he set out a tray of tartines. 'A farmer's quick meal, nothing more.'

'It's perfect,' she assured him, aware that this fragile peace between them must be handled delicately, explored carefully, encouraged cautiously. He was different out here in the vineyard, not a dour workman doing his chores, but a man who loved the land, whose passion shone through in the transformation of his face when he spoke; it transformed his tone, and it lowered his guard. Once he'd started talking about the grapes she'd had the impression that she was seeing the real man, that the workman and the gentleman at the dinner table were lesser representations of the man who sat across from her on the blanket.

It was that man who offered her the tray of tartines as he gave her a brief overview of the land's history. 'The Romans were growing grapes here long before we were and, the climate willing, grapes will be growing here long after I'm gone.' This, she thought, was the man she'd envisioned behind the thorough reports sent across the Channel. He merely looked different than the image in her mind. He looked *better*. How had she ever thought he ought to be a slender, bookish sort?

He flashed her an uncustomary smile and for an instant her thoughts were arrested by that look. In that moment, he might have been one of his Gallic ancestors walking his land centuries ago. The morning sun slanted through the sky illumining his features, the strong bones of his jaw, the curve of his cheek which softened him when he smiled, as he was now, and lit the slate blue of his gaze so that it matched the newly emergent sky. But it was the sentiment of his words that truly touched her, this idea of a legacy, of building something larger than himself.

Like Garrett.

Everything Garrett did had been motivated by thoughts for his family and what it might become.

'Is something on your mind? You're staring.' Archambeau shifted his position on the blanket, stretching out to his full length, the movement unintentionally making her aware of his maleness.

Guilt pricked again, scolding her: *How dare you be so aware of a man so soon after Garrett's death.*

She pushed the reprimand away. He was barely a foot away from her. Of course she noticed him. How could she not? It was entirely natural. It meant nothing and yet the warm heat in her blood didn't seem to agree.

'You reminded me of Garrett, just then, the way you spoke of a legacy. He always looked to the future. Even his title, which he received later in his life, was not something he thought of for himself, but for his family. He saw it as something that would be handed down generation to generation, something he'd earned.' She cocked her head, thoughtful. 'I think that was why he was so proud of it. He'd earned it. It hadn't been given to him simply because he'd been born into the right family.' She paused, a thought coming to her. The next moment she felt Archambeau's hand on hers, his gaze soft. It was a gesture of concern only, but it was also pleasant, too, in its own right, warm and comforting. Then, she understood. He thought that speaking of Garrett had made her sad.

'I'm fine.' She offered a smile as assurance. 'I just realised that talking of Garrett made me happy.' She was still processing the idea for herself. 'I think this is the first time since his death that I've shared something voluntarily and I didn't break down in tears.' It was the first time sharing about Garrett had actually felt *good*. She pondered that for a moment, staring down at her half-eaten tartine, her words coming slowly, deliberately. 'In the beginning, when it was all new, people would ask about how he died.' She looked up at Archambeau. 'No one wanted to know how he lived.'

'I'm guilty of that, too.' Archambeau gave a dry laugh. 'Even me, I asked you what happened. I'm sorry.' He squeezed her hand and then retreated, taking his hand, his touch away.

'Don't be. It's natural to want to know. It's just difficult to recount.' She absolved him with another smile. She felt the smile falter with confession. 'The truth is, I don't like to think of Garrett's last moments, much less talk about them.' She paused and slid him a considering look. 'Do you suppose that's wrong of me? I wonder if it's selfish to want to push them aside because they are too painful to consider?'

'Perhaps pushing them aside isn't so much a part of ignoring the pain as it is creating an opportunity for healing,' he offered gently, 'One can't heal if they insist on reopening the wound.'

'Perhaps,' she replied noncommittally. It was a nice
sentiment, an insightful one, even. But she was too
conflicted to believe it entirely. In the dark of night
when her demons were at their best inside her head,
she thought she didn't like to think about those moments because they reminded her that she'd chosen
selfishly that night to stay behind and play cards, and
she'd been rewarded—and punished—for her selfish-
ness. She'd survived.

She pleated the corner of the blanket between her
fingers. 'The coroner in Holmfirth told me most of the
victims died with looks of confusion on their faces, as
if they didn't have time to understand what was happening. That was supposed to make me feel better, I
guess, this idea that there was no time for pain, for fear.
I did not think Garrett looked like that.' She stopped
and hazarded a look in Archambeau's direction, suddenly horrified. 'That is too morbid for conversation.
I don't know why I said that. I am the one who must
apologise now.' Whatever had come over her to make
her share such a thing? She'd not discussed that with
anyone, not even her family.

'Not at all. You loved your husband and he loved
you. He spoke of you glowingly during his visits. You
were lucky to have such a marriage, Madame Luce.'
His gaze turned inward for a long moment. She sensed
his thoughts had moved away from her, towards another
time, perhaps another person, another place. She felt
her body lean forward in a desire to go to that place
with him, to know what thoughts were taking place behind those eyes, craving whatever he might say next.

'I think we must talk about the things we love. Words are to memories as air is to our lungs. Without it we die. Without words, our memories die. The moment we stop talking about them, we surrender them.' He gave one of his self-deprecating smiles. 'Now I am the one who has said too much. I am being fanciful, *madame*. You must pardon me.'

She was still for a moment, taking in his words, taking in the revelation that the rustic farmer-cum-gentleman was also a poet, a philosopher, yet one more side to this enigmatic man. 'No.' She gave him a slow, deliberate smile. 'I do not think I shall pardon you. No offence has been given. In fact, I rather like the idea that words are the breath of dreams. And you are right. Garrett was my dream, although at the time I may not have realised it.' She held out her coffee mug and Archambeau refilled it.

'Tell me, how did the two of you meet?' He set aside his own mug and stretched out along the far side of the quilt, the action drawing her eyes once more to the length of him, the largeness of him. 'Well?' he encouraged, tucking his hands behind his head and giving every sign of a man settling for the duration.

'It's a rather boring story,' she warned, offering him one last chance to opt out, but his blue eyes fixed on her, inviting her to tell him.

He gave a wry smile. 'More boring than a lecture on the growth cycle of grapes? After this morning, I think you owe me a boring story or two to even the scales.'

Julien Archambeau was dangerously charming like this, all smiles and dry humour. The odd thought flitted through her mind: How many other women had spilled their tales to him after such a look? Was there such a woman in his life at present? Not that it mattered. She cleared her throat and gathered her thoughts. 'We met at a political supper in London during the Season. My father was hoping to speak with an MP about some legislation that would affect tariffs on gin. It was all a matter of chance. I was seated next to Garrett. We began talking and the more we talked, the more I felt seen—*truly* seen—by him.'

She smiled, remembering how easy even those early conversations had been. 'Until I met Garrett, men treated me one of two ways: as an heiress they would tolerate and elevate in exchange for my father's money, or as someone they wouldn't even look at, who was tainted because of her father's industry; and the women were worse. Suffice it to say, the girls who came out with me were not particularly friendly.' Even years later, those memories were hard ones to suffer.

'Tell me about it?' Julien asked. 'I can hardly believe a few girls would set you back.'

'Well, not the person I am now. But back then I was bit more naïve than I knew.' She shook her head. 'I really don't want to talk about it. I was foolish and they took advantage of that.' She cringed at the memory.

Julien smiled encouragingly. 'That's all the more reason to tell me then. Does it help to know that once I gave all my allowance at school to keep the upperclassmen from beating me up? English schoolboys don't like French schoolboys, it turns out. It took me a while to learn that paying them only incentivised them to ask for more money, not to stop. The only thing that made them stop was a solid fist to the face.'

'I am sorry you were bullied,' she said sincerely. 'My bully was a viscount's daughter named Amelia St James. I couldn't punch her or pay her but I could spill wine on her dress.'

Julien laughed. 'Now you *have* to tell me.'

She settled on the blanket. 'It all started over the Earl of Redmond, the most eligible catch of the Season. Amelia wanted him and he wanted me, at least that's what I thought. He danced with me every evening, sent flowers every day. I was nineteen and quite swept off my feet. He was handsome and dashing. Then one day, he went further. He took me out driving in his curricle in Hyde Park at peak time. Everyone saw us. It made Amelia into something of a laughingstock. Everyone knew she'd set her cap for him. She couldn't ignore that I held his interest now that he'd driven out with me. She couldn't live with it either. She'd refused two other marriage proposals while she waited for him. She'd go home unwed at the end of the Season at this rate. So, she used the weapons she had. That night, she told anyone and everyone the only reason Redmond was interested was the size of my father's pocketbook.'

'That's awful,' Julien commiserated.

'It was awful but it was also true.' That was the worst part. She should have been more aware. 'My father had made no secret that he meant to have a title for me and he would buy it. I just hadn't believed it. I truly thought Redmond liked me for me. I believed it right up until the moment I confronted him. I asked him to his face if it was true and he could not deny it.'

Julien was quiet for a moment. 'You lost more than a suitor that night.'

She nodded. 'Yes, I'd been betrayed by girls who had acted like my friends, who I'd confided in. Amelia knew how much I thought I'd cared for Redmond. She knew my hopes. In my naïveté I thought I loved Redmond and she dashed those hopes anyway. What sort of friend does that? But she was no friend at all, and she never had been. Neither was Redmond. The whole world I thought I knew was a fiction.'

'But then you found Garrett,' Julien prompted. 'Surely that made up for it?'

Emma smiled. That was how she'd explained it to herself as well, that Amelia's betrayal had been worth it to find real love with a man who *saw* her. 'Garrett and I had that in common. Like my father, he was a self-made man with a fortune, a man other men had to respect because he had money and with that money he'd acquired influence. He understood my experiences because they were his experiences, too.' She smiled. 'For once, I had an ally. He called on me the next day, bringing a beautiful bouquet of spring flowers. By the end of the week, I was falling for him, improbable suitor that he was.' Emma laughed. Now that she'd started talking, she couldn't seem to stop. 'I never thought I'd fall for a man just slightly younger than my father, a man who'd already raised a family. But he didn't seem old, he never seemed old.'

'And now he never will,' Archambeau put in and she nodded.

'I've thought of that.' She offered the confession slowly. It was a somewhat risky idea to voice out loud. 'He died still very much in his prime. Neither he nor I will have to witness the slow deterioration of age stealing him from me. Maybe I am lucky in that regard. I will always be able to remember the best of him.' It wasn't enough to wish him dead, but there was consolation.

Archambeau nodded solemnly. 'My *grandpère* lived into his eighties. Most of his years were good ones. Despite his trials, he was blessed with health, but towards the end he could not do the things he loved in the way he preferred. His world seemed to shrink to the point where his dreams became obsessions. He was not quite the man I remembered growing up with. It was difficult on all of us, especially my father.'

'You were close with your grandfather. I envy you that. I never knew mine on either side. My mother's family cut her off when she married my father and my father had no family to speak of. It was always just us.'

Archambeau gave her a considering look. 'That must have been a lonely way to grow up. My family was always together; my great-*grandpère*, my *grandpère*, my *père*, my *oncle*, my cousin, we were always living with one another in some combination or other.'

'What wondrous chaos that must have been,' Emma laughed and then sobered, remembering other things he'd shared. 'How lonely it must be for you now with them gone.' Perhaps it was harder for him. She couldn't truly miss what she'd never had. She furrowed her brow trying to remember. 'Your *oncle*, is he still in England?' She could not recall what he'd said about that, only that his *oncle* had been in England during his school years.

Archambeau shifted. For comfort? Or because her question made him uneasy? 'My *oncle* is here. He returned in 1845 after my *grandpère* and my father died. My cousin and my *tante* stayed in England to look after that end of the shipping business.'

She nodded, unsure what to say. There was great sadness in those few sentences. 1845 had been a dark year for the Archambeaux. The death of the family patriarch *and* his son in quick succession. More importantly, the death of two men Julien had loved dearly.

We talk about the things we love.

She had not missed the affection that had accompanied his mentions of his *grandpère* and his father. Upheaval had no doubt followed as the family reorganised itself to fill in the gaps left by those deaths. She thought of the family left behind in order for his *oncle* to return. Had that been a sacrifice on his *oncle*'s part? She settled on, 'I'm glad you have your *oncle* at least, Monsieur Archambeau.'

'Julien.' The single word was a gunshot fired into the silence of the morning. 'Perhaps you might consider calling me Julien? Monsieur Archambeau seems so formal at this juncture.'

'Then you must call me Emma,' she replied, trying to understand what his request might mean. She might take it to mean a hundred things. Had he asked because they'd spent a morning together discussing business and pleasure? Because they'd shared stories about those they loved and those stories had left them revealed? Or because they were becoming friends? Did she dare allow that? Friendship would be complicated. Friendship between men and women always was. Friendship between a new widow and a man involved in her business enterprise would be doubly so.

Admittedly, she found herself liking the idea of befriending Julien Archambeau. Far better to have him as a friend than an enemy, especially if they were sharing a roof and a vineyard.

The voice in her head spoke sharply. *Not really sharing. All this is yours. Perhaps he'd like you to forget that. You've not yet fully discovered his role here.*

No, she hadn't. Somehow that kept getting postponed, put off in favour of other things, like walking the vineyard and learning about the grapes.

I need him for that, she told the voice in her head. *I know what I am doing. I must learn the business from him. I'd be a fool to let him go before then.*

Is that what you're doing on the picnic blanket, ogling his legs and swapping stories with your husband only gone a month? Learning the business, is it? The voice in her head was showing no mercy today.

What else would it be? came her rejoinder.

It could be *nothing* else because if it was something else, what did that say about her love for Garrett? It was not the first time she'd reminded herself of that. But it was a troublesome rejoinder because her head refused to treat it as a rhetorical question and let her be. Her mind had answers: it was a friendship that was doomed on all fronts. Men and women couldn't be friends. That wasn't how the world worked. If they liked each other enough to be friends, they were inevitably attracted to each for more than conversation. Secondly, it was a paramount rule in business not to mix the two. At least in England. Perhaps the French felt differently. Her father did not. He'd always preached that friends made the worst business partners, and her father was always right.

'I've enjoyed our picnic, but there is more to see,' Emma began, trying to put the original point of the morning back on track. 'Grapes are only one part of the process. I am eager to see the cellars. I believe they are in caves beneath the house?'

Julien gave her a curt nod, his soft gaze returning to its usual flinty hardness. 'Absolutely. I'd be happy to show you. It will take just a moment for us to be under way.' Within minutes the quilt had been folded up and the hamper stashed beneath the seats of the carriage. All signs of their picnic erased as if they'd never lounged beneath the morning sun, sipping coffee and talking of their families.

If only the consequences of those precious hours could be erased as easily. It was the one idea that floated at the forefront of her thoughts throughout the short carriage ride back to the chateau, all of them coalescing around a single word.

Julien.

He'd asked her to call him Julien. That was one inerasable consequence of the morning picnic. With that single request, objectivity had been stripped away and it could not be restored. She could not unsee the way his face lit when he spoke of the land, of his family. She could not forget the sight of him, long legs outstretched, hands behind his head as he lounged in unabashedly male repose on the quilt, his body open to her study, perhaps entirely unaware of the effect it had on her and the guilt that followed.

In the span of a morning, he'd become a man she did not want to argue against or butt heads with. She did not want to compete for control of the vineyards. She wanted to work with this man, learn from him, but without the risk of ceding control. Was such cooperation possible? Would he be able to see her as an equal? More to the point, even if it was possible, was it something he'd want, too?

The voice in her head was quick to scold, to warn. *Slow down.* But what was there to slow down about? Garrett had trusted Julien for seven years, had left him in charge of what would become her inheritance, her last gift from Garrett. He would not have risked that. If Garrett could trust Julien, by extension, so could she. She was *not* racing towards any impetuous business decisions.

In many ways, these were decisions that had already been put in place. She and Julien just needed to accept them. The more she thought about it, the more she believed Garrett meant for them to work together in some way when the time came. He'd just not planned on it being so soon. Perhaps, if there'd been more time, Garrett would have even forged the link, the expectation between them as the years passed. Garrett meant for Julien to help her. She and Julien just had to see that for themselves, help themselves find their way back to the path Garrett wanted. They'd got off to a poor start, each one more interested in defending themselves than looking at the larger picture. By the time they reached the wine caves beneath the chateau, she was sure of it. Now she just needed him to be sure of it as well.

Chapter Nine

Julien was sure of nothing as he heaved open the heavy oak doors that led to the cellars. He should have postponed the visit to the cellars even if it required making up an excuse, but he'd been loath to part company with Emma, loath to see the picnic end for reasons he was not comfortable explaining to himself. He did not want to like her, but he did. He did not want to empathise with her, but he did. He did not want to be impressed by her, but he was. He'd not wanted to discover anything in common with her, but he had.

That had been the most dangerous of all, sitting on the picnic blanket and listening to her talk about her family, how her father was a man of self-made fortune, who'd raised his children to be self-sufficient, to be tenacious in their independence, to stand up for themselves in a world that would not appreciate their ambition because of their trade or, in her case, her gender. 'Please, be careful on the steps,' Julien instructed, his free hand dropping too easily, too naturally, to the small of her back as he ushered her carefully to the centuries-old staircase.

He held the lantern up, lighting the way. This close, he could smell the scent of her jasmine sambac mixed with the earthy outdoors of the vineyards. It was a sweet torture, letting himself be overwhelmed with the feminine details of her. Was there anything more intoxicating than the scent of a woman? Especially after having been deprived of female company for a spell.

Deprivation was his fault, his own self-imposed choice. He had little to offer a woman these days emotionally or financially. If he was tortured, this was what he got for being alone, for being without a woman for so long. He'd let himself be drawn in by her stories, and now he was paying for his lapse. This was what happened when one let a beautiful woman work her wiles and a man let his imagination run away with him.

The voice in his head teased him. *But you liked her words as much as her scent, you liked the idea that her father had built his business with his own efforts, that she wants to do the same here, that she wants to learn.*

He could admire all of that in theory, even if he could not allow it to occur in practice.

Not without some heavy oversight and guidance.

That was temptation whispering now, trying to carve out a middle ground between what she wanted and what he needed.

Don't be a fool. What he ought to want was for her to remain a nuisance, a disruption to be dismissed and managed. But Emma Luce countered him at every turn. When he attempted to overwhelm her, she became inquisitive. When he attempted to bore her, she became interested. When he attempted to impress her, to awe her, she merely took it in stride as a matter of course.

It was he who had been impressed—impressed by the fortitude of a woman who'd not let herself be beaten down by the pressure of her peers. She'd been relentless today, drawing him out, asking for his stories. When he wanted to give her less, she asked for more, *and* he'd complied, talking about his family, recounting his family history, and she had hung on every word as if they were the most interesting things she'd ever heard.

They reached the bottom of the stairs and the space widened out into a large cavern. 'Stay here while I light a few more lanterns.' He moved around the cave, letting the woodsy smell of oak barrels bring him balance, perspective. Now was not the time to be swayed by a pretty face and an attractive mind. He needed to stay focused on what mattered: his land and family. Whatever feelings or reactions Emma Luce was stirring in him wouldn't last. She was novel, something new in a life that was small and narrow.

'It's enormous!' Her voice, so near, startled him.

He turned to find her standing behind him, her eyes alight with wonder as she took in the cavern. 'I thought I told you to stay put until the lights were lit.' In his shock, his words came out more sternly than intended. 'Do you want to trip and fall? These flagstones are centuries old; I can't account for how even they are.'

'I can see just fine.' She laughed off his concern, her eyes still roving about the space, taking in the shelves loaded with casks and the freestanding triangular stands holding individual bottles. 'It just keeps going and going.'

'The place isn't even full.' Julien couldn't help but show off a bit. 'It could hold eighteen hundred barrels and two hundred thousand bottles if we were at full tilt on production.'

A wide smile took her face and she spun in a slow circle. 'I will see to it that we are. I know my husband didn't focus his complete attention on the chateau, but I mean to change that. I mean to make this place into something grand. Everyone will be wanting wines from Les Deux Coeurs when I'm done with things.'

Behind her grey eyes, Julien could see her dreams were already running miles ahead of reality and it awoke an echoing thrill in him—wasn't that what he also wanted for the chateau? But those dreams also chilled him in their naïveté. It wasn't as simple as she thought. Her dreams had consequences for them both. He could not let those dreams supersede his own. More than that, he could not let her claim them.

'You've only seen the main room.' Julien gestured to an arched doorway. 'This leads down to another subterranean cellar, where the *vin mousseux* is stored.' This cavern was smaller, the three walls lined with casks.

'This place is more isolated, or is *insulated* the word I'm looking for?'

'It's just smaller.' Julien hung the lantern on a peg. 'Both this room and the grand cavern are devoid of an echo because they're so far underground.'

'How far underground?' She began a slow perambulation of the room, stopping to read the labels on the casks.

'Forty feet, not nearly as deep as Taittinger's, but deep enough,' Julien said, citing one of the other champagne houses in the area.

She stopped and faced him for a moment. 'So, everyone has wine caves?'

'Yes.' He leaned against the tall worktable set in the middle of the room, watching her continue her stroll, noting the trail of her fingertips over the oak casks, her touch slow and deliberate, a reflection of her thoughts. He'd give a small fortune to know those thoughts, to know what he was up against. 'Wine caves are a rather serendipitous occurrence.'

He was showing off now, perhaps trying to win back her attention, to see her hang on his every word as she had on the picnic blanket. 'The Romans originally dug these caves as chalk and salt mines around 80 BC. Turns out, they're perfect for storing wine.'

'Are you saying everyone stores their wine like this?' she queried, throwing him a glance over her shoulder.

'Yes. Even Reims town houses have such cellars in their basements. Those who don't naturally have access to such storage build them. Chateaux like this one, though, have been using the Roman cellars for a few centuries now.'

She paused. 'So, you're telling me that people who don't have homes built over old Roman ruins actually replicate them?'

'Yes, and why not? At these depths, the temperatures are cool enough to properly store wine while it ages.

Also, at these depths, we can protect against humidity and invasive sunlight. There is no chance of *gout de lumière* wrecking these bottles.' When she furrowed her brow he translated. 'We call it the "taste of light" or the "light strike",' he explained. 'Any exposure to light can cause it.'

She laughed and he paused, unsure what was so humorous. 'What is it? Is light strike funny?'

'No, it's you, or mainly me. I was wrong about you this morning when I said you either wanted to overwhelm me or bore me.'

'Or impress you,' he reminded her.

'Yes, that too. But it's none of those. You simply can't help it, can you? This pouring out of knowledge. Is there anything you don't know about wine?'

'There's probably very little.'

'And humble, too.' She laughed at his arrogance and he laughed, too, and for a moment they were at ease again, as they had been on the picnic blanket.

'Is my husband's special vintage in here?' She bent down to peer at casks stored on a lower shelf. 'This was the year he was going to reveal it.'

'It's not in a cask. It's bottled, over here.' Julien pushed off the table. 'I'll show you.' That was just the metaphoric bucket of cold water he needed to come to his senses. He was fantasising over a woman who'd recently lost a man she'd loved, a woman who was emotionally and professionally off-limits to him. He'd told his *oncle* as much. So, what the hell was wrong with him? That was a rhetorical question. He didn't need to answer it to know. Oncle Etienne would be disappointed in him. He'd set out to overwhelm her and he'd ended up being the one overwhelmed.

Marry her and claim it all in one fell swoop.

Oncle Etienne's words tempted. What a temptation it was—to marry her and share this life with her, to have the partnership he'd once hoped to find with Clarisse, to experience the partnership Garrett Luce had claimed with her. Perhaps she need never know the motivation, the deception…

Julien stopped his thoughts right there. That was how his *oncle* thought, not him. Shortcuts and easy solutions were dangerous. Such thoughts did his own principles no service and they did Emma even less. She was a smart woman. She would find out. And it would hurt her. He'd heard the undertones of vulnerability on the picnic blanket and in the kitchen when she'd spoken of her past, of how she'd been treated by Society. It had made her tough, but at a cost. He would not be the reason she opened those wounds again. Nor would he be the maker of his own woes, the opener of his own old wounds. She wouldn't be the only one who was hurt. He would not knowingly set himself up for such disappointment.

He joined her at the wooden rack showing her the casks, all neatly lined on the racks that ran the length of the wall each vertical rack twenty bottles high, stretching to the ceiling. 'There are—'

'Two thousand bottles,' she breathed, finishing his sentence, impressing him with the speed of her calculations and their accuracy. 'I'm surprised they're already in bottles.'

'Already? There's no "already" about it. Champagne takes time. It must "rest" at least fifteen months at this point,' he explained patiently. 'This batch started its journey seven years ago. It came from the harvest that fall. It went through fermentation and spent three years in a barrel, it was blended carefully with grapes only from that same year.' He'd insisted on it. Sir Garrett hadn't known better, but Julien did. If this was going to be a special bottling to commemorate an important event, it was going to be done right. 'It's been through second fermentation, through riddling, and now it is finishing its ageing process right on time.'

She trailed her fingers over the bottles. 'Gin is much less complicated. It takes two weeks to make a decent batch of gin. Gin lasts whether it's in an open bottle or not. An open bottle of gin might last a year or more without losing its flavour or potency. Champagne is decidedly more…delicate, more fragile.' She gave a sigh. 'Which makes it a double shame that all these bottles have been bottled for naught.'

Julien cleared his throat and took the plunge. What better way to get his thoughts back on track than to discuss a little business. 'The champagne was meant to be served to guests on the occasion of your seven-year anniversary this year. I believe your husband intended to have most of this shipped back to England after your visit this summer.'

She nodded, her face solemn, and he felt like a cad for bringing up such delicate reminders of her loss. 'Yes, we were going to have a big party at Oakwood.

Garrett had been looking forward to serving this and making party gifts of it for guests.'

'We can still celebrate, if you felt up to it,' Julien began tentatively. He wouldn't push her into doing anything she wasn't ready to do, neither would he allow Oncle Etienne to push her. But he would make the offer and see what happened. There was no harm in that, and in fact there might be a lot of good, he justified. 'We could host an event here at the chateau in June and unveil it as a tribute to him, as a way to celebrate his life.'

It would also be the perfect opportunity for unveiling other vintages, like the one he and his *oncle* were counting on, his new champagne blend. 'If we did it quietly, discreetly, no one would complain. It would be a commemorative beverage put out by the chateau on your behalf.' He paused to let her think before adding, 'You needn't even be at the unveiling if you felt it was too public and too soon.' He was counting on that reasoning having some sway with her. He needed her to keep a low profile at least until after the harvest, solidifying this year's sales with the buyers, which, if received well, would go a long way in smoothing concerns about what was happening at the chateau in regard to any potential change in leadership and the debut of the new vintages. There was no time like the present to have her start thinking about how a widow behaved. Circumspection on her part, would definitely help things on his.

'I love the idea, but I'd want to be there,' she said, her quicksilver eyes coming alive. 'It would be a chance for me to meet the growers' consortium and other im-

portant figures in the local industry.' She brightened at
the prospect of an event. 'Planning an event would be
a good project for me.'

They could agree on that at least. If she was busy
planning an event, she'd have less time and less interest in wanting to see the ledgers, where certain truths
would quickly become self-evident to her. Once they
did, she might be less interested in…him. Unless she
was already on his side. If she thought this event was
her idea, which she would if she was in charge of it, she
might be less likely to feel undermined. *If* they were on
the same side by the time everything was revealed. It
wasn't entirely honest of him, but it was honest enough.
For now.

*Once everything is settled, once the land is safe, I'll
tell her everything*, he vowed.

Until then, it had to be this way. This was perhaps
the best reason of them all he had to curb his fantasies
about the Widow Luce.

He did not see her again until after supper that night,
and that was by accident. He'd not intended to see her
again. He had, in fact, intended to give himself some
distance from her and the potency of their day spent
together. He'd fabricated an excuse to skip dinner and
took a tray in his offices, sending word that he had
correspondence to catch up on after a day in the field.
He'd been careful not to imply that falling behind was
somehow her fault for having put demands on his time,
though, while re-establishing an appropriate business-
like distance between them. It would be a good re-

minder for both of them. Friendly was good; he did need her on his side. But *too* friendly was not and that was what they'd been today, conversing over their families and building empathy.

Despite his best intentions, the fates were against him the moment he walked into the library and saw her sitting before the fire, a glass of brandy at her elbow, a book in her lap, her dark head bent in avid interest as her elegant fingers—fingers he'd spent too much time watching today—turned the pages. She was reading fast and intently.

The soft closing of the door gave him away and she looked up in his direction. 'I am educating myself,' she announced rather happily, holding up the book. 'Chaptal's *Treatise on the Culture of the Vine and the Art of Making Wine*,' she read the rather elaborate title. 'He's got it down, quite literally, to a science. There's even an equation about the relationship between sugar, alcohol, and fermentation.' She smiled, obviously pleased with herself. 'Pretty soon, I'll know as much as you.'

'Science.' He frowned, finding the word displeasing, and strode to the shelves. 'That's the problem with Chaptal. He thinks anyone can make wine if they know the recipe. It takes more than just mixing ingredients. There's a certain *je ne sais quoi* to winemaking that he overlooks.' Julien pulled several tomes from the shelf. 'If you want to read about wines and grapes, read Godinot's *Manner of Cultivating the Vine*, Bidet's *Treatise on the Nature and Culture of the Vine*, perhaps a little of Diderot's encyclopaedia, or the work of your pioneering countryman Christopher Merret.' He piled the teetering pile of books on the side table next to her brandy. That brandy was a subtle reminder that Emma Luce was not a traditional woman.

'I've never met a woman who likes her brandy.'

She grinned and took a swallow. 'That's because you'd never met me.' Her gaze rested on him and softened from her teasing. 'Did you get your letters written?'

His letters? Oh, yes. His little lie to avoid dining together. 'I did, thank you.' He needed to remove himself from the room before he found he was sitting down with his own glass of brandy and engaging in a conversation that might go any direction, all of them dangerous. 'It's been a long day and I want to be up early, if you'll excuse me.'

'Of course.' Did he detect some disappointment in that? Had she wanted him to stay? All the more reason to get out while he had his wits intact. She gestured to the book pile. 'I will read the books. Thank you for the recommendations.'

He left her with a short bow but at the door her voice called him back. 'Julien, thank you for today.' It was softly said, seriously said. He did not doubt she meant it and he wasn't sure he could let such sentiment stand in its entirety for fear it might irrevocably change the balance of their association.

He gave a nonchalant wave to the stack of books and a wry grin. 'You might want to delay your thanks until you're through the reading pile. You might not thank me then.'

Chapter Ten

Emma was thankful for the days that followed. She'd never known days like these. Days that were entirely her own to do with as she liked, to spend as she pleased. And it pleased her to spend them with the books Julien had suggested. The weather cooperated, turning March into a damp, rain-soaked month that was best passed indoors in a comfortable chair pulled near the fire.

Her days took on a rhythm of their own; mornings she would take tea and breakfast in the library, her nose buried in the texts as she busily filled notebooks with information, writing questions lining the margins to ask Julien at dinner. For every one thing she learned, it sparked something new to ask. In the afternoons, she went walking. She visited the cellars, studying the inventory, learning the names and amounts of the wines that made up the chateau's catalogue. She planned the June event, making lists of supplies and jotting down ideas for decorations. Her days were full, but her industriousness was self-assigned. She did what she wanted when it pleased her.

It was one luxury she could not lay claim to during her marriage to Garrett. They were always on the move, always going somewhere to meet someone, to make a deal or close a deal. To inspect a factory or to meet with a banker. She'd liked being included in his projects. Inclusion had led to consultation, and she'd been flattered to be asked for advice, which was often taken. That was flattering, too, to know that she had her husband's respect and his trust.

But she saw now how her time had not been her own. It had been the price of being absorbed entirely into Garrett's life. She'd liked their life, but she was liking this new life of hers, too. She had a chance to discover who *she* was, and who she was becoming. This was an unexpected gift, something she'd not known she wanted.

Women were passed so swiftly from man to man there was seldom time for them to know their own minds. A girl left the schoolroom at eighteen to enter Society with the express purpose of finding a husband so that she could be transferred from a father's responsibility to a husband's. Should that fail, as it had in her case when Garrett died, a girl would return to her family's care once more. But Garrett had freed her from that cycle with this chateau. He'd given her a place where she could be herself, whoever that might be, and it touched her deeply that he'd understood her so well as to recognise her need to be her own person.

Her vision blurred at the thought of her husband's kindness. It was an extraordinary gift he'd left her, but it was also extraordinarily lonely. Was she meant to spend her days alone? To never know the comfort of companionship that she'd known with Garrett? She'd always appreciated him, but in hindsight, she saw how truly rare their marital friendship had been. It set a dilemma for her. How would she find another man to equal Garrett? And if she did, how would she honour the relationship she'd had with Garrett by putting another in his place? Would that diminish Garrett's memory?

She swiped at the tears that stung her eyes and set aside Bidet's treatise. She'd read well past lunch and clearly her thoughts were beginning to wander. Emma moved towards the wide library windows that looked out over the vineyards, noting that the sun had come out from behind the clouds at last. Movement in the vineyard caught her eye. It was Julien, strolling the vines, dressed in his work clothes, a battered hat on his head. Perhaps *strolling* wasn't the right word. Strolling implied a sense of laziness and there wasn't a lazy, idle bone in Julien's body. If her days were her own, his days were ruled by the grapes.

Julien was up with the sun, walking the vineyards each morning, something she knew only because she asked, *not* because she'd witnessed it first-hand. He was up and gone long before she took her breakfast. Their paths would not cross until the afternoons and only if she went to the cellars. His afternoons were spent in his offices there, something she'd discovered on one of her many visits to the wine caves beneath the chateau. He would come out and greet her as she toured the caves, but he never invited her into his space.

She told herself it was because the space was small and cramped and he was a busy man. To prove, one had only to know that he spent his early evenings walking the rows again. She told herself she should not begrudge him his afternoons when she had his evenings.

Supper was fast becoming her favourite time of day at the chateau, the one time of day when their worlds merged, the one time they were together. She enjoyed those evenings more than she probably ought to. She thought he enjoyed them too, although probably not as much as she. After all, she was the one who'd initiated them. She'd sent the first invitation the day following their picnic, on the grounds of wanting to discuss the reading he'd recommended.

She'd started with Diderot's encyclopaedia and read his description of the influence of land on winegrowing, her mind filled with questions prompted by the reading. She wanted to know more. As she read Diderot, the voice in her head became Julien's, reading the entries out loud just as he'd lectured her on the grapes the day of the picnic. She'd read the books but what she really wanted was for Julien to harness the extraordinary amount of knowledge he possessed in that dark, tousled head of his and teach her himself.

Those dinners became the high point of her days. After mornings and afternoons of self-guided learning, the evenings were a time to practice her knowledge. Dinners turned into tastings. She prepared menus that required her to broaden her scope of wine knowledge, to challenge her palate, to become more discerning, all under Julien's guidance. Then, the debates would begin, sometimes at the table, sometimes in the library, where she had her books and notebooks at hand.

They might debate tasting rules: Could someone serve a red wine with fish? Or they might debate wine lore: Did the English really discover champagne first? She rather thought there was decent evidence to suggest that was true. The English had imported still wines and deliberately added sugar to it for fizz. She proudly cited the Christopher Merret treatise in support. But Julien insisted champagne's origins were French even if the process had been codified in England before being refined back in France. It had been a rousing discussion, one that made her smile even now, days later.

But despite those meals followed by those wondrous evening debates, Julien made no further overture to partnership. Each evening the connection between them would surge in the enjoyment of one another's company and her hopes would surge along with it. She would think: perhaps tomorrow would be the day he'd want to discuss the June event, or show her the books, or discuss the business he'd been running for Garrett. But each morning, he was gone from her again, out walking the fields, conducting his business without a thought for her until evening.

Sometimes she felt as if she were living a fairy tale where the princess lived in a lovely chateau of her own, the master of the house only appearing for evening meals to quiz her. She did not carry those stories to their conclusions where, based upon scintillating dinner conversation, the princess fell in love with the ogre despite his looks. Julien's looks were fine—quite handsome when he took the time, and quite appealingly rugged when he did not.

It was his aloofness that she struggled with. If she'd not invited him to supper, would he have ignored her entirely? That gave her pause. Perhaps the mistake was hers. Perhaps she should not wait for an invitation to take part in the day-to-day running of the vineyards. She'd already been waiting several weeks. It was nearly April. How much longer should she wait? There were consequences for not waiting; not waiting would risk the perception that she was shouldering her way into his territory, something he'd been sensitive to since the first night.

It would be far better if he invited her in, which was why she *was* waiting. But at some point, she could wait no longer for him to do the inviting, even if barging in would hurt both their feelings. This was why one did not mix business with pleasure. She had imagined the beginnings of a friendship and had imagined such a friendship entitled her to certain considerations while he clearly did not, indifferent perhaps to whether they spent their evenings together.

She watched him stop to study a vine, then his head bent, leaning against a nearby post, and his broad shoulders sagged. At this distance, he seemed tired, vulnerable, as if the weight he carried had suddenly broken him. The thought taunted her, her mind unable to tolerate the idea of a defeated Julien. Julien was strong and contrary, a stone wall to batter away at endlessly with her ideas and questions.

Was something wrong with the vines? Was there a

blight? That was the word, wasn't it, for grape diseases? Did blights happen before the grapes even blossomed? But there was no time to look through her notebooks. Whatever was happening down there, he wasn't going to face it alone. She took a final look out the window and raced for the stairs, stopping only to grab a shawl. These were her vineyards; she ought to face whatever was down there with him. And it was the perfect time to delicately remind him who was truly in charge.

'Julien!' The sound of her voice startled him into lifting his head. He spun around to see Emma, hatless, pelting towards him, skirts lifted high to show bare legs and half-boots, the ends of her shawl flapping wildly. 'What is it?' She panted breathlessly, her words coming out in a worried rush as she bent, a hand clasped to her waist. 'I saw you from the window.'

'You were watching me?' He smiled, in part because she looked so delightfully mussed compared to the usual perfection of her, the usual control.

'I was looking at the vineyard, you just happened to be in it.' She straightened, her breathing evening out. She shot him a dagger stare with her quicksilver eyes. 'That is beside the point. You looked distressed. What has happened?' Ah, there it was, the sharp tongue, the feistiness he'd become used to over their supper debates. She'd taken to her reading assignments with gusto, ingesting the tomes at an impressive speed and with an even more impressive level of comprehension. She wasn't afraid to test him with her new knowledge.

'But you *were* worried about me.' He couldn't resist one further tease.

Her brows scrunched. She was starting to second-guess her conclusion. 'Are you not in distress? Is something not wrong with the grapes? You bent your head, your shoulders sagged.'

She'd been studying him in detail. Her observations rather stunned him, touched him. When had someone paid that close attention to him? Had a woman ever? Usually, a woman's attention went as far as his title, assuming he was in possession of it. And when he didn't have the title…well, the last four lonely years were proof of how that went. But Emma Luce had watched *him*.

'No, I am not in distress. You could say I am in relief.' He directed her attention to the vine. 'Look, there's sap.' He couldn't stop grinning now that the initial relief had passed and reality had settled. 'Do you remember what that means?' It was his turn to watch her now as she bent towards the vine, her eyes riveted on it.

She flashed her gaze at him, a smile taking over her face as she proudly announced, 'Budburst.' He watched laughter bubble up in her, watched it bring a spark to her eyes, a light to her smile, and he thought he'd not truly seen her alive until this moment. 'It means spring is beginning, the vines are alive,' she quoted him. 'The grapes will start growing.' Her enthusiasm was infectious and rivalled his own. He'd been worried for a week now; budburst had come much later than he'd anticipated. He'd begun to believe something had happened in the winter to kill the vines.

'How wondrous,' she breathed, and he had the sense that she meant so much more than the wonder of the grapes, that the wonder extended to celebrating not only the grapes, but life, and simply being here. Her gaze held his, her smile widened, dominating her features until she shone like a dazzling star. 'We will make wondrous wine this year, Julien, I just know it!'

The moment got the better of them. She was in his arms, her face turned up to his, her arms twined about his neck in what could only be termed as a hug. Emma Luce was *hugging* him, and he was hugging her back. He may even have given her a little spin around in his enthusiasm over the grapes, over her. She laughed up at him, the sound full of life, just before she kissed him, on the cheek of course, an enthusiastic peck of celebration. It felt good. It felt right, and that made it not only wrong, but perilous. How did one come back from this line once it was crossed?

Chapter Eleven

'What shall we discuss tonight?' Julien spoke the usual words as they made their way into the dining room that evening, but she did not miss the forced casualness with which those words were infused. She'd overstepped herself in the vineyard and they'd both felt its effects.

'I thought we might discuss Chaptal now that I've completed reading his treatise, and because you seem to dislike the fellow.' She strove to match his casual tones, strove to set aside what it had felt like to be surrounded by the strength of his embrace, what it had felt like to look up into his face and see another man entirely— a man open to joy. He'd looked younger in those moments. Of course, he was still young, not yet forty.

How old was he? Thirty-five? Thirty-eight? Julien had a rather timeless quality to him. That she was trying to pin down a specific age spoke to her growing curiosity over him on a more personal level, a curiosity that had been piqued the day of the picnic, hearing stories of him as a schoolboy in England.

You think about him too much, came the scold. *Face the evidence. You know his schedule, and you look forward to the evening meal because those debates are with him.*

Early on, she'd told herself he was merely objectively handsome, that she needed to get to know him if she wanted to navigate him, manage him, solve him like a puzzle, and claim the prize of full access to her vineyards.

After weeks of dinners and debates, that was less true now than it once might have been. Now her curiosity was piqued for itself, not for any extrinsic gain. Since the picnic, his appeal had started to shift to something more personal, and today she'd rather spontaneously acted on that shift. She'd like to say it was much to her regret, but that would be a lie. She did *not* regret it even if it left her with complicated emotions. The thrill of being in his arms had been tempered by a sense of guilt, that being in Julien's arms was somehow disloyal to Garrett.

'It's not that I don't like Chaptal,' Julien began after the food had been set down *à la française* so that they could serve themselves from a tureen containing a creamy vichyssoise soup, and a platter of pork loin drizzled in a *poivrade* sauce. The footmen retreated and Julien continued as he served her a plate. 'Chaptal's chemical calculations are a wonder. There's no debating that his formula takes the guess work out of winemaking. A winemaker can reduce his margin of error in the addition of sugar needed to increase the alcohol content to the right levels. It's the consequence of that information being widely disseminated that bothers me.' He shook his head and Emma laughed.

'You don't mind Chaptal's findings, you only mind who gets to be privy to them. What might those *devastating* consequences be? That wine be democratised?' The gentleman in him was showing through tonight.

'What I *mind* is being rendered redundant because everyone has a recipe and no one needs my expertise.'

'But that's not true, though. It would take more than a recipe to make your knowledge obsolete,' she began, but he interrupted.

'Certainly, there's more to winemaking than adding sugar, but people will *think* it's true.' He tapped his temple with a forefinger, his voice taking on an edge of intensity. 'People will *think* they can make their own wine, that *anyone* can make wine. *Alors*, they can, but not everyone can make *good* wine. Too many people making bad wine is not a help for the reputation of the industry.' He stopped to taste a sip of his wine, a chilled chardonnay with oaky notes. 'This was a good choice tonight.' He nodded his approval.

'I chose it myself, although I had Richet approve it,' Emma said calmly, aware that inside her, a warm flame of appreciation had flickered to life at his praise.

Julien held the glass up to the candlelight. 'This is what I'm talking about. A month ago, you had the same access to the wine that you have today, *non*? But you chose a wine that was too heavy, too rich. Despite proper wines being at your disposal, you still chose incorrectly.'

She studied him for a long moment. His usual stoicism was firmly back in place. But perhaps it had been wrestled there with great effort. And she knew better now. The stoicism was a mask for something more, something he tried very hard to hide from the world, from her, from himself. Here was a man who was passionate about his grapes, his wine, but made great efforts to keep that passion under lock and key. Still, it leaked out when he talked of his vines, as it had today when he'd discovered the sap. Why did he try so very hard to be something he was not?

'So, winemaking should be for an elite few?' She gave him a questioning look over the rim of her glass. 'Where is the famed French *égalité* in that?'

Julien turned serious. 'I am no lover of the mob.' Instinctively, she recognised she'd crossed yet another dangerous line. She ought to retreat, ought to seek the safety of Chaptal's fermentation process instead of plunging headlong into French politics. The first rule of good business was never to discuss politics, but it seemed today was a day for breaking rules.

'Why is that? I would think, as a man of your background, that democracy would suit you.'

'My background? What do you know of "my background"?' His slate-blue eyes had become hard flints; his hand had stilled on the stem of his wine glass. Every muscle in his body tensed beneath the fabric of his evening jacket. She had him on the run from something, but what? She'd not meant to corner him any more than she'd meant to kiss him in the vineyard. It was a pattern with them. All sorts of things not meant to happen occurred when they were together: fights when they meant to be friendly, discoveries when they meant to be wary. For two people who prided themselves on control, they didn't seem to have a lot of it when they were together.

If he wanted her to apologise for her statement, he'd be disappointed. 'I meant that as a man who has an obvious love for the land and a talent for it, you must aspire to having your own land as opposed to working another's. Surely, there are better opportunities for a man to be self-made now that the land is not tied up in noble holdings.'

'Opportunities at what price?' The look he gave her was almost a glare. 'I might caution you to not speak about that which you do not fully understand.' He rose, the gesture declaring dinner was over, but she was not ready to let him go, to simply walk away.

'Perhaps we might adjourn to the library, there are other things I want to discuss like the vintage reveal party.' She offered the topic as a peace offering, a promise of détente, a promise that she would take care not to venture into politics again for the moment.

In the library, the conversation did go well for a while. She managed to talk about the event; what they might serve, where they might hold it—perhaps in the gardens. She asked for his input on the guest list and it seemed as if they might end the evening on an amicable note. *Falsely* amicable, if she was being honest.

Emma sipped her brandy, acutely aware of the man who sat in the chair opposite her by the fire. They'd fallen into silence after having exhausted the topic of the wine gala, each of them apparently content to simply be still for a moment. What was going on in his head? Surely, his mind was not as still as his body if her own mind was any measuring stick. Her thoughts were busy debating whether or not she dared bring up the subject of her taking next steps with the vineyard, of asking for an introduction to the growers' consortium. On the one hand, talking about the gala was the perfect conversational entrée for the topic, but on the other, the events earlier today and this evening had fraught their discussion with a sharp edge. When she asked, she didn't want to be turned down. If she was, she'd have to ask again and again until he gave way; the issue would become a battleground. The last thing she needed was more contention between them.

Emma knew how to read a room and she wasn't convinced circumstances were quite right tonight to get a yes from him. And yet, if her entrée to the growers' consortium must go unaddressed, perhaps there were other issues that could not. Not all the tension that simmered beneath their quiet sips of brandy and fireside silence could be attributed to a dinner conversation gone sideways. They might have made their peace with her political remarks but not with the issue of the vineyard. The forced normalcy had still been there when they'd talked of the gala. Julien had been overly polite as he'd poured their drinks, careful to not let his fingers brush hers when he handed her the snifter, and that she noted those nuances was proof that the effects still lingered hours afterwards for both of them.

'Are we not going to talk about it?' she ventured in light tones. 'The kiss in the vineyard?' she offered for clarification.

'It was hardly a kiss.' Julien set aside his brandy and rose, going to the long windows and looking out into the dark, his hands clasped behind his back.

'Then why does it bother you so much?' she challenged, turning in her chair to keep him in sight.

'It doesn't.'

'Yes, it does,' she argued. 'You've not been quite yourself tonight, not that you're ever "quite yourself",' she added as a goad. He had himself on a tight leash at the moment and she wanted to snap his control, make him admit to what he was feeling.

That earned her a growl and a sharp look tossed at her from over his shoulder. 'What is that supposed to mean?'

'Well, since you asked, it means that you work so hard to ignore that you *feel* anything, and yet I think you feel *everything*. Deeply. But you believe you must hide it. Why is that?'

The growl became a harsh chuckle. She recognised the sound. He was going on the offensive. He was the king of the dry chuckle. It was his strategy, his way of dismissing people and topics he didn't want to discuss. She braced. Would his response be denial? Deflection?

'You seem to have spent a lot of time thinking about me while you've been here. Perhaps overthinking. I would not encourage that, although I certainly understand it. We are isolated out here and you are…lonely.' Ah, so it was to be deflection then.

'And you're not?' she challenged. 'You, sir, are lone-liness personified.' She would not sit there and let him patronise her.

He'd overplayed his hand. He'd meant to chase her from the room with his insult, not draw her closer. Julien didn't need to turn from the window to know she was coming for him. Emma Luce would not take being patronised sitting down. He could hear the rustle of her black bombazine skirts, smell the jasmine scent of her as she closed in on him.

'You know nothing about me.' He put up his last defence, hoping to drive her off. It was a lie though, he very much feared that she *did* know him. He'd not meant for that to happen. Oh, she did not know certain things, like he was sometimes a *comte* depending on the government's current attitude towards titles. She didn't know his family had once owned these lands seventy years ago, a legacy that had been built over centuries and stripped away in minutes all for the sake of the mob, for *égalité*. But she did know *him*. She saw his passion, saw his heart, and that scared him. He'd not shown that to anyone since Clarisse. He'd not meant to show it to Emma Luce.

'I could say the same,' came the fierce retort as she took up a position beside him, staring out into the darkness, both of them acting like there was something to see. 'What makes you think you know anything about *me*?' She might be surprised there. He watched her when she thought he wasn't looking. He saw the efficiency with which the house was run, the quality of the meals that made their way to the table every night, courtesy of her menus, the extra level of neatness the house took on under her care. Because he saw how much the servants enjoyed working for her. Petit sang her praises, saying how delightful it was to have a mistress who understood the delicacies of cooking. Mrs Dormand appreciated the burden of decision making that was lifted from her shoulders with a mistress present.

Oh, he knew quite a bit about her and he wished it made her less likeable. It would be far easier if she'd hid away in her room, crying her eyes out. But she'd done none of that. She'd thrown herself into her new life, her new role, as best she could. That made her impressive and interesting and absolutely more difficult to manage.

'I know more than you think,' he answered, edging his voice with a hint of challenge. 'I know that being alone and being lonely are not the same. I am *alone*. You are *lonely*.' She could not hide that behind her constant busyness. It was *because* of that loneliness that she was a force constantly in motion—reading her wine books, working with the staff, planning the gala, walking the cellars, learning her wines. All of it was a cover for what really plagued her—how to combat her loneliness. Embrace it and endure, or move on, even if that meant moving past Garrett Luce's memory? He wasn't the only one hiding certain truths. Her eyes flashed with anger and something else—admission perhaps? Sadness?

'Yes, I miss him,' she confessed. 'It helps to be here. At Oakwood, I kept expecting to come around a corner and see him or enter a room and find him in his favourite chair. There were reminders of him everywhere; his clothes in the wardrobes, his toiletries still on the bureau where he'd left them before our trip, everything just waiting for him to come and pick them up again. It was like even our life together was waiting for him to return to it. But not here.'

She drew a deep breath. 'Here, I am free to start again on my own.' She tried for a smile. He could see what it cost her. She was being brave. His heart went out to her and in that moment, he yearned to tell her that he understood, that he knew a little something about starting over without the person you loved. That he knew there was no such thing. There wasn't really a clean slate. The ghosts still followed; the past could never be entirely left behind. No one knew that better than he did. But such a disclosure required he tell her other things; that the woman he'd loved had lived in his family's chateau while three generations of Archambeaux had not.

The Archambeaux had not lived in their home for seventy years. Now he lived here on Garrett Luce's generous sufferance, sharing the residence with the ghosts of his past and his family. That could end. If Emma asked him to leave, if Emma refused to sell, it would all have been for naught. He'd spend his life like his *oncle*—living a stone's throw away from unfulfilled dreams. So, he did what he always did when conversations became too personal, too painful: he deflected.

He softened his tone. 'There's nothing wrong with being lonely, Emma.'

'No, there isn't,' she said staunchly. She pushed back a strand of hair that had come loose. 'It just takes getting used to.' Yes, he could agree to that. Being alone took practice. There was an art to spending all of one's time with one's thoughts without letting those thoughts become overwhelming.

She faced him, giving him a full glimpse of her beauty, her strength. 'Just to be clear though. I did not kiss you because I am lonely.'

'Oh?' He arched a brow, trying to be cool. That was too bad. He could have understood a kiss out of loneliness. Now he'd have to find other explanations and the path those explanations might travel made him uncomfortable. He wasn't sure he wanted to discuss what she called a kiss. If they did, he'd have to admit to his reaction—admit that he'd liked the feel of her in his arms far too much. He'd have to admit that he'd hugged her back, swung her around. That normally, the person he'd have wanted to celebrate budburst with was his *oncle*. But today, the first person he'd wanted to tell was her, and there she'd been, with him in the vineyard at the exact moment he'd wanted her to be there. They'd been reckless and he'd loved it.

He'd thought of nothing else since. He'd been prickly with it, snapping at her at dinner, trying to ignore the intensified awareness that hummed in his blood despite his best efforts these past weeks to keep his distance. The picnic had been a warning and he'd heeded it. But today proved his efforts were for naught. She'd destroyed his defences in moments. 'Do you care to enlighten me, then? Why did you kiss me?'

'To celebrate the good news, to celebrate being here, and for the first time in a while, to celebrate the sheer thrill of being alive in springtime.' The truth of those words shone on her face. 'Because it fit the moment.' She paused, something flickering in her eyes as her gaze held his, something that set undeniable tendrils of desire flaring within him. 'Because I *wanted* to kiss you.'

'I do not think you know what that word really means.' He should not have said that. He should not flirt with disaster. He should put an end to this conversation immediately. He should remind them both there were limits to their association despite the close proximity in which they lived. But he did neither. The distance between them closed. Her gaze became the colour of mist and fog. He traced the fullness of her bottom lip, his gaze dropping to that luscious mouth, his voice husky. 'The English may think that was a kiss, but I assure you, the French do not.'

'What, pray tell, is a kiss then?' Her own voice was reminiscent of smoky brandy, throaty and coy, her teeth nipping at the pad of his thumb as it passed over her lip.

His mouth hovered, a whisper away from hers as he breathed his seduction. 'A kiss is the meeting of mouths, the press of lips, full and open, it is the tangle of tongues, the taste of souls.' He took her mouth in demonstration, the smell of jasmine filling his senses, obliterating all reason, as passion slipped its leash and ran amok.

Chapter Twelve

At the press of his mouth, chaos reigned; want ran like wildfire in her veins, hot and engulfing, her senses splintering like a tree at a lightning strike. Good God, this kiss was desire unchained, and it ignited a rough hunger of her own. She answered with a new fierceness that left her own need naked and known. She knew already that in the aftermath there could be no misinterpreting this kiss, with its unbridled, wild warfare, this duel of mouths, of hands, of bodies. Her hands were in his hair, her teeth tugging at his lip even as his own drifted down to nip at her throat—a throat she'd wantonly exposed, her body begging even as she laid siege to his.

She moaned her madness, her hips pressed hard to his, the physical evidence of his desire unmistakable against her skirts. She wanted, she wanted… The two words thrummed through her with the heat of his kiss, her mind unable to complete the sentence. It was enough to simply want, to let that want rip through her with the intensity of an inferno, devouring reason and anything else that stood in its wake. 'Julien.' She gasped his name, her hands ripped at his immaculately tied cravat and moved onto his coat, his waistcoat, the buttons of his shirt, and each barrier fell before the frantic speed of her hands.

His hands did not reciprocate with such delicacy. He seized the bodice of her gown with two hands and rent, sending buttons scattering while wild laughter welled up her throat. Had anything ever felt so delicious? So freeing? Her chemise and undergarments fared no better. Julien was rabid in his frenzy, and so was she. She wanted to devour him, claim him, as much as her own body cried out for the same.

Claim me. Mark me. Know me. Drag me from the abyss of aloneness. Bring me into the light.

Her breasts were bare in his hands, his head buried between them as he knelt before her, his hands futilely, frustratingly working the string of her pantalettes. He swore and brought his mouth to bear, ripping the string with his teeth, his hands roughly pushing them down, his mouth at her mons. She could feel his breath coming warm and fast against her nether thatch. Desire, honest and raw, surged in her, rising fast, riding her hard. Then he tongued her seam and she thought she'd lose her mind. 'Julien, I can't.' She would fall if he kept this up; her legs had no strength.

'Hold on to me,' came the response, his own desire making him terse. And she did. Her hands dug into his shoulders, nails digging into those muscled depths as his mouth did wicked things to her most private places until release claimed her and her vocabulary was reduced to sounds. How he found the strength to carry her to the fireplace was beyond her, but then, in the moments following that oral decadence a lot of things were beyond her—thought, speech, basic motor functions. And yet, she was by no means sated. Her wildness had only been tempted by his mouth, not tamed.

'How are you?' Julien's voice was a sexy tease, his eyes hot blue flames as he laid her down.

'We are not done yet.' She reached for him, working his elegant evening trousers down past lean hips with quick, adept fingers, freeing his phallus to her gaze. 'You're magnificent.'

He gave a possessive growl, his body fitting unerringly to hers like a puzzle solved. 'I was hoping you'd say that.'

She wrapped her arms about his neck, drawing him down so that the hard length of him pressed against her thigh. 'Don't be gentle, don't be nice. I won't break.' She didn't want to lose the tempo, the heat and the speed that fed the fires of chaos in her, that didn't let her think, only let her feel. If she took time to think she might not like where those thoughts led.

'I was hoping you'd say that, too,' he laughed, low, at her ear. Dear heavens, this man was rough seduction personified and her body was craving it, perhaps even her soul was craving it, needing the ferocity of him, needing the connection with another. It was a potent combination. He entered her hard and swift and she cried out, revelling in the power of the joining. She wrapped her legs tight about his hips, lean and powerful, her own hips rising to meet his.

Please, please, please, please... The words became a gasped litany as her body met his in the old rhythm. *Please* for the pleasure, *please* for the obliteration...just *please.* And then release came, a thunderclap, a powerful storm of its own, its deluge dousing the fire. Passion contained, docilely returning to its leash, chaos caged.

She was vaguely aware of Julien pulling a soft blanket over them, of his warm body curving about hers as they dozed by the fire. She could feel the deep rise and fall of his chest against her back, the strength of his arm as it draped about her, his hand warm and possessive at her hip. This was a new kind of wild heaven, a new kind of wickedness, and it was positively divine. Her pleasure-addled mind flickered to life for a moment. Was it possible something could be both wicked and divine? At present, it didn't matter. But it would. That particular thought was unfortunately already waking up in her mind even as she drifted off to sleep.

The dying fire woke them both shortly after midnight and he draped her in the blanket and took her hand, leading her on a mad dash through the house to her bedroom, stopping once to silence her laughter with a kiss. 'You don't want Richet to hear you, do you?' he chuckled, pressing her to a wall.

She closed her hand around his rising phallus. 'He might hear me, but he'll *see* you.' She had the meagre protection of the blanket, but he had not even that. Julien was striding the midnight halls of the chateau in his altogether.

At her chambers, Julien hesitated. She tugged at his hand. 'Will you stay? Please? We could try something a little slower, perhaps a little more comfortable, like in a bed.'

She gave a laugh and he smiled. 'How can I possibly refuse?'

It was her turn to seduce him, with her mouth, with her touch as she savoured the man in her bed, riding him astride in a slow, grinding trot that teased them both to the edge of exquisite pleasure before she allowed them to claim it. But perhaps the most exquisite pleasure was the one she watched on his face, the way his neck arched, pleasure welling up the muscled column of his throat and taking the form of masculine groans, his eyes going wide, locked on hers as she felt his body clench and prepare inside her. It was her cue to let him go, to take him in her hand at last.

He drew her to him and she tucked herself against his side, her head nestled into the hollow of his shoulder. 'I think this is the wildest, most decadent, divine night I've ever had,' Emma whispered.

'Don't,' Julien breathed into her hair. 'Don't think. There will be time enough for that later.'

She woke much later and knew immediately that he was gone before she even opened her eyes. She could feel the light dawn against her eyelids, could feel the emptiness of the bed, its coolness, the absence of a man's weight. In a practical sense, she understood why he was gone. Her maid would be in to help her dress. Catching the land steward in the mistress's bed would spark all types of rumours, add to that the mistress had only been widowed a short time, and she'd never be able to hold her head up. She'd have scandal attached to her name before she'd even introduced herself to the neighbours.

The last hit her especially hard. She groaned as the reality of the morning settled on her. What had she done? She'd slept with Julien. She'd done wicked things with Julien, behaved decadently with him in ways she'd never behaved with Garrett. More than that, she was supposed to be in mourning. She'd behaved like a hussy. What did that mean? Should she feel riddled with guilt? And if she didn't, should she feel guilty for not feeling guilty enough? It was not her behaviour she felt guilty over. She couldn't care less what Society thought. Society had never done her any favours. The guilt was on Garrett's behalf. Should she feel guilty for moving on so quickly? Or was this exactly what she needed to do *to* move on? Oh, she'd really opened a Pandora's box on this one. What was wrong with her? Why had she acted so impetuously?

She knew what was wrong with her. She *was* lonely. Julien had not been wrong there. She missed Garrett. She missed the simple pleasure of having him present in her day. She'd not realised how much Garrett's touches, a casual touch on the shoulder as he passed her desk, the fifty little conversations they'd have throughout the day, had meant. There was a void in her world that no amount of work could fill. She'd been hungry for a human connection, and not just someone to talk to—after all, she talked to the staff all day. Menus with Mrs Petit, housekeeping items with Mrs Dormand and Richet. But those interactions didn't count. They had to listen to her. They were not her equals. They didn't dare get to know her, disagree with her, probe her secrets.

And Julien should do those things? The voice in her head was quick to point out the flaw. *He is the land steward. Why does he get to be special? Isn't he also an employee of the chateau?*

The explanation was proximity. They spent too much time together. It was an unfortunate but perhaps inevitable situation. She'd been lonely and he'd been there.

Emma cringed at the description and drew the sheets up over her head as if she could block it all out. Was that really all it was? An outlet for her loneliness? A different way to grieve the loss of her husband? Perhaps that was the best explanation she could offer herself. She should leave it at that. And yet, to do so would be to buy into a lie. It had not all been about her last night. She'd not been in it alone. She'd not even been the one to start it. *He* had kissed *her.* Ravenously, like a starved man. She'd not been the only lonely one. They'd been equal participants in what had followed. Dear heavens, it had been rough, uninhibited, and thorough and…new.

Romantic intimacies with Garrett had always been satisfactory, pleasant, comforting, meaningful. No complaints. He'd been a considerate and decent lover. But last night had been beyond any previous experience— both physically in the sense of the things she and Julien had done, but also emotionally in the things she had felt.

Emma blushed at the memories; literally tearing

at Julien's clothes because she could not get at him fast enough, Julien using his mouth to bite through the stubborn string of her pantalettes before using his mouth on her. She'd heard of such things before, but never had she experienced them. Sleeping naked, skin to skin beside the fire afterwards, racing through the house nude, nearly having him against a wall in the hall. It was the stuff of wild fantasies. She'd thrilled to it, and so had he. At some point, it had stopped being about loneliness.

Now she was lying in bed reliving that decadence and comparing Julien to her husband. That did not speak well of her, to compare the two men. What sort of woman did that? Well, she thought she knew the answer to that. The sort of woman who was loose with her favours. By definition, to compare, one must have at least two items to weigh against one another. She'd not ever thought she'd be a woman with more than one lover.

But now you are, came the rejoinder.

She'd not thought to be a lot of things; childless, a widow before the age of thirty, owner of a French vineyard. Alone. Confused.

Get a hold of yourself! her inner voice scolded. *You had a one-night affair with a handsome man, it does not have to mean anything.*

Was that what she wanted? For last night to exist as a moment out of time? An antidote?

She could certainly choose to shape it that way. It would make it easier to ignore. Julien would like that. He'd been fully willing to ignore the kiss in the vineyard until she'd pushed the issue. But she did not think last night could be as easily ignored. Which meant, option two: she had to go on living her life with last night a part of the new reality between her and Julien. There could be no pretending that they hadn't ripped each other's clothes off, seen each other naked, and made mad love in the library and in her bed.

She threw off the covers. It was suddenly too hot to stay underneath them. What did one say to their lover the next morning in those circumstances? Did one simply go downstairs, butter their toast, sip their tea, and ask about plans for the day, and had they read anything interesting in the news?

And, oh, by the way, did we perhaps want to try the library again but in the afternoon with the sun coming through the windows?

Or, *Did you happen to retrieve our clothes from the library floor before the servants were up this morning?*

She rather hoped he had. It would be difficult to explain petticoats and waistcoats and bodice buttons scattered on the floor. She groaned at the thought of one of the footmen or one of the scullery maids who laid the fires finding the detritus of their evening. Emma squeezed her eyes shut. How would she ever face Richet again if he knew? It would be bad enough facing Julien wondering if he regretted it while she recalled everything that had happened. How could she look at him again and not think about last night?

There was the bigger question, too. Was last night one-time only? Or would it happen again? If it was only one time, she might justify it to herself as a bid against loneliness or even an experiment. To repeat it would be to admit to something more. Did she want it to happen again? Did *he*? That came with a host of other questions like: If it did happen again, what would it mean? Where did this lead? She looked up at the ceiling and let out a sigh. Those were only the practical implications. There were more philosophical ones, too.

Why did Julien stir her so deeply when she'd loved Garrett utterly? The guilty dilemma flooded again. Was the speed at which she'd taken a lover unseemly? Or a natural part of the process of moving on? This—all the uncertainty, all the questions—was the price of that one night of pleasure. What had she been thinking? But she knew very well that in the moment, she *hadn't* been thinking—that was the problem. From the moment his eyes had dropped to her mouth and his thumb had stroked her bottom lip, she'd stopped thinking entirely and started feeling. And it had felt good, right up until now.

There was a rap on her door and Emma quickly pulled the covers up. Her maid, Chloe, entered carrying fresh linen. *'Bonjour, madame.* You've slept late, I hope that means you've slept well. The sun is out today. We shall have some pleasant weather at last.' Emma watched Chloe for any tells that she knew what she'd been up to last night and who she'd been up to it with. Chloe was chatty today, but Chloe was always cheerful, always chatty. There was nothing new there. Emma reached for the robe she kept near the bed and started to relax. Perhaps she might be able to keep this…indiscretion…between her, Julien, and her conscience.

'Monsieur Archambeau asked me to relay a message, *madame*. He wanted me to tell you that he's gone out today.'

'Did he say where?' Emma took a seat at her dressing table, letting Chloe brush out her hair.

'No, *madame*, only that he did not know when he'd be back. He said not to wait supper on him.'

She ought to feel relieved. She didn't have to face Julien today. By the time she did see him, she'd have herself together, her mind organised instead of her thoughts flying in a hundred different directions like a heart-struck young girl. But she did not feel the relief she'd expected at this reprieve. She felt disappointment, and dismay. Her mind immediately dissected what it could mean—did he leave because he didn't want to face her? Because he regretted what had happened?

Did he regret it because he'd let his guard down, allowed someone to see him at his most vulnerable? Or did he regret it because of what he'd done with her? If it was the former, she could manage it, they could come back from that. But if it was the latter, if it was her, or their actions, he took objection to, that could ruin everything. How would they ever work together then? If she'd known this would be the outcome would she still have done it? If the opportunity arose, would she do it again? She feared the answer would be yes.

Chapter Thirteen

He should not have done it. After a day of brutal exercise in the fields trying to work himself into forgetful exhaustion, that was the conclusion he'd reached. There were, in fact, quite a few things he should not have done. He should not have taunted her, should not have flirted with her, should not have pushed her, because he knew by now that when she was pushed, Emma Luce pushed back. He'd spent all day enumerating his sins. But that had only made the torture worse.

Using the last of the daylight, sunset falling, Julien kicked his horse into a hard gallop along a flat stretch of road that lay between the chateau and his *oncle*'s farmhouse, hoping that if he could ride hard enough he could exorcise the heat from his veins, and convince himself to regret last night, because logically he *ought* to regret it.

But that was only logic talking. He seemed to have little use for such a commodity in the last ten hours and it was a hard sell. He could not persuade any part of him to regret last night. His mind was full of images of her; her hair falling down, the heat in her eyes when she looked at him, the way she'd looked when pleasure claimed her—pleasure *he'd* given her—her back arched, her head thrown back, her hips pressing into his, legs wrapped about him as if she never wanted him to leave her, but of course he had to. He could not spend within her. There were other images, too—her atop him in her bed, riding him like Godiva with her dark hair draped over her breasts.

That had been exquisite. Leaving her bed had been much more difficult than he had anticipated. His body still reverberated with the echoes of their lovemaking, every wild, wonderful minute of it. The ache in his body asking the question *when*? When would they be together again? Not *would* there be a next time—his body had leapt right over any circumspection. His body was not bothered by more sophisticated issues such as the relational implications of last night.

He did not fool himself that he could simply pretend last night had not happened. For one, he did not think Emma would let him treat it so callously, and for another, he did not want to. His body ached for hers, to repeat it. But what would that mean? An affair with Emma Luce? It would have to be hidden. From the servants, for the sake of her reputation, and from his *oncle* for the sake of his. The farmhouse came into view with its green shutters, like the chateau's, and Julien slowed his horse. If his *oncle* saw him racing up the road, he'd know something was wrong. In the yard, Julien dismounted and schooled his features. He must not give away anything. His business with Emma was between him and her, not his *oncle*. His *oncle* had already hinted that intimacies could be strategically used to advance their cause.

That had not sat well with him when his *oncle* had originally introduced the idea, and he liked the idea even less now that he knew her better.

That's because you've become attached, that's what empathy will do for you, his inner voice scolded. *You did not heed your own warnings, your own advice.*

He wanted to dismiss the self-directed scold. Just because he'd slept with her didn't mean he was attached. They were two consenting adults who'd been keen to stave off loneliness. Sex *could* be just sex. Goodness knew he'd tried 'just sex,' trying to find relief, trying to obliterate the pain of the past.

He wasn't doing a good job of selling the argument to himself. In this case there was no 'just sex' about it. It had been physical, and primal, rough and riotous, but emotion had been there bubbling underneath. They'd both been desperately seeking something: belonging, connection, and for a few short hours, they'd found it in each other's arms. He wanted to find it again. With her.

His *oncle* was in his office, sitting behind his desk, poring over reports and ledgers, dressed immaculately, and looking out of place, something that struck him more strongly than usual. His *oncle* dressed well for town, but not for the countryside. His office was also well-appointed with an expensive desk from Paris and all the accoutrements that adorned his bookshelves—the scales, the globe, the leather-spined books with the gold gilt letters that came from a Paris bookseller monthly. This was an office to rival a noble's town house. It was not an estate office of a man who lived in a country gentleman's farmhouse. But his *oncle* had never aspired to be a simple country gentleman, had he? His life, all sixty-two years of it, had been dedicated to the pursuit of something larger—restoring the Comte du Rocroi's land.

His *oncle* looked up and smiled. 'Julien, welcome. You are in time for supper. It will take no time at all to set an extra place.'

Dinner was a pleasant affair; one could always count on eating well at the farmhouse, breakfast or supper. Perhaps eating a little too well. Only a nobleman ate like his *oncle*. They talked of the weather and of local news in the neighbourhood, making a two-hour meal of it, which alternately soothed and chafed at Julien's nerves. It was not until they'd adjourned back to his *oncle*'s office that there was a shift to business.

'I suspect you haven't just come to catch up on the news. You've come to tell me something.' His slate-blue eyes, so like Julien's own, twinkled, and Julien froze. How did his *oncle* know? Then he remembered. The other news.

'Yes, we've got budburst. The vines are showing. Another season is under way.' That's what had started everything yesterday. Julien took his usual seat across from his *oncle*. Budburst seemed a lifetime ago, and far less significant than what had followed, a sure sign that logic had deserted him. When had anything been more important than the vines? 'Now we just need to hope the winter weather is gone for good. I don't want a cold snap bringing a frost and killing us off before we truly get under way. And your vines here? Are they showing?'

'*Our* vines, you mean,' his *oncle* corrected. 'Yes, buds showed a couple days ago. It took them long enough this year. They're as unpredictable as a woman.' He chuckled. 'Speaking of which, how is the situation over there? Has Madame Luce given up on her fantasies of being a vineyard manager?'

Emma. He'd not thought of her as Madame Luce for quite a while now, not since their picnic. 'No, in fact, just the opposite. She's become an ardent student of viniculture.'

His *oncle* scoffed at the idea. 'Assign her some hard reading like Merret's treatise. The science will put her to sleep. Have her read Chaptal.'

'I *did* assign those.' Julien took a bit of satisfaction in informing his *oncle*. 'She devoured them and she debates me nightly. Ask her who invented champagne at your own peril.'

His *oncle* arched a white brow, catching his slip. 'Then, I'd say you are not trying hard enough. The goal was to make her disinterested in the process, not to have her become intrigued by it.' He gave a sly look. 'But perhaps if you debate nightly, her interest isn't so much in the wine as in the instructor? Perhaps she wants to impress you?'

Julien took refuge in chagrin. 'She is a woman in mourning. I doubt she even looks at a man with such thoughts.' But she'd looked at him with want and desire last night. He'd not let himself contemplate how much of that want and desire was for him and how much was a want and desire to assuage her loneliness. Had she simply used him? Could he blame her when he had used her for his own needs as well? And yet, somehow in the riot of passion, they'd transcended those needs.

His *oncle* gave a shrug, unconvinced. 'Well, *I* won't debate with you. Perhaps an invitation to the chateau might be in order? I could come to dinner and discuss the wine gala with her. I do admit to some curiosity about this woman who seeks to unseat us.'

'She doesn't seek to unseat us,' Julien corrected swiftly. His *oncle* was being hyperbolic. 'She just wants what is hers, what her husband has left her.' He realised as he said the words that he believed them. The resentment he'd felt upon her arrival over a month ago was absent. How had that happened? *When* had that happened? Last night or before? How long had he felt that way?

His *oncle* was silent for a long while, his gaze fixed unblinkingly on him. 'Oh, my, *mon fils*, she's really got her hooks into you if she's got you thinking about throwing away the family legacy. No woman should come before your family,' he cautioned. 'A woman is nothing but trouble. You should know that by now.'

'It's her chateau, Oncle.'

'It's your inheritance, it's what your great-*grandpère* lost his head for, what your *grandpère* lived in exile for, what he and your father came back for, what you were raised for. We have all lived for this moment, invested for this moment, and now it's up to you to see it through.' He waved a beringed hand. 'I am an old man. But you are the Comte, you are the next generation.' If his *oncle* was trying to make him feel guilty, he was doing an excellent job. When had he moved away from his old dreams?

His *oncle* sighed. 'Maybe it is easy for you to care less because you live in the chateau every day, surrounded by our family's artefacts—the art collection, the furniture that's been acquired over the centuries. You can pretend it is yours. I have never lived there.'

'It is not truly mine either. It has not been ours for seventy years.' Julien gritted his teeth. He would not be made to feel guilty about not wanting to steal a woman's inheritance from her. Nor would he allow himself to feel as if he were betraying a man who'd been like a second father to him. He and his *oncle* had always been on the same side, always shared the same ambitions.

But today, he felt caught between his *oncle* and Emma and it was not necessarily his *oncle* he wanted to favour. The Archambeau dream seemed too expensive if it cost Emma her home. And yet, such a thought disconcerted him greatly. Was he really willing to protect Emma from his *oncle* at the expense of not restoring Archambeau land? What end did that serve? What did he get from playing Emma's hero? What would he be left with? An alienated *oncle*, a lost family dream, and quite possibly hurt by a woman yet again if he let himself keep falling.

His *oncle* smiled. 'Ah, to be young again, *mon fils*, and to feel spring running through my veins, blood pounding, and a woman to share it with. You think I don't know how you feel, but I do. Take my advice, even though you are not in the mood to hear it. If she's got your blood boiling, marry her, have it all—the woman, the land, the house.'

'It's not like that, Oncle.' Julien prepared to make the old arguments about dishonesty and the morality of such a strategy, realising even as he did that he was making the arguments for different reasons than before. He had decided to defend Emma. His arguments now were not so much for him but for her—to protect her. Every lie he told his *oncle* was told to protect what had happened between them last night. 'As I said when you first suggested it, it is the dishonesty that I cannot countenance.' This time, it was not the dishonesty of his feelings, but using those feelings to lead her down a dubious path. He cared for her; he did not want to use his caring to trap her.

'But is it still dishonest? It is only dishonest if you feel nothing for her, *if* you lie to her about those feelings. I know in the beginning, that was your worry, but now it seems that perhaps there *is* feeling between the two of you.' His *oncle* had a serpent's own tongue.

Julien scoffed. '*If* that were true, do you think she'd believe in those feelings once she found out all I stood to gain? She would never believe it was love alone that motivated me and I would have way to prove to her otherwise.' He shook his head. He was uncomfortable even naming that feeling. *Was* it love that he felt? That seemed a rather strong, rather incautious word for a one-night affair. 'You surprise me, Oncle. You of all people know that love is a fiction, simply a name we give to an emotion. It only exists because we call it out of thin air.'

'I didn't call it love. I called it "feelings". I said only that now you have them, whereas before you didn't. It solves your concern over duplicity. It doesn't matter if you or I believe in love or not. It only matters if *she* does. If she does, she will believe you.' It was entirely obvious to his *oncle*. But Julien did not think it was that simple.

'I think you forget she has already had a great love in her life. She will be hesitant to believe she gets to have two.' Last night had nothing to do with love. Other emotions perhaps, but not love. 'She is not in love with me any more than I am with her. One night does not require marriage especially when one is a widow.' And she was a smart widow. She knew how the world worked. She had lived in that world, been on the receiving end of its cruelty. She would not let her guard down easily. She *would* question his motives. What would he say then? It was a deuce of a dilemma he was faced with. In the beginning, he'd been concerned because the strategy required false feelings. Now he was worried because it didn't. His feelings had become very real, real enough to want to protect her at the expense of his own gain.

His *oncle* laughed when he might have been angry at his nephew's stubbornness. 'Ah, Julien. You don't have to say anything about what happens at the chateau. I have eyes. You look like a stag in rut, worn, ragged, and hungry for more. I am a patient man, *mon fils*, and I believe in you. Go home, watch your grapes grow and sort it all out. Strike while the iron is hot because when it cools, she may not find you as attractive.'

There was a fearful wisdom in that, Julien thought as he swung up on his horse a few minutes later and set off for home. He'd not fooled his *oncle*. He'd not even fooled himself into thinking one night with Emma wouldn't lead to another. All he could think of on the way home was how quickly he wanted to reach her, to lose himself in the passion, to let the hunger obliterate his dilemma. She would not thank him for it if she knew his motivation in seeking her out was to drown his conflicting thoughts. If she discovered the truth of him and his connection to the land, she would think the worst even though it wasn't true: that he'd manipulated her for the benefit of his own inheritance at the expense of her own. Love words, even spoken in truth, would not be compelling enough then. The question was, how would he convince her otherwise if she discovered the truth? Did he really think his secrets would keep for ever?

The moment she left the chateau, she would learn he was a *comte*. Whether or not the French government *du jour* recognised his title or not, his family's nobility went back to the fifteenth century. If she learned about the title, it stood to reason she would learn about the land and that her inheritance only existed because his family had lost theirs. It was not a matter of if but how long he would have before she knew. Before she'd want to make herself known to the neighbourhood. Already she was asking questions about the consortium, already planning the June gala. But he didn't think he had until June.

He ought to be the one to tell her, but he did not relish the idea of it. Still, if he didn't tell her, there were plenty of people who would. Everyone around here knew the Archambeau story, knew about the tragic love story, the Archambeau-Anouilh feud that followed, and the broken-hearted, defeated death of his father. If he didn't tell her, someone would let something slip in passing and pique her curiosity or tell her outright. That decided it—he couldn't let her leave the chateau without him to gatekeep, to make sure no one let anything slip until he had his chance to tell her. But not yet. Not before the passion between them had its chance. He wanted a little more time before he had to risk what it was that lay between them with the truth. He spurred his horse as hard as he dared in the darkness and headed for home, for Emma.

Emma took a tray in the library for dinner with the intention of continuing her reading. She was trying to get through a brief overview of a history of *vignerons* in the Champagne region, written in English. She'd found it lurking on the shelves and wondered if it had been one of Garrett's purchases in an attempt to learn more about the property and industry he'd bought into. Two pages in, she was ready to admit defeat. Not because the treatise was too difficult to follow, but because she'd chosen poorly. This had been a mistake, dining in the library without Julien, with no one to talk to, or argue with, with noth-

ing to distract her from reliving last night in the room
where it all happened, from reminders of exactly why
her body was deliciously sore and her mind sorely exercised with the emotional implications.

Each ache reminded her of Julien and those reminders prompted questions: Where was he? What was he
doing right now? Was he on his way home? Or was he
immersed in business with people she hadn't had the
chance to meet yet, the passion of the previous night
already taking a back seat to his precious grapes and
the impending growing season? Surely not, and yet his
absence was indicative of how much last night had disconcerted him, perhaps left him with the same questions it had left her. Had it also left him with the same
wants as well? She might not have arrived at all the
answers today, but she had come to a place where she
would not let herself feel guilty about the passion, about
the need to feel something with another.

These were not the only dilemmas on her mind. Another dilemma mingled with the interpersonal, reminding her that in bedding Julien, she'd conflated business
and pleasure. In an attempt to distract herself from Julien's absence and her tendency to overthink last night,
she'd gone down to Julien's office in the wine caves
thinking to retrieve the accounts. After all, now that
she had a basic grasp on the winemaking process, it
was time for her to turn her attentions to the books.

It was something of a surprise to realise she'd been
here several weeks and hadn't once looked at the vineyard accounts. To be fair, she'd had a lot of other things
to sort through: household accounts, the accounts of

the home farm, and the various other budgets that supported the running of the chateau. But now, it was time. Only it wasn't. When she'd reached Julien's office, she found it locked and a key nowhere in sight. She'd made a mental note to ask Julien about getting the ledgers, adding it to the other mental note to ask Julien about meeting the members of the consortium. If she remembered correctly, they'd met at the beginning of March near the time of her arrival. If so, they'd be meeting again very soon. It would be the perfect time to introduce herself and take up her place among them.

So much to do, so much to talk to Julien about. But not tonight. Tonight, there were other things to think about. Emma sighed and curled into the deep seat of the chair. If indeed she had thought of taking a lover, this would have been rather sooner than she'd imagined it would be, but she was certain Garrett would not begrudge her. He'd want her to carry on, to claim her happiness. She closed her eyes and let the warmth of the fire bathe her, let the memories of what they'd done in front of that fire flood her mind and lull her to sleep.

'*Ma cherie*, wake up and make love with me,' Julien's words, followed by the gentle, inviting buss of his lips against hers, woke her shortly before eleven. 'What were you dreaming of, *ma cherie*?'

She smiled up at him, her body coming alive from its slumber. 'You, what else would I be dreaming of?'

'Let's go upstairs and make some of those dreams come true.' He kissed her, long and slow, making her wonder if going upstairs was really their best option.

The fireplace wasn't a terrible choice, as they'd proven last night.

'Only some?' she teased, her body warming to memories of the pleasure and wanting to repeat it more than her mind wanted to offer caution.

'Well, if we made them all come true tonight, what would we do tomorrow?' He reached for her then, scooping her up in his arms, and carried her to bed.

Chapter Fourteen

If she'd thought the prior night had been an anomaly brought on by the heat of a fight and the excitement of a challenge realised, or that such bone-shattering love-making only existed as a moment out of time, not to be repeated, tonight was proving otherwise. One did not need rough, ravenous sex to claim the luxury of a shuddering climax. One apparently only needed Julien to carry them to bed to put one on the path.

'A proper bed and a proper night tonight,' Julien murmured in muted tones that sent a delicious thrill of anticipation down her spine.

'Not too proper, I hope.' She felt the mattress take his weight as he sat beside her.

'No, but perhaps gentler.' He raised her hand to his lips. 'Tonight, I want to notice everything about you, everything that I missed last night.'

'And if I want the same?' she murmured, playing along with this rather sophisticated flirtation of his.

'Then you shall have it.' He stepped away from the bed, his gaze intent on her, a reminder she ought to take care with what she wished for. That gaze alone was burning her alive, raising her desire to a fever pitch, and this was just the beginning.

He shrugged out of his long riding coat and she realised belatedly that he still wore his outerwear. He'd come straight to her in the library, not stopping to even take off his coat. He'd been thinking of her, wanting her. The knowledge that he'd come to her primed for passion carried its own thrill and whittled away her doubts. He wanted *her*, not the madness—the person, not the emotion.

This was all for her, this wicked, decadent show of masculinity revealed. He drew his shirt over his head and her breath sucked involuntarily at the sight of his sculpted torso exposed in the soft flicker of firelight. She had a sudden urge to run her hands over the planes of his skin.

'Later, *ma cherie*.' He gave a low laugh, reading her thoughts. Her face had become glass. 'This is for your eyes only. Later will be for your hands, your mouth if you would like, and we'll both enjoy that very much.' His hands dropped to the waist of his trousers and her eyes dropped with them. Whoever thought a man could not be a temptress—or was that *tempter*, her riveted brain could not decide the right word—did not know Julien.

His trousers dropped and he gave them a gentle kick aside with a flick of his foot. He was all bare now, all for her. She'd thought him gorgeous last night, thought she'd seen quite a bit of him, that she'd paid attention. But it was nothing compared to now, to seeing the manly sculpture of him, the carved definition of his upper arms, the chiselled symmetry of his abdomen, the squared angles of his iliac girdle, tapering downward, leading the eye to the magnificence of his phallus jutting upward, the divine architecture of man on perfect display. 'I doubt Michelangelo could have done better,' she breathed.

He came to the bed and for a moment her heart leapt and she reached for him. But he laughed, drawing her up to her feet. 'It's your turn now, *ma cherie*. Shall I instruct?' He took her vacated place on the bed, lying on his side, a leg propping up a hand dangling dangerously near his erect phallus. She had sudden, erotic visions of him pleasuring himself as she undressed. Perhaps he meant to—perhaps that was part of this feast for the eyes.

His hand wrapped about his phallus and gave an experimental stroke. 'Would you like that, *ma cherie*? Would you like to watch?'

She blushed, her body prickling with an embarrassed, wanton heat. 'How did you know?'

He laughed. 'You give yourself away too easily tonight. Every thought is written on your face.' He dropped his voice. 'I love it. I want to know what you want.'

She moved to him and disengaged his hand, pushing it gently aside, taking him in her hand instead. 'I want it and I don't want it. If you spend yourself now, I will have to wait that much longer for you to spend yourself for me.'

He leaned forward and nipped at her neck. 'You're a

selfish minx, and a tease, too. I thought you were supposed to be getting undressed.'

'You expect me to be able to concentrate on undressing when you're putting on quite a show just lying
there?' she scolded. She lifted a leg, resting it on the
chair near the bed, and pulled back her skirts to reveal
a stockinged expanse of long, slim leg. Then she began
to roll.

She was killing him with her slow seduction. Women
wore too many damn clothes, especially English
women. Julien bit back a groan as she finished with her
stockings and instead of releasing her skirts, she moved
to her hair, taking out one pin at a time. Vixen! She was
going to make him pay in anticipation for every inch of
skin revealed and he was loving every moment of this
exquisite, seductive torment. But what he was loving
more was Emma's confidence in her sexuality. He had
had a taste of that last night when she'd taken the lead
in their lovemaking, riding him astride. Tonight was yet
another course in the feast that was Emma Luce's sensuality and he meant to see that they both ate their fill.

At last, she discarded her dress, a plain, dark work
dress that buttoned up the front. She'd not dressed for
dinner and he gave a silent thanks for that. There'd not
be layers upon layers of petticoats and fancy corsetry beneath a work dress. He did not think he could
have withstood an elaborate siege to his senses tonight.
He'd been aroused before he'd even reached home. That
arousal had only ratcheted at the sight of her drowsing
in the chair. Coming to this room, watching her watch-

ing him remove his clothes, had done nothing to diminish it. Now he was flagrantly rock-hard on her bed, and she was teasing him with every button.

At last, the dress fell from her body and the firelight played with the thin fabric of her chemise and pantalettes, outlining the high, full curve of her breasts, hinting at pebbled nipples beneath the linen, lining the flat plane of her belly between her hips, the trimness of her waist. Emma Luce was a woman who kept herself in good shape. Over her head went the chemise and the pantalettes fell with far less resistance than last night, no teeth ripping required.

He went to her then, when the last garment fell, to hell with his self-imposed rules about no touching. That part of the game was over now. He wanted his hands all over her, wanted to scoop her breasts into his palms, to feel the weight of them in his palms, wanted his mouth on them, his tongue on her skin, tasting the salt and jasmine of her.

She wanted it too. There was no demur from her when he picked her up and carried her back to the bed; no cries of unfair play when he laid siege to her body with his mouth. She begged just the once, dragging him over her, and he complied. There was nowhere he'd rather be than inside her, pushing them both towards that incredible place they'd discovered last night.

'Help me get us there,' he whispered, his mouth against her throat. Her legs closed around his hips, her hips rising to meet his own in welcome. He felt the sweet clench of her muscles squeezing around him, the silken slide of her channel as his phallus entered. A soft moan escaped him, a sound to mirror the relief that came with being inside her. The fanciful notion swept him that somehow when he was with her, he was home, that there was a completion he could find nowhere else, with no one else. It was nonsense, but it fit the moment and he didn't challenge it, he went with it, followed it, gave himself over to it as their bodies picked up the rhythm. It was slower than last night. There was a poignancy to this lovemaking, his body aware of every nuance from the rise and fall of her hips, to the little adjustments of her body to accommodate his, to the catch in her breath as her body gathered itself.

He lost himself in the prelude to climax. They were in a world of their own making, a world they were building moment by moment, a world where there was no time nor room to think about the vineyards, about his *oncle*, about his secrets. There was only the two of them, only their pleasure. Nothing else mattered. Nothing else existed. Climax took him like a thunderclap, sudden and strong, a cacophony of the senses that overwhelmed him. He let himself be overcome, carried along the current of release. Peace would come later. For now, he let himself revel in the unbridled explosion of pleasure coursing through him and her.

If a man could climax twice in succession, watching Emma claim her pleasure would have sent him over the edge yet again. She met her pleasure head-on, eyes wide open as it took her, and tonight there was a special sense of manly pride in knowing he'd given this to her, that it wasn't a product of the night, of unleashed emotions out of control. Tonight, everything they'd done had been by deliberate choice and still the ending had been spectacular.

Peace came, the hard current of climax releasing him into a quiet pond where he could float. With her. He gathered her to him. She made a soft sound in her throat, her head resting in the hollow of his shoulder, a place that seemed uniquely made for her. This was what had haunted his day. This was what had brought him home tonight.

'This is new for me,' she whispered after a long while, her words an intimate confession in the dark.

'What is?' he felt compelled to ask, although he could guess, with some trepidation, where the conversation might go. He'd had widows as lovers before. There was always that moment of comparison, that brief glimpse into the marital bed and how their husbands had failed them by contrast. He'd rather not have that moment with Emma. Garrett had been a friend. But more than that, he wanted this to be just between himself and Emma. He wanted no intruders.

'Being reckless, letting myself be overwhelmed, caught up in the moment.' Her answer surprised him. 'I never thought…' Her voice trailed off. 'I never thought a lot of things,' she started again. 'I never thought I'd be a widow before I was thirty. Never thought I'd be facing so much of my life without Garrett, without a family of my own. I thought there'd be plenty of time.'

That was not what he'd expected to hear. He ran an idle hand down her arm in a gentle caress. 'Do you feel guilty?' He hoped not. It would taint the pleasure and he didn't want that for either of them. If she felt guilty, he would feel guilty, too.

'No. I've squared my conscience with that. There is no shame in seeking comfort or consolation.' She sighed. 'May I be completely, bluntly honest with you?'

'Yes,' he said solemnly. 'Please do.'

'It is the overwhelming pleasure I am having trouble countenancing. I had not thought to feel that way so soon, or to feel the pleasure so deeply with someone else.' She paused here and worried her lip. 'If I am being truthful, it's not just that I felt the pleasure deeply, but that I felt it *more* deeply.' She gave a long exhale and Julien waited, patient. He could guess what she wanted to say, but he would not say it for her. It was something she needed to say for herself.

'That's where the guilt comes from: feeling with a stranger what I did not feel with my own husband whom I loved with all my heart. Or at least thought I did.' Her gaze met his. 'What does it mean about the quality of my love if I found pleasure so soon with another? It is something of a surprise to me to be swept so entirely away by someone I didn't know a month ago, and I don't know where it leads or what it will accomplish, and all of that unnerves me.'

Of course it would. The pleasure, the planning, the purpose—or lack of purpose—in their lovemaking. She was a planner and Garrett had been all that was good and stable, the personification of reliability. But what was happening between them bore none of those trademarks. 'Is it any consolation to know I don't know where this leads either?' Julien offered. If she needed the consolation of promises, or the reassurance of a future together, he could give her neither. They were not his to share with any surety. All he could give her was the moment. At some point in the future, she would turn from him. She would hate him, feel betrayed by him. Perhaps these moments would offset the depth of that hurt, unintended as it was, when it came. Perhaps she would know that he'd not meant to hurt her.

She sighed and drew a circle around his nipple with the tip of her finger. 'When one is married, one takes a lot for granted without realising it, because imagining anything else is too horrifying. I assumed Garrett would always be there for a long time because anything else was unthinkable. A stable marriage blinds one to the reality that nothing is guaranteed; not for tomorrow, not a year from now. We had dreams and we never thought we wouldn't get to them.' He felt her smile against his chest. 'But this is hardly seemly conversation for bed. I'm sorry.'

'No, it's the perfect place. This is our cocoon, our safe place,' Julien assured her.

'What about you? What are your dreams, Julien? Has there been anyone?'

No intruders. He didn't want anyone here but the two of them. 'There was someone, a long time ago. We did not have the same dreams. She needed more than I could give her.' Let that be a warning to Emma. He had his limits. She couldn't say he hadn't said so.

'She broke your heart?' He could hear chagrin on his behalf rising in Emma's voice and it touched him that she sought to be his champion. Then she quieted. 'I'm sorry, Julien. I am sure you didn't deserve it.'

'Are you though? How do you know I didn't deserve it?' he teased lightly. 'I'm argumentative, and stubborn, according to you.'

'And don't forget contradictory,' Emma added. She rolled to her side and fumbled in the drawer of the bedside table.

'What are you doing? Come back.' He reached for her, not wanting the idyll to be over. There were hours yet before dawn and he wanted to spend every one of them right here.

'I'm still here. I haven't left. Now, roll over. You promised me I could touch you, later. Now it's later.' He watched, entranced, as she poured oil from a vial into the palm of her hand and blew on it, warming it. 'I've wanted to give you a massage ever since you took your shirt off. Lie still and let me.'

It was the most decadent proposal he'd likely ever receive. He rolled onto his stomach and felt the weight of her across his buttocks as she straddled him, felt the warmth of the oil, then the competence of her hands as they rubbed the oil into his skin, into muscles he hadn't realised were tired until she kneaded them into relaxed submission. This was heaven, to be here with her in the dark. Something deep in his soul cried out, wanting this for as long as it could last.

Over the next weeks, that one thought sprang constant in his mind. If spring could last for ever, he would be the happiest of men. Spring was the perfect season—

a season of hope, a season full of potential, all things were possible. There was promise everywhere Julien looked—the land promised renewal after a long winter: trees with leaves, fields of green, flowers in bloom. Overhead, the skies were blue with the promise of mild weather, warmer weather, to come, the vineyards burgeoned with the buds of new grapes. It would be May soon, there would be leaves and flowers on the grape vines, the buds of April having blossomed.

He spent his days in anticipation of that. He showed Emma how to trim out unneeded growth, how to structure the buds so that they produced quality grapes. These were heady days, filled with walking the vineyards with Emma beside him, showing her the work of raising grapes. There were picnics aplenty, sitting on the south-facing slopes of the vineyards, making love in the afternoon sun, telling stories, learning one another. He told her stories of attending school in England. He loved listening to her talk of her family, of her brothers; he railed on her behalf when she talked of her miserable debut in London and how the other girls would have nothing to do with her because of her father's 'dirty' money.

In the evenings, he loved to pull a stool up to the kitchen worktable and watch her as she cooked. Petit had acquired several nights off in order for them to have the kitchen to themselves. He treasured those meals prepared by Emma and eaten at the kitchen table. And always the lovemaking. No honeymoon could have been finer. But like with all honeymoons, he was acutely aware there would be an end. The gala was drawing closer and he could not keep her here at the chateau for ever. But out there, beyond the chateau walls, his secrets waited to destroy his happiness one more time. One more day, he told himself each morning, and then the next. One more day, before all of this unravelled and Emma learned the truth. One more day before it would all end. The only question was how and when.

Chapter Fifteen

When it ended, he was naked on a picnic blanket caught quite literally with his trousers down, Emma lying beside him drawing her circles on his chest while the early May sun beat down on them. 'I've had a note,' she began in drowsy tones. 'From Widow Clicquot. She's invited us to tea at Boursault.' It was said so casually, Julien did not at first grasp the full import. 'Well, she's invited me, but I assumed it would be fine to have you come along. *Would* you like to come? I didn't stop to think that you might be too busy here with the grapes.'

He didn't hear the last. His brain had finally caught up with the implications. Dear God, Emma was going to have tea with the Queen of Reims. The widow knew everyone and everything, and that boded ill for him. He levered up on his elbows, the sudden movement dislodging Emma rather abruptly. 'Why did she invite you for tea?' How had this connection come about? He certainly hadn't prompted it.

Emma looked bewildered. 'I wrote to her last week

to introduce myself and to let her know we would be holding a gala in June. She is a living legend. I figured if I was going to run my own vineyard I needed to know her.'

Julien felt his gut clench. He tried to keep the panic out of his voice and only partially succeeded. 'Is that what you told her, that you were running the vineyard?' Good God, if the Widow told Edouard Werle, her business partner and currently the Mayor of Reims, and if he told any one of the consortium, it could lay waste to his plans. That was just the beginning of the damage, what one wrong word could do to business. That wasn't counting what one wrong word could do to him, to them and the relationship they were starting to build. It would annihilate them.

'Julien, what's wrong? I just wrote to her and told her I was new to the chateau at Cumières, that I was newly widowed, that my husband had left the chateau to me, and that I was interested in learning about wine.' Two little creases formed in the space between the slender arches of her brows. 'Is it because she's the competition? Is that why you're upset? I can't figure you French out sometimes. One moment the consortium is a council of your friends and the next it's a cabal of competitors.' She gave a light laugh. He had to be careful not to overreact.

'It is a competitive business first and foremost,' he reminded her. 'Clicquot-Werle is so far above the rest of us, they aren't really the competition. We just compete amongst ourselves. I once saw their cellars in Reims.

They have cranes to lift the barrels up to the bottling rooms. We have three presses, but they have eight.'

'Perhaps *we* should have eight,' Emma hypothesised.

'We don't dominate the Russian market,' Julien pointed out, reaching for his trousers. 'Her champagne does.'

Emma laid back down on the blanket and looked up at the sky. 'We need to dominate a market. What about the British market? Surely with the Season and all the balls and parties there's room to expand.'

Julien frowned. 'Not even the big houses sell more than a few thousand bottles a year to Britain.' He tried to tease, 'The English are too busy drinking your father's gin.'

'Do you wonder why that is? It seems to me that you should do some research. Why is it that the Russian court consumes thousands upon thousands of bottles each year but the British do not? Is it the taste? If so, what about the taste? Can we cater to that taste with a particular blend? For instance, is it too sweet for the British? The Russians love sweet things, but the English are more of a savoury people, wouldn't you say? They like their beef and gravies.'

She kept saying *we*. It was an intoxicating and dangerous little word. It conjured up all sorts of fantasies of what it would be like to build a champagne empire with her. To teach her all he knew about the grapes and the growing, the blending and the bottling. All she had to do was give him the land. *Marry her.* His *oncle*'s grand strategy echoed in his mind, taking on a different tone than when his *oncle* had first floated the idea.

It was no less palatable than it had been the first time, but it was becoming shockingly more tempting and harder to resist. Perhaps because it was less dishonest than it had been in the beginning. To seduce her, to feign love for her in order to trick her into marriage all so that he could claim the property through her, had smacked of dishonesty—a dishonesty of feelings, and a dishonesty of agenda. He would not entertain such an idea. But now the idea wasn't based entirely in dishonesty. His feelings would not be a lie. He cared for her. He wouldn't be feigning his desire. That part of it was honest. Getting the vineyards back was a benefit by association. Would she ever believe though that that wasn't his primary motivation?

You're going to lose her in the end. She'll hate you if she thought you married her for the vineyards. But she's going to hate you anyway when she finds out you've been dishonest about who you are and what your purpose is here—that you want the chateau and the lands for yourself. You don't have to lose the vineyard, too.

'Julien, are you even listening to me?' Emma punched him on the arm, a playful scold. 'I'm rolling out a whole new marketing plan for us and you're somewhere else. I'm going to write to my father and see if he can investigate reactions to champagne for us. I was also thinking, we could set my brother Gabriel up as an agent of sorts. He already travels for my father, selling gin. Why not have him travel with our champagne? We can send him cases for sampling and he can meet with all the hostesses in London, at least get their feedback about the taste. He could also go to restaurants. Why limit oneself to just private parties?'

Us. We. It was too much. 'You are aware that Garrett was not turning a profit here. You act as if this place were a growing concern.'

'Because he was not serious. This was a hobby to him. He loved having his vintage shipped to him, to tell everyone the wine on the table for the evening was from his own vineyards. That's all he wanted it for. Now we could really make something of the place. You've kept everything in immaculate shape. You just need a marketer, and that's me. I might not know as much about grapes as you do, but I do know how to sell things. With your guidance, I am sure I can put this place on the map, so to speak.' She sat up and reached for his hand. 'But I *will* need your guidance. I can't do it without you, you needn't worry. I need you to introduce me to the consortium, to be my liaison with them until I'm more familiar.'

The way she talked was everything he'd ever dreamed of, what he'd wanted with Clarisse. A partner by his side. But he had to tread carefully here. They weren't partners. He owned nothing here. She talked as if they were equals but they were not, for so many reasons. And yet, beneath the sun on a picnic blanket, or lying in her bed in the dark of night, they were equals for a short time when they made love. He was desperate to hang on to that, desperate to appease both his *oncle* and her without hurting either of them.

He pulled on his shirt and she made a pout. 'I miss you already, Julien,' she teased. 'I like you better naked.' She pulled him down beside her. She smelled of jasmine and sunlight. 'Shall I tell the Widow we'll accept her invitation?'

'Yes.' He would go and be on hand for damage control, if needed. There was always a chance the Widow would be discreet and not bring up anything personal. He might survive the interview. The Widow was a businesswoman first and foremost. Perhaps she would not stray too far from that.

'And the others? Shall I invite them individually to the chateau or shall I expect to meet them at the next consortium gathering, which should be fairly soon. They meet the first part of each month, yes?'

His *oncle* would say he wasn't doing a very good job of distracting her. Perhaps he'd put his shirt on too quickly, after all. He leaned over and tendered a soft kiss. 'You have a lot on your mind today, Em. Should I do something about that?'

She looked up at him with clear grey eyes. 'The note from Madame Clicquot was a reminder that I can't just sit around watching grapes grow. I've been idle too long.'

He made a playful grimace. 'That is not an endorsement of my skills. I shall have to try harder to keep you entertained.' He dropped a kiss to the column of her throat. He nipped and she laughed but she also batted him away. 'No, seriously, Julien. I've been decadently lazy. It's not that I haven't enjoyed these past weeks. But there's work to be done. Do you realise I've been here two months and I haven't left the estate? I haven't met anyone. I haven't minded it, but if I remain a recluse any longer people will think I'm rude.'

'They will think you're an English widow in mourning. They will understand.' Julien took refuge in the old argument. 'No one expects you to be entertaining.' He still wasn't sure how her presence would impact the gala. The event he and his *oncle* were counting on was exciting in its possibilities as well as frightening. There was so much that could go wrong.

'I'm a businesswoman. The vineyard business never rests, as you've told me. I cannot be idle in the spring. I must prepare for the harvest, for the marketing that comes afterwards.' She cocked her head, smiling at him, unaware of how much her conversation unnerved him, of how much her words were bringing everything to a head. 'I think if I were to ask you when the busiest time of year is, you would tell me spring through the harvest. But I would tell you the hard work is autumn through spring, getting our bottles into the hands of clients.'

Julien tried one last time to dissuade her, although he was already recognising it solved nothing, only delayed the inevitable. 'You cannot be her. You cannot be Madame Clicquot. I have to be honest with you, *ma cherie*, if you're thinking to replicate her personal trajectory to the top of the champagne industry, it cannot be done any longer.'

'What do you mean by that, Julien? Do you doubt me?' He hated seeing the smile fade from her face, the spark in her eye turn to something harder. But she had to be told the truth for her own good.

Be honest, it's for your own good, too. His conscience stabbed hard. *You have a stake in this. Don't you dare forget about that.*

'Don't be angry, Emma, because I am willing to point out some not inconsiderable truths to you,' he replied hotly. There was a long silence, he could almost feel her bristling beside him, then he felt the tension ease from her, felt her eyes upon him. A look of apology passed between them. They'd both behaved badly, quick to snap, quick to temper. While it made for good lovemaking, it also made difficult conversations that much harder.

'All I mean, Emma, is that the times and politics are against you in a way they were not against her. One could argue that she was successful because she slipped through the cracks and succeeded when no one was looking.' It was in fact an argument his *grandpère* had repeated from his father, Julien's great-grandfather, who had indeed been a contemporary of the Widow. Champagne was a tight knit region, Julien explained to Emma. Everyone from Epernay to Cumières knew everyone, and for a long while there were no outsiders. The industrial revolution that had swept Britain and parts of France had been slow in coming here. That, too, had worked in the Widow's favour.

'If anything,' Julien concluded, 'the coming of industrialisation has not freed women, at least not middle and upper-class women. It has done just the opposite. Those women are expected now, more than ever, to occupy the private sphere of the home. It is the one distinction that sets them apart from their lower-class working girl counterparts. Those girls must earn their bread.'

'Like the distinction of a gentlemen, hmm?' Emma replied languidly, but he was not fooled by it. There would be a sharp barb nestled in her response. 'The only thing that defines a gentleman is that he does not work for his income. Others do the work for him.' That barb hit rather too close to home for Julien, and in ways that she would not have meant to target.

'Yes, I suppose so. So, you see, as Lady Luce, the wife of a baronet, you cannot possibly dabble in trade or business.'

'But as the daughter of a gin merchant?' she countered easily. 'Perhaps then I might.'

Julien frowned. 'Not even then. You're an heiress in that regard. Be honest. Is your father leaving the running of his gin company to you?' They both knew the answer already. The company would go to her brothers when her father retired. They both knew as well that even now, her mother was not involved in the day-to-day running of the business. Her mother's role was to throw lavish parties and help sweet-talk politicians, but nothing beyond that. 'Don't hate me because I'm right, Emma.'

Oh, no, he thought sardonically, *there will be plenty more and much better reasons to hate me, just wait.*

'I see.' Emma gave him a hard final look and jumped up from the picnic blanket. She brushed at her skirt, her voice calm. 'You're not as much like Garrett as I thought. He was never intimidated by my ideas.'

'Since when has disagreement been a sign of intimidation?' He got to his feet. His temper was starting to rise again. 'I have offered you my opinion because I respect you. I am *not* intimidated by you. If I was, do you think I'd tell you things I know you don't want to hear?'

'Yes, I think you might.' Her grey eyes flashed. Emma Luce in a temper was as formidable a sight to behold as Emma in a passion. 'It would depend on your motives.'

'What would those be? I can't think of a single thing I'd gain by making you angry at me.' Julien made sure his voice was well infused with just how ridiculous he thought the assertion was. There was a long pause and for a moment Julien was hopeful that the pause meant she saw the flaw in her reasoning. But when she spoke, it was with calm, measured tones and chilling words.

'I can. To keep me in the dark.' She gave him a hard look before turning to walk away.

That barb hit too close to home. 'About what, Emma? What do you think I'm hiding?'

'I don't know. Something.' She paused before spearing him with a stare. 'I notice that you don't plead denial. That says a great deal, that my worries aren't baseless, after all.' She did leave him then, striding away to begin the long trek home.

'Emma, wait!' he called after her. 'We're too far from the house. We'll drive back together. I'll have the picnic things cleared up quickly. Just wait.'

She turned back long enough to say, 'I have been waiting and I'm done with that now. I'll walk back. I need time to think, and so do you.'

Every fibre of his being urged him to go after her.

No good could come of Emma being left alone too long with her thoughts. She would imagine all sorts of perfidious things. But what would he say? Were there any words, any arguments that could make things better? He shook out the blanket and folded it, watching her retreat into the distance. This was not going well at all. He would not be able to contain her much longer. Nor did he want to, and that was as much a problem as anything else.

He loved her ideas, loved her desire to engage in the business of winemaking and selling. But those were the very things that kept him and his *oncle* from their dream. If she were to succeed, she'd have no motive to sell. And if she were to fail, he and his *oncle* didn't have the funds yet to make an offer on the place. Julien climbed into the gig and gave a desultory cluck to the horse. Everything had been going so well until she'd come along, and now his quiet world, a world that hadn't made him happy but at least had been a world he understood, was on fire. She was burning him from the inside out. At this rate, he'd be nothing but ash when she was done with him.

Chapter Sixteen

She was done with waiting. Emma strode through the fields that abutted the road, her steps wide, her pace angry. She was angry with herself, angry with Julien. She'd waited because she'd wanted to. She'd chosen this affair over pushing forward with the vineyards, all the while knowing deep down that the two were not mutually compatible, that it *would* come to a choice. She could not have both.

She'd not expected, though, that it would come to a head over an invitation to tea. She'd actually expected a very different reaction from him. She'd thought he'd be excited about the initiative she'd taken and about the doors this invitation could open. But he'd reacted as if it were the worst possible thing she could have done.

Emma picked up a stick and swatted at the tall grasses as she walked. A few bumblebees buzzed in irritation at the disruption. Julien's reaction was proof that she didn't know him as well as she liked to believe. She'd felt they'd grown close over the past weeks. They'd told each other stories of their childhoods, of their families. They'd made love exotically, erotically, on picnic blankets, before fireplaces, even once on the kitchen worktable after a homemade supper. She'd never known the depths of pleasure that she knew in Julien's arms. Surely such pleasure could not be feigned or fabricated without there being genuine feeling, sincere caring for one another.

She knew that was true on her part, which was why this current impasse cut at her so deeply. She liked Julien, perhaps more than liked him. It was hard to use the word *love* so soon after losing Garrett, mostly because she'd not expected to ever fall in love again. But here Julien was, showing her a different passion than the love she'd shared with Garrett, showing her that a person might have more than one meaningful relationship in their lifetime. And yet, there was a price for that. He was not Garrett. She'd keenly felt that today.

Julien had not supported her today. It had all been subtly done. Someone less aware might not have even noticed, but she had. He'd looked for any opportunity to undermine her ideas, and her ambition. She'd not understood it. Didn't he see that her success with the vineyard was his success as well? She heard her father's voice in her head: *It's never just one thing.*

Businesses or relationships didn't succeed or fail because of one single incident. Some might say they'd won or lost a fortune on the turn of a card, but it was never that clear-cut. There was always something underneath, something that preceded the watershed event. The quarrel today had been that—a watershed event—

bringing to the fore issues that had existed from the beginning between her and Julien, issues that she'd not bothered to resolve. Mainly, the issue of who was in charge here. That had been between them from the start. Julien was still trying to be in charge.

Emma made a list in her head of all that she'd not yet done since arriving: she'd not seen the books; she'd not met the consortium; she'd not driven around to the various domains and introduced herself; she'd not gone into Reims and connected with the bankers. Ideally, these were things Julien should have helped facilitate. But he'd never once offered. It prompted questions she didn't want to ask: Had he deliberately blinded her? Kept her here? Distracted her on purpose? Was there something he didn't want her to know? Without her in the open meeting neighbours and the growers' consortium he could maintain the illusion of being in charge. And she'd let him. In hindsight, she could see the pattern. Each time they'd got close to issues of her being in charge, he'd found ways to divert the conversation with a story, with an argument, with sex. And she'd allowed that, too. She'd chosen to pursue the pleasure he offered.

The chateau came into view, its majestic turreted wings and steep skyline demanding her attention. This was Garrett's gift to her. She needed to be worthy of it. That would require taking a stand against Julien if he continued to block her way forward. It would mean letting him go as a lover.

You knew it would end, her conscience taunted.

Had it been worth it? To fill the loneliness, to experience something new? To remind herself she was alive? These were no small things. But now it was time to move forward with or without Julien. If he was a man who could not support a woman's success, then she was better off without him. But that didn't stop the idea from hurting.

He was in the cellars when she returned, in the room he claimed as his office. The door stood open. The only time the space was unlocked was when he was in it. It had not struck her as odd at first, but it did now. *Was* there a reason he kept it locked when there was essentially just the two of them here? Field workers were not up to the chateau and the house servants could be trusted implicitly. Keeping it locked meant she had to ask him for access to the room and to all the room contained even though the room and its contents were technically hers.

Julien looked up from the desk that was crammed inside; it wasn't a large space. It seemed more like a closet hollowed out from the cave walls. There were no windows, just the desk, a chair, and shelves lined with books and ledgers. He also looked crammed inside, a man too big for the space. His eyes met hers, his brow lifting in challenge, in question, as if to say, *You're in my space, what do you want?*

'I would like to see the books from the last seven years.' She was pleased her words came out cool and polite. 'Please have someone bring them to the library right away.' What could he say to that except yes? They both knew he had no grounds on which to refuse her. This was her house, her books, her right.

'Would you like me to join you?' he answered her with equally polite tones. 'I would be glad to show you the books.' They both knew that was a lie. If he'd been glad to show them to her he would have done so already. The fact that he'd not voluntarily offered to show them to her weeks ago when she'd first arrived, coupled with the recent reality that he hadn't pled denial when she'd accused him of hiding something this afternoon, hung palpable between them, gilding the interaction with an air of suspicion.

'No, thank you. I will let you know if I have questions.' She wanted to see the books with her own eyes and form her own opinions first without seeing them through whatever lens Julien might want her to view them through. The idea that she could potentially not trust that lens made her stomach clench. She did not want to believe that but she *must* consider it.

The books were waiting for her on the long library reading table when she arrived after a short detour to her chambers to change from the picnic. She'd traded her outdoor clothes for a loose gown of dark blue. It wasn't quite black but she wasn't seeing anyone, and she wanted to be comfortable. It was going to be a long night and likely an uncomfortable one. Soon she would know if Julien was hiding anything from her, or she'd know she owed him an apology for her thinly veiled accusation this afternoon. If she was wrong, would he forgive her? She'd attacked his honour. Even so, she'd prefer to be wrong than to discover some perfidy on his part. If there were lies, it meant there were also other, difficult, realisations she'd have to face as well and she'd rather not, especially when they'd all rotate around the knowledge that she had been duped.

There was something wrong with the books. This was the only conclusion Emma could come to after running through all seven years twice. The books were not complicated: money in, money out, and this was not a busy chateau dealing with countless exports, just one man's delight in having wine from his own property. She did not think she'd overlooked anything. But two problems were staring her in the face.

First, there weren't enough grapes accounted for. The chateau had more acreage than there were grapes being recorded. Second, Julien wasn't drawing a salary. Not once in seven years had any money been paid to him and yet Garrett had always talked of having hired him. Hired people were paid. Other wages not attached to the household budget were recorded here—like the payments made to the grape picking crews that came through every harvest.

An awful fear took root in her stomach as she stared at the ledgers. Had Julien stolen from Garrett? Was that what he was trying to keep her from discovering? It would be impossible to know how much he'd taken. Had he also taken the grapes and sold them, pocketing the profits? It would be so easy to do without someone here to oversee the overseer.

And yet it felt wrong. A man like Julien, who loved the land, who spoke of this place with such passion for it, would not steal from it. People didn't steal from those they loved. She couldn't stop her mind fast enough. What did that mean for them? Nothing good. Emma left the table and began to pace. Whatever was happening here, he'd not felt enough for her to tell her. Why was she so surprised by that? She'd been betrayed by so-called friends before and Julien had at least left her plenty of hints. She should have been on alert for that pattern to repeat itself since the day he'd left word with Richet about his whereabouts but not bothered to share them with her.

Her mind might understand those conclusions but her heart did not like them. It refused to believe she was that inconsequential to Julien, that he could be so callous. She glanced at the clock on the mantel. It was just after eleven. She'd worked through supper and well into the evening. It was late but not too late. How would she ever sleep tonight? She'd been angry and hurt when she'd started the process, and now she was angrier still, her hurt magnified by what might very well be a truth she could no longer hide from. There was nothing so embarrassing as self-delusion. Especially when it wasn't the first time. She was supposed to have learned her lesson.

There's no time like the present.

She wasn't going to sleep. She might as well put her questions to him. Ask him about the missing grapes and the non-existent salary. She would see his true colours. She made for the stairs. This time of night, he'd be in his room—a room that was actually guest chambers. Quite nice quarters for someone who worked for the chateau. No attic room or below stairs dormitory for him. Garrett had treated him like a king with those rooms.

Or did Garrett know? Perhaps Julien had self-assigned those rooms because there was no one to gainsay him?

Oh, how she hated such negative thoughts. Even more, she hated that sometimes they were necessary. One didn't get ahead in the world by walking around with blinders on.

She halted at the door to Julien's room. Suddenly, knocking on the door became a litmus test. If he was worried about what she'd find in the ledgers, how could he be asleep? He'd be awake, concerned. Surely, that boded better? Only a man who didn't care would be able to sleep after the quarrel they'd had. She rapped on the door and waited.

'Come.' Relief flooded through her. He was awake. It was a sign of concern, a sign that perhaps the quarrel had left him restless and dissatisfied, too. Perhaps it was also a sign that all might not be lost.

Emma stepped into the room. It was a distinctly masculine space. Tall leather wing-backed chairs were set before the fire. Julien occupied one of them, dressed in banyan and trousers. The banyan gaped open, exposing a glimpse of his torso. He was such a handsome man. Just this afternoon they'd been… No. She must set aside such thoughts. Until she got to the bottom of this, there could be no more of *that*.

'I have questions. I didn't want to wait until morning.'

'So, you've come for a bedtime story.' Julien's eyes

were like glacier shards as he watched her progress. She took the empty chair, feeling the coldness of his gaze.

She cut right to it. 'Were you stealing from my husband?'

'Why would you think that?' His fingers played with the stem of the brandy snifter on the table beside him.

'Because there is no record of your salary in those books.'

'And that makes me a thief?' He was unbearably aloof. He was making her do all the conversational work here. But what had she expected? That he would be in tears, begging her forgiveness, on his knees declaring undying devotion for her? There she went again, conflating business with pleasure, assuming that he cared for her and that caring would spill over to how he treated her as a business partner. She had to stay resolute.

'It makes you dishonest. We can start with that and go from there.'

It hurt to look at her, to see the stony shards her eyes had become, a gaze that had so recently looked on him as if he were the focal point of her world. He wanted *that* Emma back. He wanted to be on a picnic blanket with her, touching her, smelling her, talking to her, listening to her spin impossible dreams. He wanted to feel alive, the way he felt when he was with her, as if he could conquer the world, as if the world had not beaten him down but instead had marched him towards this moment.

Julien reached for his glass and took a swallow to give himself something to do besides watch her. He'd known she'd come. She was a woman who didn't like to wait. That she'd waited this long to make her discoveries was something of a miracle. He'd had plenty of time to come up with explanations and he had nothing except the truth to offer her. He did not think the truth would go over well. But if she was going to hate him, it would be for the truth, not a lie.

'The truth might not suit you. Are you sure you want it?' He poured some brandy into the spare glass and pushed it her way. 'You'll need this.' He let her take a swallow before he started. 'I am not stealing from you and I never stole from Sir Garrett. I do not draw a salary because I do not take a monetary wage from the estate, although your husband did offer me one.'

He gave her a moment to digest that, her sharp brain working. 'The grapes,' she breathed. 'There is a certain quantity of grapes missing each year.' She paused. 'You took your pay in grapes?'

'And in investment in wine futures—the predicted sale of upcoming vintages,' he supplied.

'Is that why the estate doesn't appear to be making money on the wines? Because the profit is paid to you after Garrett breaks even and gets his money back?'

'Yes. Of course, I roll quite a bit of my profit back into the estate. You could say I'm something of a shareholder. Garrett and I treated the estate like a joint venture. He put up the money, I put up the time and effort. It's been an experiment, we started small. Like you, he wanted to study the industry before he fully committed.'

She nodded. 'This year was important to him. That

seven-year vintage was to be a turning point for him.'
A turning point for them all. He'd hoped to increase
his level of investment in the estate and then in a couple years make an offer for it with his profits from the
estate and his other venture with Oncle Etienne. 'And
the grapes?'

Julien to a deep breath. 'My Oncle Etienne and I
blend the grapes with the grapes on his property to
make a *couteau champenois*, but we need the *pinot noir*
grapes from here. We don't have enough of our own currently.' Because his *oncle* had not been able to acquire
the *pinot noir* vineyards yet.

She seemed to give that some thought. 'That works
for now, but what happens when the chateau is up to
full bottle production and needs its grapes for itself?'
He'd hoped to own the chateau by then. 'The wine must
be very good then for you to live off the proceeds.' He
could see her running the numbers in her head.

'The *couteau champenois* is good, more importantly
it is becoming somewhat rare. People aren't in want of
the "red champagne" like they used to be. It's for an
exclusive club of wine drinkers.' Who paid large sums
for the bottles, an example of how important it was to
control supply and demand.

She was silent, gathering her thoughts. 'Those are
not damning things, Julien. I do believe they're true,
as far as they go. But they don't go far enough. They
make me wonder why a land steward would eschew an
income and choose to invest in the estate he works for.'
She took a thoughtful swallow of her brandy and stared

into the fire. 'These are not the actions of a land steward, are they, Julien?'

'I am very entrepreneurial.'

She gave a hard laugh. 'My husband may have believed that but I don't. Nothing about you has added up since the first day. You were nothing like what I expected.'

'You were *exactly* how I imagined you.' Julien poured a half glass.

'You were part farmer but only part because your manners were too fine. That made you a gentleman.' She was getting close now and Julien tensed with the knowledge of it. Any moment now she'd make the more difficult of the two connections and then the other would follow.

'Gentlemen don't earn money, it's what sets them apart.' She reprised the discussion from the picnic before spearing him with a look and a verdict. 'Julien Archambeau, are you a gentleman? Is that why you wouldn't take a wage from my husband?'

'A man has his pride, Emma.' It was untrue. He and his *oncle* made enough money from the *couteau champenois* to keep themselves afloat, and his *oncle* had the funds from their small shipping company, although much of that was kept in savings for the day when they could buy the rest of the vineyard. Still, he wasn't about to take coin for work. The Archambeaux had not sunk so low as to take wages for working their own land. It was all right for his *oncle* to have the shipping money—he was a second son. He'd always been expected to make his way in the world. But Julien's father had been the Comte. The title might mean nothing now, but there was pride.

She was studying him again. 'You would do all this work—walking the land, pruning, harvesting, all to attain some grapes?' She was prodding, prompting, and prying. Her instincts were telling her it didn't make sense, didn't quite add up. He could see her mind working. 'There's only one reason a person would make such a commitment to a place and that is attachment, love.' She fixed him with her stare and he met his fate bravely. 'Julien, tell me the truth. Did this chateau once belong to you?'

Chapter Seventeen

She sat frozen in place by her own revelation, disbelief and shock rolling through her even as her mind acknowledged that it made sense. The manners, the haughtiness of him, his willingness to challenge her, unlike any servant she'd ever encountered. The next question naturally asserted itself. 'Who are you, Julien?'

'The Archambeaux were gifted this land by the king in 1455.' Julien's voice was quiet in the dimness as he calmly delivered his *coup*.

'Then there must be a title that goes with it.' She would not let him sneak any detail past her, although her stomach was starting to tighten.

'Comte. Comte du Rocroi. But it doesn't matter any more. Titles come and go in this new France. Did you know they were suspended again four years ago? If a new government is voted in this year, there's rumour titles will be restored once again.' He shrugged. 'Not that it would mean anything. It would most likely just be the restoration of hereditary titles, which our family's is,' he added. He gave a sardonic smile. '*Et voila,*

I am the Comte again.' This was followed by a harsh chuckle. 'No privileges though, just the words. Just the title.' She recognised he was trying to mitigate the revelation, and her heart, most regrettably, warmed to it, prompting her to wonder even now—was he trying to protect her?

'The purported land steward is a French *comte*.' She repeated the words, starting to feel silly now. All the things she'd accused him of seemed ridiculous.

'As I said, it doesn't matter. Titles are meaningless now in France. We lost the title in the Revolution and then we lost the land when my great-*grandpère* lost his head. Great-Grandpère sent his son, Matthieu, my *grandpère*, and my father, who was only an infant, to the safety of England, as I've mentioned before. But when the decree went out that all emigres must return in order for their families to keep their lands, my great-*grandpère* refused to bring his son home. He knew it wasn't safe. It cost him everything.'

'But when it *was* safe,' Emma picked up the story. She knew this part to some degree from what he'd shared during one of their many long, lazy afternoons. She spoke slowly, piecing it together. 'Your grandfather returned, leaving his younger son behind in England to continue running the now legitimate shipping company. But he had nothing to return home to. The lands had gone to someone else by then.'

'Titles were restored by the Bourbons so he had that to come home to. He established a second branch of our shipping business in Calais. He began saving his profits and making enquiries. It took time. The land had been broken up and it was owned by several different people. Once my grandfather was able to secure one of our old parcels, one with a house on it, we moved to Cumières and left the shipping office in capable hands. I was still quite young when we came here. Cumières is the only home I know. All I know of the time in Calais is in the stories my father told me. I grew up walking the land beside them, learning from them.'

'Until you were ten,' she prompted when Julien fell silent.

'Yes. It was hard to leave. I didn't want to go but Grandpère insisted that I have a foot in both worlds. He wanted me to learn the shipping business from my *oncle*. Just in case, he said. France was unreliable. The Revolution changed my *grandpère*. He lived with the knowledge that his country had killed his father, taken our family's property, forced him into exile not knowing if it would ever be safe to return. For a man who loved the land, it was a heavy fate. He lived with a strong sense of betrayal and distrust after that. Land and family were all a man could rely on, he would tell me.' The little boy he'd been had learned those lessons well, perhaps better than he thought, Emma mused. Julien kept his cards very close to his chest, as Garrett might say. People knew only what Julien wanted them to know. She was starting to see his omissions not as lies but as protection. Unnecessary protection, perhaps. He could trust her.

'As you know, I spent my winter holidays with my *oncle*. The trip to Cumières was too long to undertake for Christmas and the Channel too unpredictable. But

I had the summers here. I looked forward to those all year long.' There was a hint of a smile on his lips and a softness to his gaze, as if the words had conjured memories of fairer times. This Julien was irresistible, and he was dangerous to her resolve. Some of the fight went out of her. The longer he talked, the harder it was to remember why she was angry.

Her father's lesson came to her again: *Everything has two sides*. Perhaps she would have been less angry with Julien, perhaps they would be in bed right now if she'd applied her father's lesson sooner. The explanation was so simple. Julien didn't draw a salary because he was a gentleman, because he couldn't let go of that part of himself, of what his family had been. There was nothing nefarious about that or about the missing grapes.

'I am sorry for all your family has suffered,' Emma said quietly, aware that she'd have to do better than that for an apology. She had reparations to make. Julien wasn't the villain here. But quite possibly, she was. It had not gone unnoticed, although Julien had delicately not mentioned it, that she was now the owner of a piece of his estate, a very large piece, including a home that had been in his family for centuries before it was taken away. 'Julien, am I the enemy?' She didn't want it to be true. If it was true, why befriend her? Why teach her? Why make her his lover? These were implications she'd so far avoided pursuing because they led down unpleasant paths.

'Why would you think that?' His tone was more guarded now and she sensed he was trying to protect them both by evading her question. But she could not let it go.

'I am living in your house. *Your* house, *your* land is my inheritance from my husband.' How it must gall him to be the caretaker of this beautiful land and yet have no legal rights to it, to make decisions regarding its future. The only rights he had were given to him by Garrett to act as his man of business. With such freedom to act, perhaps it had become easy for Julien to pretend the place *was* his in all ways that mattered. Until she'd shown up. 'You must resent me.' How ironic that she'd feared being the one who would be betrayed in all this, when it was really Julien who was the one betrayed—by his country and in some ways by her and Garrett, albeit unintentionally.

'I don't resent you. Just the situation,' Julien said quietly. 'You had nothing to do with the circumstances.'

'I am part of those circumstances now, though, and I *do* affect them simply by being here, by having my own ambitions.' She thought about that for a long moment—something didn't seem right. There was another piece still missing. 'Julien, did you not try to buy the place from Monsieur Anouilh?' This place had been available seven years ago. Had it been a lack of funds? Chateaux and land didn't come cheaply, but surely they might have applied for a loan in Reims, especially if they already had some land established. They would have had collateral and a shipping firm to vouch for their solvency.

Julien gave a bitter laugh. 'We tried. Monsieur Anouilh refused to sell to us.'

He paused and she prompted, 'There's more, I sense it. I can handle it. It seems odd that a Frenchman would choose a foreigner over a neighbour.'

He shot her a swift glance before returning his gaze to the fire. 'Garrett outbid us. His pockets were end-lessly deep and he was determined to have the place for his new bride.' For her. Her heart sank even as Julien tried to pass it off. 'Your husband had no idea of our history with the place. He didn't know us or anything about the property.'

'You never told him? You let him hire you think-ing that you were just a convenient neighbour to watch over the property while he was away.' She was trying to figure out if she thought that was dishonourable be-haviour or not.

His gaze turned to her and lingered. 'You think it was somehow a lie to not tell him, don't you? But what could I do? This was the only way I could get close to the land, to take care of it. Then, Garrett offered me rooms here. My *oncle* and I decided it would do for a time.'

'Until you could make an offer to Garrett? Hop-ing perhaps he'd run out of enthusiasm for a place so far away?' Never guessing that Garrett would never let go of it, that the place had been consigned to his bride as part of her widow's portion. How it must have stung when she'd walked in, upending Julien's long-held hopes.

Julien nodded. 'That was the plan. We realised we'd need more money to make an offer to Garrett. He'd paid more than the place was worth but he didn't care.

He had money to burn. We'd have to at least match that amount when the time came. But meanwhile I could take care of the land and make sure it would be fruitful when another chance came.'

'But I came instead,' Emma put in.

'Do you really want me to say it, Emma? Yes, you were somewhat of a wrinkle in those plans.' The wrinkle being she was not interested in selling. She was interested in staying. She had nowhere else to go that allowed her the freedom and independence she was used to, the chance to build something of her own.

Guilt swamped her against her better judgement. She was now part of an untenable situation for Julien, for his *oncle. She* stood in the way of the family dream to restore the Archambeau lands and legacy, generations of work. She had no intention to sell. Surely, Julien must know that by now. There was no way he could get his hands on the land as long as she owned it and she *would* own it unless circumstances changed. Unless…

One of her father's lessons: *If something seems impossible in one environment, change the environment.* Julien could change the environment. He could chase her away, make things so unbearable for her that she would sell. That strategy seemed unlikely at this point given the time he'd spent coaching her on viniculture. Although, she wondered in retrospect if it was merely a failed strategy. Had he in truth been trying to overwhelm her with all the books, the long walks filling her with knowledge, and she'd thwarted his attempts? If that failed, there was another option even less savoury.

He *could* marry her. The land would become his upon marriage. She felt sick to her stomach. Was that why he'd taken her to bed? When all else failed, seduce it out of her? No. She would not believe it of him. She'd kissed him first. He'd been a complete gentleman right up until that day in the vineyard. He'd made no inappropriate overtures.

'Emma, say something. You've been silent too long and I can see your mind working.' Julien's low voice interrupted her thoughts.

'That's just it. I don't know what to say.' Emma rose. Anything she said now would be driven by emotion and confusion. She would regret it come morning. 'I think it's best that I leave now.' She needed to be somewhere he was not, somewhere she could think without those slate-blue eyes on her, where she wasn't driven to subjective empathy for this man. 'I have tea with the Widow tomorrow. You needn't come. I can manage it on my own.' Then, to restore a touch of the professional to a conversation that had begun that way and then severely veered off course, as so many of their conversations did, she added, 'Thank you for your time. Be assured, I will not make a habit of importuning you at such a late hour.'

That was too bad, he'd like to be importuned by her at this hour quite frequently, but for different reasons than awkward, secret-spilling conversations. Julien slumped in his chair after the door shut behind her. Now she knew. As predicted, the knowing had been disastrous. She wanted nothing to do with him beyond what she needed for the vineyards now. If she wasn't so inexperienced and in need of his expertise, he had no doubt she'd have asked him to leave. He'd not been dishonest with her, but he had not been truthful either about his attachment to this place. Should he have been? Would things be different if he'd told her from the start?

He stared at his empty brandy glass and debated a third glass. No. Another drink would not make it better. He feared nothing could. His family's legacy of loss had made him hard-bitten. He'd inherited quite a lot of his grandfather in that regard. He might have shaken that off if it hadn't been for Clarisse's betrayal, which had resulted in a broken heart and the loss of the land. His grandfather had been right. You could trust no one, and no one should be entrusted with the things you hold dear—one's heart, one's family, one's land. These precious items must be protected, locked away. He'd lost his heart to Clarisse, and his father had died of a broken heart over the double disappointment, defeated after a life of striving. How much more proof did he need?

And yet.

Those two simple words reminded him of his stupidity. And yet he knew all this and he'd still managed to lose his detachment when it came to Emma Luce. Julien ran a hand through his hair and let out a sigh. She'd done a number on him with her voracious appetite for knowledge, her intoxicating idiosyncrasies—he didn't think his mind would ever quite erase the pictures of her in the kitchen, rolling out dough with a smudge of flour on her cheek, or stirring a pot and bending over it with her eyes shut, sniffing it. He'd never had a woman cook for him before. Clarisse wouldn't be caught near the kitchens.

The two women couldn't be more different. Clarisse, blonde and diminutive, who loved to shop, who'd never worked a day in her life or known how to. How he'd loved pleasing her with a trinket or sweet. He'd lived for the sound of her laughter; the sparkle of her smile turned his direction in a crowded room. She'd been surrounded by beaux but she always found her way to his side—the young handsome heir to the Comte du Rocroi. He'd been a good dancer in those days. She'd loved that about him and his kisses, too. He'd not minded it had been hard to keep up with her tastes on his limited funds.

Emma was pleased with quieter pleasures. She'd immersed herself in the chateau, buried herself in reading, took delight in debating him where Clarisse had no interest in disagreeing with him. That would have required a discussion of things she had no knowledge of or desire to learn about. Whenever he'd talked about the grapes she'd laugh and say he sounded like a farmer. And of course, sounding like a farmer was definitely a bad thing according to Clarisse. She would teasingly remind him that a future *comte* didn't prune vines and walk the land in dusty boots. There would be servants to do all that for him once they married. She'd been keen to remind him of that, too. He'd have to start living like a *comte* after they wed.

Their marriage would never have worked. He would

have been unhappy within months. But he would have had his land. Oncle Etienne would have been happy. As soon as Julien produced a son in that marriage, the universe would be righted. The Archambeau line would inherit the chateau and all the vineyards between the chateau and his *oncle*'s farmhouse, the damage of the Revolution undone, the family avenged. No sacrifice, not even Julien's happiness or integrity, was too much to ask for when it came to *famille et terre*. Only he'd not understood it that way at the time.

He was different now, too. The young man who believed in love, who was hungry for a taste of it, was gone. He was approaching middle age, jaded and used to being alone, used to disappointment. He was not used to getting what he wanted. It always slipped away in the end. He and Emma had never stood a chance. He was too ruined. Ruined by a broken heart, ruined by a family legacy that was on the brink of becoming poisonous. It had defined four generations of Archambeau males, been the sole driving purpose of their lives. Now it had cost him Emma, a woman he had…feelings… for. He didn't dare call it falling in love. That was for fools. But he had feelings for her. Together, they might have made a passionate partnership—they might have built something remarkable if they'd had the luxury of a clean slate between them. That was gone now. Perhaps it had never existed.

He closed his eyes, leaning back in his chair, the wicked thought coming to him: At what point did a dream become a nightmare? At what point was he entitled to live his own life? To set his wants over those of his family? And if he could do those things, what would that life look like? He'd lived with the Archambeau legacy for so long he wasn't sure if he could live outside it.

Chapter Eighteen

It was the first time she'd been outside the estate since her arrival and the day couldn't be more different. The carriage top was down, the sun was on her face, and the countryside was in bloom, a far cry from the closed carriage she'd arrived in, the landscape as barren, as grey, as her mood. Grief had been her constant companion in those days. And yet her mood today was not as light as it might have been.

She was making the five-mile journey to Boursault by herself, without Julien beside her. The visit should have brought her great joy. What a thrill it was to meet the great champagne widow, Madame Clicquot, but that thrill was lessened by the tension between her and Julien. Last night's revelations had clarified some tensions but instilled new ones.

As a result, she'd not slept well, dozing off only at dawn for what turned out to be a dream-plagued nap. She probably looked like a hag between her black widow's garb, pale face, and dark circles beneath her eyes. This was not the sort of drama she was used to over a man. She and Garrett had never fought, never kept secrets, not even in the beginning when they'd been trying so hard to impress each other as new couples do. With Julien she was out of her depth. It was a new and uncomfortable experience.

She liked being in charge, liked knowing what came next. With Julien she did not know. Now, when she ought to be focused on the Widow and making a good impression, all she could think about was Julien. What was so terrible about what he'd done? He'd done nothing illegal. She'd come to the conclusion that what grieved her the most was simply that she hadn't known, that he hadn't felt he could tell her. He could take her to bed but he couldn't tell her who he really was or about his family's association with the estate.

Because it would have altered everything.

But why not after they'd begun the affair, when, surely, he was more certain of her? She had no answers for that, at least not answers she liked.

The Chateau Boursault came into view and Emma cleared her mind, focusing on the details of the building with its squared wings on either end and the rounded turrets, the steeply pitched roof, all done in the neo-renaissance style, and then there were the windows— so many windows! She began to count them to put herself at ease. She'd got to twenty when the carriage stopped in front of the steps leading up to the white six-panelled door. The place was magnificent and her first thought was that she wished Julien was here to see it with her.

She was expected and shown into the entrance, her

heels tapping on polished parquet flooring. The foyer was a room unto itself and decorated accordingly with a nod to Italianate styling. Columns set into the walls framed trompe l'oeil murals. A crystal chandelier hung from the ceiling, reminiscent of her own. This chateau was a palace, an homage to elegance. But it wasn't as old as Julien's. Where his had the patina of centuries, this one was new, barely lived in for two years. *Julien's.* She needed to be careful with that word. Was she really thinking of the chateau as his? That boded ill if she was already mentally ceding it to him. It echoed back to her earlier fear that perhaps he saw marriage as a way forward if he could not get what he wanted through business avenues. If she'd not had that revelation, would she have fallen for his ploy? Had she been that close? A footman led her through a series of interconnecting rooms to a small sitting room that overlooked the back gardens. The glass doors were open to let in the fresh breeze and Madame Clicquot was already there.

'Madame Luce, welcome. Forgive me if I don't get up. Age and my bones don't always agree with me.'

'Please, I would not have you bother on my account.' Emma crossed the room and helped herself to the chair adjacent to Madame Clicquot's. Seventy-five was indeed an august age and in ways the woman looked it. She had the double chin of a life well-fed if not well-lived, and Emma thought there was a resoluteness in the set of her jaw that came from perhaps the accumulated fatigue of carrying on, perhaps too often carrying on alone. Especially when there were burdens to be borne. Would she look like that at seventy-five? Worn and shaped by the pressures of her world? The aloneness of it? It was a sobering thought. But everything came with a price. Just different prices.

'Am I not what you expected?' The woman's eyes were shrewd. Whatever fatigue Emma might have detected was absent from her gaze. Her speech was certainly direct.

'I did not know *what* to expect. Thank you for receiving me. I am new to the area and I am desperate to learn everything I can.' Emma smiled. 'And desperate to meet you because you are a legend.'

'Hmmph.' Madame scoffed at that. 'Or was it that you wanted to meet because we are alike? You see some similarity between us? Both of us widowed at twenty-seven, trying to make something out of nothing? Like you, the wine was a side business for my family when Francois and I married. It was still a side business, really, when he died.' A maid brought in an enormous silver tea tray and set it down between them. Emma moved to do the honours.

'How do you find the Chateau?' she asked with a gimlet eye as Emma passed her a teacup painted with delicate sprigs of lavender. 'It has a ridiculous name, it should be a *domaine*. You should think about renaming it,' Madame hinted broadly. 'Nothing says Englishman like a poorly named vineyard. Aside from that though, your husband was a good sort. I met him once. I *am* sorry for your loss.'

'Thank you.' Emma sipped her own tea. 'I wanted to ask you about your *vendangenoir* and your presses.'

It was a good enough question to set Madame off

on her favourite subject, champagne. One question led to another, which led to a second pot of tea and another plate of cakes. The woman was impressive. Emma could have listened to her talk all day but it was clear the older woman was tiring. Emma immediately felt some guilt over that. She'd been enjoying herself so much. 'I must apologise for keeping you so long.' Emma set down her teacup as a hallway clock chimed five. Dear Lord, she'd been here two hours!

'Nonsense, I've enjoyed it immensely. There are not many women to talk with about the industry these days.' She waved a plump hand. 'In the old days, when I first began, there were several female *vignerons*.' She paused. 'Do you know the term? A *vigneron* is a grape-grower, someone who grows grapes expressly for wine. There were even women who blended the wines. Many of them widows who had to see to themselves. They took over their husbands' businesses and with success in most cases. But these days, there's no room for a woman unless she's already in position.' Madame gave her a strong look. 'I don't envy you trying to break into the business these days. There's machinery to think of now. Which of the new inventions can we use that will make the process efficient while still maintaining the integrity of being hand-crafted? It is a delicate balance to consider.'

And yet the House of Clicquot managed to turn out thousands of bottles a year. Emma thought industrialisation hadn't stumped Madame at all. But perhaps it hadn't been maximised to its fullest. Emma leaned forward. This was her moment to impress the Widow, to give back a piece of knowledge for all the woman had given her this afternoon. 'Industrialisation is not only changing how we can produce wine but also the markets it can reach. With railroads, we can reach far more potential customers without having to contact them directly. Right now, we need agents to represent the products to a select few. But with railroads, we can connect with people faster and farther. There's already a railroad in Epernay, more will be coming. I think the future is in labelling. The right kind of label can market a product as well as any agent. My father is in the gin business in England, and he's already using that technique to good success.'

'Is that so? We have labels already,' Madame countered.

'But are they labels as recognisable as the product? As if the label were its own product, one might say. Maybe not just a label with words on it, but a label with a picture of something people could associate with the product. A grape vine, the silhouette of a chateau, a glass, anything as long as it's a consistent image the buyer can count on seeing.'

'It's a very interesting idea. What does Monsieur Archambeau think about it?' Her eyes sharpened and she laughed. 'You did not think you'd escape today without us talking about Julien Archambeau? I'm surprised he didn't come with you.' And a little disappointed, too, Emma thought.

'He's busy with the grapes,' Emma improvised.

Madame lifted a brow. 'He's always busy. Too busy for a man his age. He needs to get out and meet people.

By people, I mean he needs to meet women. A handsome man should be married. Oh, I see I've shocked you. Age has nothing to do with appreciating a fine figure of a man. I've known the Archambeaux for ages. My family knew his back before the Revolution. Of course, Julien wasn't around then, but our families knew one another. My family wasn't noble so the Revolution posed a lesser threat to us and my father knew how to play the right sides. But it destroyed the Archambeaux. Matthieu, that's Julien's grandfather, never got over it. Etienne carries the family torch now.' She offered a stern look, 'I'm sure you know your chateau used to be theirs. Seventy years ago, to be sure. But French memories are long and they carry a grudge.'

'Yes, I know,' Emma said tersely, but it occurred to her that she just barely knew. The news was not even twenty-four hours old. Was this what Julien feared about tea with Madame Clicquot? That the old woman would unpack his family history without his permission?

'You'd best watch yourself. Julien is a persuasive man. I'm surprised he hasn't married you already. That's one sure way to put the chateau back into Archambeau hands.'

The old woman, legend or not, was outside the pale with that comment. 'I lost my husband only a couple months ago. I am not looking to remarry.'

'Well, one doesn't need to marry to enjoy the pleasures of Julien Archambeau,' the widow said sagely. 'But it does put one on the path towards marriage, just thinking of having him all to oneself for a lifetime.' Emma hoped her face didn't give her away. Did the widow guess that she'd already succumbed to Julien's charms? What an embarrassingly easy conquest she'd been.

'All I'm saying, *ma cherie*, is to watch yourself, if you don't mean to marry again. He was willing to marry for the chateau once before. There's no reason to think he wouldn't try to marry for it again, especially if there's no other way to get it.'

'Marry for it?' She stopped the widow in mid-story. 'He said he had his heart broken once.'

'Oh, indeed he did.' The widow shifted in her seat, settling her plump form in for a good telling. 'Seven years ago, before the government suspended titles yet again, he was the son of the Comte in those days. He was engaged to Clarisse Anouilh. Her dowry was the chateau and its vineyards. But her father broke the engagement off. He found someone better for his ambitions. Hers, too, truth be told. She never would have satisfied Julien. She was pretty enough, but she was a girl. Julien was a man and he needed, still needs, a partner, not a pretty doll.'

Emma barely heard the last of the widow's opinion on Clarisse Anouilh. What a stupid fool she'd been. Now she had her answers, her real answers. What hadn't made sense last night became clear. She rose. 'I must take my leave, Madame. Thank you again for your time and your…insights.'

'It was nothing. I wish you all the success over there.'

Emma nodded and departed, thankful for the footman who saw her back through the warren of rooms to her carriage. Her mind was too full of other things to spend any energy on how to find her way back through the house.

By the time she reached home, she was furious. Furious with herself for having been duped and furious with Julien. How dare he sit there last night playing the wounded victim against her accusations while he'd been using her all along, manipulating her into getting what he wanted, which wasn't her after all—a thought that was a bit lowering—but the chateau. He'd offered himself in marriage once before in order to get his land. She could no longer pretend he wasn't above doing so again. Last night she'd not been willing to believe it of him, but Madame's revelation about Clarisse Anouilh was incontrovertible proof.

'Where is he?' she ground out, breezing past a stunned Richet.

'In the cellars, *madame*. *Madame*, there's been a delivery for you—'

'Not now.' She shook her head and was off down the long stairs to the wine caves. Good. The cellars were soundproof. That suited her. There were things she needed to say to Julien she didn't want anyone else to hear.

He heard her coming before he saw her. There was the loud thud of a heavy oak door shutting, as if it had been heaved to with considerable, rapid force. Then there'd been the sound of her feet on the flagstones, staccato clips. If anger had a stride, that would be it.

That damn tea was today. Something had apparently gone wrong. That worried him. One did not upset Widow Clicquot without reaping consequences. He should have gone. He could have at least smoothed things over. He did not need a boycott of his wines.

She stormed into his little nook of an office, eyes bright, face flushed, hair coming down from beneath the little hat she wore. She'd be magnificent if she wasn't aiming all her ire at him. She slammed her reticule down on his desk with a solid crack. 'You used sex to seduce the chateau out from under me. You rotten bastard!'

'Slow down, Emma. What are you talking about?' Julien said carefully, easing back from the desk lest he become a casualty of her anger. He scanned the desktop, thankful to note he'd put away the letter opener. He didn't fancy a stabbing.

'I am talking about Clarisse Anouilh. You were going to marry her for the chateau! Save yourself a pile of money. Why buy the place outright when you can just marry for it? It was only when that didn't work out that you tried to buy the place.'

Julien held up his hands. 'It was arranged by my father and her father. It was meant to be an alliance. Our ancient name in exchange for the return of our lands.' He paused. 'If it's any consolation, I did care for her and it broke my heart when her father called off the engagement. Does that make you feel better, to know I didn't come out on top?'

'It does not change the fact that you were going to try that ploy again with me when it became clear I was not going to sell.' There was the tiniest of cracks to her voice, that's when he heard it. She wasn't just angry. She was hurt and he had hurt her. The sheen in her eyes was tears and he did not want a single tear to fall, did not want to be the reason Emma Luce cried.

She faced him across his desk, her features stark with loathing. 'The two questions I asked myself all the way home were how could I have been so stupid to let myself fall for a man I barely knew, and how could you be so cruel? Julien, I trusted you with my grief, my stories, my hopes, my wants, my passion, I gave myself over to you entirely in ways I'd not given myself to anyone, not even Garrett. You exploited every last piece of me.'

Could someone *feel* ashen? Julien felt as though if he looked in a mirror in that moment he would look pale, entirely drained of life. 'Such a man would be a despicable creature indeed. But that creature is not me, Emma.' Against his better wisdom, he came around the desk and knelt before her, reaching for her hands, desperate to touch her, to comfort her. He wanted nothing so much as to take her in his arms and kiss away her doubts. But she snatched her hands from his.

'Don't you dare touch me again. That's what started this trouble.'

That was unfair. 'You started it, in the vineyard,' he shot back and immediately regretted it. He rose and went back to his seat. 'That is not why I made love to you, Emma,' he said in slow, patient tones. 'I did not make love to you out of pity or to manipulate your grief or to lead you down the path of a whirlwind marriage.'

'Those are the only reasons that make sense.' Emma glared at him, anger the only thing keeping those shiny tears of hers at bay. 'You hardly knew me and it all happened so fast. I should have seen the signs, should have known better.'

Julien interrupted, overriding her with his words. 'I made love to you because you are the most intelligent, irritating, beautiful, capable, interesting, and stubborn woman I've ever met. And if given the chance, I would make love to you again and again and again because you challenge me, you've brought me back to life. And I don't want to go back. I need you, Emma. You've turned my life upside down, but it will never be right side up again without you.'

Her face registered shock and disbelief. 'That is conveniently the perfect fallback position. You can deny the "strategy" while still advancing your cause. That is rich. You've lied about who you were, you've hidden information from me about the chateau and your history with it, you tried to distract me from meeting people in the area and announcing my presence. At this point, why should I believe anything you have to say?'

'Because I love you. Because I didn't want you to be hurt, to feel that somehow what happened between us was no different than what you'd experienced with Redmond. All of this was to protect *you*.' He made the confession with a new confidence. He did love her. It was entirely true even if he had not named it to himself until this moment. And in this moment, he felt powerful and yet vulnerable. What would she do with his confession? Would she throw it back in his face or would she embrace it and open a path for them? He hoped for the latter but braced for the former. His Emma was a fighter.

She rose. 'No, you don't get to say that.' Ah, so she was going to fight. 'I've been in love before, with a *good* man, and *this* is not what love feels like. Love does not hurt; love does not tie one's stomach into knots. Love does not make a person decide between two things they care about deeply.' Her quicksilver eyes flashed with deep emotion and her jaw clenched, her words tight and terse as if she could barely restrain herself long enough to civilly grind them out before she left the room. So, it was to be a two-fronted battle, Julien thought. She was fighting him and a past she couldn't quite let go of.

Chapter Nineteen

Julien loved her. The thought followed her all the way upstairs to her chamber, unwilling to be kept out by her door. She could leave the room but she could not leave the thought. Emma pressed her head to the door. How dare he say those words when he knew she'd been made a fool of in love before and when he knew how difficult it would be for her to believe them. How did she dare *believe* them? How could she when she knew what he stood to gain? Did he think her naïve? Willing to take a handsome man at his word? Worst of all, how dare her heart side with him when it ought to know better.

But could you do it? Could you love Julien? came the whisper.

To love Julien in return would be an enormous leap of faith across a wide chasm filled with doubting fingers that reached up from her past to clutch at her at every opportunity. Once more, she was the one with the money, the property. How could she be sure Julien saw beyond that? Or even wanted to see beyond that? How could she be sure that he saw *her*? The answer was, she couldn't be. To love Julien would be a true act of blind faith, both in him and in her own intuition. Such an act had not been required in loving Garrett. There'd been no risk, no cost, just reward. It had made her choice easy. This choice was not easy.

There were so many reasons not to make it. It was too soon; it was too good to be true. Men used her for money. She should not expect Julien to be different when he openly had so much to gain. But she wanted him to be different. Her heart wanted a reason to believe, a reason to leap, and that was a dangerous place to be. 'Whose side are you on? You are supposed to be on my side,' she muttered to her traitorous heart as she got ready for bed, acutely aware that she need not sleep alone tonight—that too was her choice.

'Who side are you on these days?' Oncle Etienne's tone was sharp and scolding, the same tone he'd used when Julien and his cousin were eleven and had been caught with the brandy at the Christmas party. It was all Julien could do to not feel eleven again now as they strode the Archambeau vineyards. It was perhaps a warning to him just how angry his *oncle* was that they were outside walking the land, something his *oncle* usually left to his workers. He suspected they were walking the land now in order for his *oncle* to make a point. Although Julien was not certain what point that was. The summons had been sudden and unexpected.

'Are there any sides, Oncle? I'm afraid you have me at a disadvantage.' Perhaps word of his quarrel with Emma had reached his *oncle*'s ears. No one would have actually heard the quarrel but the icy atmosphere at the chateau the last few days would hardly leave anyone in doubt there'd been a split between them. In the evenings, the dining room was dark. There were no more elegant meals that lasted hours. No more retreats to the library to finish those discussions. Emma had been sure to keep her distance. She'd not come out to the vineyards when she knew he was walking, or down to the cellars when he was in the office, and he'd felt the absence of her keenly.

'There's our side, *mon fils*. I feel as if you've forgotten that.' His *oncle*'s tone relented slightly as he clapped a fatherly hand on Julien's shoulder. 'I thought you had Luce's widow under control.'

The thought of controlling Emma was almost laughable. 'She's not a woman to be manipulated. She's too smart for that,' Julien cautioned. Despite the words she'd flung at him and the things she thought of him, he felt compelled to protect her. He might not be her enemy, his intentions had been honourable, but his *oncle* would do anything to regain the lands. His *oncle* was more than capable of doing the things Emma had accused *him* of doing. That was the difference, he realised, between him and his *oncle*. He'd always admired his *oncle*'s business sense. His *oncle* ran a successful regional shipping company, he had acquired some of the Archambeau lands, but Julien had never seen the cost of that up front like he was seeing it now.

'Your widow went to visit *the* widow at Boursault earlier this week.' His *oncle* slid him a sideways look. 'Without you in attendance.'

'She asked me not to come,' Julien replied simply. 'I cannot keep her captive at the estate.'

'You should have been with her to control the conversation,' his *oncle* chided. Silently, Julien agreed. If he'd gone, perhaps he could have prevented the widow from spilling the tale of his engagement to Clarisse, from suggesting to Emma that he was the sort of man who'd sell himself in marriage for an estate. He'd taken a gamble there, thinking the women would limit themselves to business only instead of making his personal history a primary topic of conversation. But that wasn't something that would have upset his *oncle*. Something else had happened as a result of the visit.

His *oncle* stopped to study a vine. 'Everything bloomed a little later than expected but it's making up for lost time. I think we might have an early harvest.' He smiled and Julien felt the tension that had been building between them ease. Whatever happened, they had the grapes between them—the grapes kept them together. 'The old widow told her agent and the agent told Charles Tremblay, who has made it his business to share with everyone he can find, that Madame Luce is at the reins of the estate, that she's running the vineyard. A woman, and an outsider, is at the helm of the chateau, not Julien Archambeau, a man who implicitly had everyone's trust and subsequently their money.' That was the rumour they'd feared the most, the idea getting out that Julien was no longer in charge.

'Her being in charge doesn't affect what's already in production there. She won't even have a harvest to call her own until next year, and there won't be a vintage that can be attributed to her management for a few years yet.' Julien tried to soften the blow. 'If you're worried about the consortium, we can reassure them of that.'

'And your position there? Is that guaranteed?' came the pointed question.

'I do not know,' Julien answered truthfully. He would have felt more secure in the position if his *oncle* had asked this question last week. This week he wasn't so sure. 'She's not asked me to leave.'

'But she might?' His *oncle* sounded worried. 'You have to be indispensable to her, Julien. She has to be made to see that her success relies on keeping you there.' His *oncle* shook his head. 'I don't like it, Julien. Our fates are too intertwined with hers. She has us trapped. If we support her and help her succeed, help her retain the good faith of the consortium, then she will not sell and we are no closer to getting those lands back than we were seven years ago. But if she asks you to leave, and tries to go it on her own, she'll ruin the land, and if we ever get it back, it will be a mess to re-build the chateau's reputation from there. But the latter is a future concern. I am more concerned with the immediate fallout from the Widow's gossip. We are losing money, *mon fils*.'

'What?' Julien straightened from his examination of the vines. 'Why?'

'Can you really not guess? A few of the consortium members who'd bought futures on our *couteau champenois* have asked for their money back. They are concerned about the grapes that come from the chateau if you are no longer the one making decisions over there. I suspect once word gets around people have asked to pull out, others will want to do the same.' That would be devastating. They'd put all they had into expanding the production of the highly sought after *couteau champenois*. 'There's more. I received this just this morning.' His *oncle* reached into his coat pocket and withdrew a letter. He passed it to Julien. 'It's from the Growers' Consortium Bank, the one that holds the loan we took out for the acreage we were able to buy back last year. They are concerned that the "changes in our circumstances" make us a high risk. They want to foreclose on the loan.'

Julien stared at the letter. He knew what foreclosure meant. If they didn't pay the loan in full, the farmhouse, the vineyard which they'd put up as collateral, would be lost. He handed the letter back to his *oncle*. 'Can we pay it?'

'If we bankrupt ourselves. It would take everything we've got. We would have to use the funds we'd set aside so far for buying the chateau. We'll have to dip into them already to return the money on the futures. In short, it will take all of our reserves.' Which meant it would take years to put money aside for the chateau—again. It also meant a significant setback in their ability to run their own vineyard.

'But our vineyards would still function because I'd be there. We could slowly rebuild, find a new source for the grapes in the *couteau champenois*. Tremblay's been wanting in on that and his grapes are good.' Julien spoke slowly, thinking out loud. He didn't want to believe it, but it was possible Tremblay had started the rumour on purpose to force them to turn to him as a source for the grapes.

His *oncle* nodded and let out a sigh. 'It is what I was thinking as well. Pay the damn loan, scale back production to what we can afford, perhaps support the vineyard from funds from the shipping company until our coffers are restored and create a new partnership for the *couteau champenois*. But dammit, Julien. We'll lose the chateau. We won't have the lands back in my lifetime.'

For the first time, Julien saw true age in his *oncle*'s face. There were wrinkles and lines, a bit of sagging at the jaw. 'Oncle, perhaps what we have is enough. There's the farmhouse, and there's the land we do have. It was Archambeau land before and now it is again, because of your efforts and my father's efforts.' Today, his *oncle* looked defeated, a warrior who'd fought his whole life for an unattainable goal, but also a man who'd been so set on his dream that he hadn't enjoyed what was right in front of him. Julien thought there was a cautionary tale in that for him. Would this be him at sixty-two? Alone, obsessed? Oncle Etienne looked like a successful man on the outside, but he'd given up so much, including his marriage, compromised so much, and each compromise asked for another and another.

'I made *mon père* a promise on his deathbed.' Oncle Etienne shook his head. 'Do not give up now, *mon fils*. We must stay strong. I think the way forward is to distance ourselves from Madame Luce. The consortium will come around if we show we're good for the money and that we'll support them, not an outsider.' He gave a shrug. 'Who knows, once she has no place with them, she might give up, and perhaps the consortium would help us buy the chateau as a reward for *our* good faith.'

Julien's blood chilled. His *oncle* meant to drive her out. If his *oncle* couldn't have the chateau, he wasn't going to allow her to have it either. 'Mutually assured disappointment, then?' Julien asked.

'Unless you marry her?' his *oncle* asked, too hopefully for it to be taken as a joke.

'I don't think there's any chance of that,' Julien said. Even if their latest quarrel hadn't taken away some hope of that, this latest conversation did. Refusing to marry her was a sort of protection for her. If he married her now, no matter what his own motives, he'd be his *oncle*'s puppet. That would create a shadow over their marriage before it started and Julien did not think it was a shadow that could be overcome even with time. Emma would question every decision about the vineyard. Was this decision for the good of them or his *oncle*? It would destroy them. She would doubt the truth of his feelings and that would destroy *her*, to say nothing what it would do to *him*. Trust was everything to her. She'd given it once and been betrayed.

His *oncle* gave him a final clap on the shoulder. 'Well, that settles it then. The consortium meets tomorrow. We'll announce our decision there and you can find the right time to tell Emma Luce you'll be leaving her to devote yourself full-time to your family enterprise.' He drew a deep breath. 'I feel better already, *mon fils*. I knew talking to you would help me organise my thoughts. With luck, Widow Luce will have been nothing but a small detour in the road to our success.'

Julien offered a tight smile and wished he could say he felt the same. But no, that wasn't quite right. He didn't want to wish Emma gone from his life. He didn't want to leave the chateau. He'd spent seven years of his life managing those vineyards with the hope they'd be his someday. Maybe one day they still would be.

He said goodbye to his *oncle* and made the ride home, taking the long route so he could think. Did he tell Emma about the consortium meeting? It was the monthly meeting, and as the head of the vineyards she was entitled to a spot among them. She should have been invited once Madame Clicquot had let the news circulate that she was in residence and planning to work. There'd been plenty of time to send her an invitation this past week. That they hadn't was further proof they meant to ignore her, shun her for being an outsider. She was a woman and English. Julien reasoned this was perhaps not much different than the reception she'd received when she'd made her debut in London. His heart had gone out to the young girl she'd been and the courage it must have taken to keep showing up even when she was obviously unwanted. That pattern was about to repeat itself.

It was clear, too, that his *oncle* knew she wasn't invited and he was expecting Julien to keep the secret. He was not to tell her. That was the dilemma he chose to focus on as he rode home. Did he tell Emma? It felt unfair and dishonourable to decide her fate without giving her a chance to defend herself. The consortium was casting her out without even meeting her, judging without even hearing her brilliant ideas for the future of marketing wines. These were ideas that all of them could benefit from. One didn't need to be a *vigneron* or an expert blender to be a good marketer. She would be an asset to them if they would give her a chance.

Why the hell did he care so much? She'd made it clear what she thought of him. She stood in the way of his family attaining their ancestral lands. He ought to want to see her pack up and leave, to have things go back to how they'd been with Sir Garrett—a few letters a year and a yearly visit to check in. But he found it was the last thing he wanted. What he wanted was for her to stay and fight. If he kept this meeting from her, it would be one more thing she could add to the list of sins against him, one more secret he'd kept. It would prove that he was everything she thought he was.

If he told her, she would go to the meeting and his *oncle* would know he'd chosen her side. The cost of that would be great. To lose his *oncle*'s trust, his *oncle's* pride in him, was no small thing to Julien. His *oncle* was all the family he had left here. He'd hardly seen his cousin and aunt after he'd left England. By contrast, what did he gain by telling Emma that would be worth that? Would she thank him for telling her about a meeting meant to drive her from Cumières? Would she understand what this act would cost him? Would it be enough to earn her respect? Her trust? Her love?

Does it matter? his conscience whispered. *Does it matter what you gain or lose? You need to do the right thing regardless of cost. She did not ask for this. She did not ask to be thrown into the midst of your family drama. All she did was come here to heal and start a new life, a new life that your* oncle *and the consortium want to make impossible. She has no ally but you. You say you love her—is keeping the meeting a secret how you show the woman you love that you care for her, even if she doesn't love you back?*

Emma's last words to him whispered. *'I've known the love of a good man, and this isn't how love feels.'* Damn, but he hated it when she was right. He left his horse at the stable and went to find her, his decision made.

He didn't have to look far; she was in the foyer giving directions to footmen busy with ladders and pulleys hoisting a gigantic crystal chandelier. 'What is this?' For the first time in days, Julien felt a smile creep across his face.

She turned and her own smile faded at the sight of him. That hurt. She'd not forgiven him yet. 'My crystal arrived. I hadn't had time to get the chandelier up yet. But I definitely wanted it up for the gala.' He wondered if the pronouns were intentional. *I wanted.* A reminder that she was in charge here. This was her home. The gala was her event. 'It's only three weeks away.' Julien wondered if after tomorrow there would even *be* a gala. If there was, would he be invited? Would he even be a part of her life come June? His heart cracked a little further at the thought of being sent into exile, from this place, from her.

'It's beautiful.' Julien raised his gaze to the chandelier being slowly lifted.

'We bought it on our honeymoon from Baccarat.

Garrett was impressed with his work. It's not old, of course. His son's wife thought it too nouveau for Oakwood Manor. She always hated it. But Garrett thought—'

Julien didn't want to hear any more about Garrett. Garrett, the good man she'd been married to, the man who knew what love was. 'Let me help,' he interrupted, taking the stairs two at a time to assist with the pulleys.

The chandelier had granted him a reprieve, one last opportunity to rethink his decision, but at last the big chandelier was securely in place and everyone had a moment to come ooh and aah over it. The servants scattered, talking excitedly, and the footmen removed their ladders. Julien could put off his conversation no longer. 'May I have a word, Emma.' She gave him a cold quirk of her dark brow at the familiarity, but he refused to call her Madame Luce, refused to take a step backwards. They'd been lovers, and if it were up to him they'd be lovers still—more than lovers.

'You may say anything you like. I trust the grapes are progressing well. It looks greener and greener out there every day,' she said crisply, politely.

'In private,' Julien replied when it became clear she meant to have this conversation in the foyer where anyone could hear. 'Perhaps in the sitting room.' He gestured to the room closest to the foyer.

Once inside, he closed the door. 'I have some news. It is not pleasant but I thought you should know. The growers' consortium is meeting tomorrow. You should be there.' He'd done it. The secret was out. His *oncle*'s trust in him broken.

'Of course I should be there.' Emma's response was tart. 'I should have a seat on the board as one of the larger growers in the area.'

'There are other reasons you should be there. They mean to shut you down. Not literally,' he explained, 'they just mean to make it impossible for you to carry on without their support, support they plan to withhold.' He watched Emma stoically take in the news. Was this how she'd looked when she'd learned about Garrett? Staunch, pale, the only sign of distress being the clench of her hands in her lap, her knuckles white.

'On what grounds? They've never even met me,' she countered.

'You're an outsider and you're in the way of the goals of some consortium members,' he admitted plainly, although it hurt to do so, hurt to see the betrayal in her eyes.

'I suppose by that you mean you and your *oncle*.'

'My *oncle* is the one leading the charge, you might say.' Then he added, 'My *oncle* is losing money. Madame Clicquot let it drop that you were at the reins here and now some of his—our—investors with the *couteau champenois* want to pull out due to a lack of confidence,' he explained briefly.

She fixed him with one of her grey stares. 'I suppose I could make it all right though if I agreed to marry one of the consortium. That might restore their confidence in what was happening here.'

'No, not at all.' In all of his imaginings he'd never once thought of that, of applying public pressure in order to attain her hand. 'Why would you think that?'

'Because I can think of no other reason why you'd tell me about a meeting I wasn't invited to and at which men will attempt to decide my fate. I am either to marry and become acceptable through my husband's reputation, or I am to be pushed out because my own is lacking. Either way, you win. You get what you want.' She glared at him, 'Don't celebrate too soon, though, because I don't go down without a fight.'

He wanted to yell that he didn't want a fight, that all of this was for her, that he'd taken a huge risk in telling her, that he'd jeopardised his relationship with his *oncle* for *her*. He wanted to grab her by the arms and look into her eyes and tell her that what he wanted was her, that he didn't give a damn about the chateau. Not any more, not when he'd seen the cost, not when it meant losing her. But Julien did none of those things. She'd made it clear she would not believe his words. He could only hope she'd believe his actions. He'd un-burdened himself completely. Would she understand what this would cost him when she showed up at the meeting tomorrow? Because she would be there. He knew Emma Luce and she could not be in possession of this information and stay away.

Chapter Twenty

Emma exited her carriage and smoothed her skirts, taking in the landscape So, this was the Archambeau farmhouse and the ancient Archambeau land. It commanded a view of the Marne in the distance, and it was neatly kept, hectares filled with rows of grapes spreading around the house in all directions. Even the drive was lined with grapes. One had to go past them to reach the house.

The drive was full of carriages, and grooms walked the horses of those who'd chosen to ride instead of drive on this glorious May day. She was definitely in the right place. Or the wrong place, depending on how one looked at it. She'd come here to confront those who would keep her down and lock her out. It was a place where she was not wanted and yet after what Julien had told her last night, how could she not come? She had yet to decide how she felt about Julien's disclosure. Had it been done as a bid to win back her trust? Or had it been bait to a trap? Did he want her to come because he knew the odds of her succeeding here were slim? Had he told her as a way of setting her up to fail once and for all?

She didn't want to believe it, but she had learned the hard way about the costs of naïveté. She may not want to believe it, but she had to consider it. The reality was she was walking into a den of her enemies, and yet she could not stay away. From the house, the camaraderie of low voices spilled out, punctuated by male laughter and chuckles, a subtle reminder that she was outnumbered here and in uncertain territory.

Well, she'd been outnumbered before by the likes of Amelia St James and her wicked coterie. But she'd triumphed. She'd risen above their pettiness. She'd been the one to make a love match with Garrett Luce and when Amelia and the others had looked down their unwed noses at the two of them the following year, Garrett had been willing to bulldog anyone who was out of line.

Emma walked towards the house, making sure to lift her head and square her shoulders. Today, she was on her own. She'd have to be her own bulldog. She couldn't even count on Julien. What could she expect from him? Would he support her? Why should he support her after the way she'd spoken to him on the last two occasions? She'd been rough with him, blunt and honest, but she did not regret the words. They needed to be said. If they weren't, they would fester.

He told you about the meeting, her conscience prompted. *That counts for something. He said he loved you. Those are not easy words for a man like him. Love has hurt him, too.*

She still hadn't quite processed that. The argument that had kept her up all night swirled relentlessly in her head one more time, as if she had not just considered it. Why tell her about the meeting? After her harsh words, he owed her nothing, unless he wanted her there so he could press his marital suit, turn her failure to his triumph.

Or maybe he is trying to prove his words. He loves you. Why would you think he'd pressure you when he's never once spoken of marriage to you?

Technically, it was a fairly large leap to marriage. She and Julien had never spoken of the future during their affair. They'd lived in the present. It was Madame Clicquot who'd brought up his previous engagement and what had been involved, who'd warned that perhaps Julien was leading her down a path that ended at the altar. And Emma had ran with that. Because it made sense. Because it answered the question: Why would he want her? Because he wanted the land and she was the key.

Inside, Emma handed her straw hat to the footman. A footman? At a farmhouse? She wondered if Etienne Archambeau lived so well or if the footman had been brought in by the consortium for the occasion. She opted to believe the latter. '*Madame*, everyone has already eaten,' he began, unnerved by her arrival. She was not on his guest list.

'I am aware.' She smiled at him to put him at ease. She'd arrived late on purpose, in part because it was a good strategy—she wanted to take them by surprise—and in part on principle. Jesus might have eaten with

Judas but she wasn't that magnanimous. She could not stomach the thought of sitting down for a meal among those who would persecute her, see her destroyed. 'If you could just show me where they are?'

The hired footman directed her to the dining room where the men were gathered around a long, old, oak table, set at odds with heavy silver and china containing the residue of lunch while a few continued to peck at leftovers.

She stopped in the doorway and raised her voice to be heard above the din of male conversation. 'Good afternoon, gentlemen.' Conversation stopped, forks dropped along with jaws, and the room went preternaturally still. She found Julien at the table and allowed herself a quick glance, careful not to risk too much for either of them. Perhaps Julien wouldn't appreciate the glance here in front of his friends and colleagues. She wasn't sure what she expected to see in those cool blue eyes of his. Strength? Support? She saw a glimmer of both, although she knew she didn't deserve it, not from him. They were ill-fated lovers, caught in an impossible situation.

A silver-haired gentleman rose. 'Madame Luce, I presume?' He was all gracious manners and had blue eyes like Julien's. 'We weren't expecting you.' He found an empty chair and pulled it up to the table.

'You should have been.' She swept the table with her gaze, including everyone in the scold. 'I am the owner of the vineyards at the chateau.' She smiled to indicate she'd be candid but friendly for as long as she could. They needn't be enemies. 'But I am here now.

By good fortune, I found out about the meeting, so no harm done,' she said cheerily. 'I believe the business meeting is about to begin?' She was rewarded with the man at the head of the table—Etienne perhaps— shifting uneasily in his chair, the table remaining silent. Julien had been right. They did mean to see her deposed. She decided to help them out. It would be the last favour she'd do them. 'I see, gentlemen. I *am* the business meeting. Well, let me start the conversation. It has come to my attention that there is some concern about my ability to run the vineyards at the chateau.' She'd spent quite a while last night thinking through her position. How she might establish her own credibility while also shoring up Julien's losses. 'I want to allay those concerns by letting you know that while I will be overseeing marketing and many of the back-end aspects of the business, Julien Archambeau will remain at the helm of the agricultural and blending aspects. You all respect his reputation, so there should be no doubt about the quality of wine that will continue to be produced at the chateau.' It was a difficult concession for her to make. She'd debated it hotly with herself all night. But she would not allow her business to suffer for the sake of her personal feelings. She would have to find her way past that. The chateau needed Julien.

A man at the end of the table cleared his throat. '*Madame*, allow me to introduce myself. I'm Charles Tremblay. I own Domaine Arnaud, my wife's property, but I understood that Monsieur Archambeau would be working exclusively at his family's vineyards.' He shot a look at Etienne Archambeau, apparently waiting for Etienne to confirm it. She shot a look at Julien. Was that true? Her whole solution hinged on having him with her.

But why would he stay when you have accused him of terrible things? Did you really think he had nowhere else to go?

The silence stretched out at the table, all eyes turning towards Etienne. She might have overplayed her hand, unwittingly. It was a dangerous thing putting a man on the spot where he felt cornered in front of other men whose admiration he needed. Cornered men and animals were dangerous, unpredictable creatures. She'd cornered Julien, too, she realised. Her eyes darted to where he sat, his eyes cool and calculating, directed at his *oncle*. Why didn't he speak up? His hesitation was telling. Why wouldn't he defend her?

Because he knows you want to defend yourself.

But she couldn't defend herself at present. While it did not suit her to give in, sometimes one could talk too much and make a situation worse. A good cook knew it paid to let the stew simmer before stirring the pot. That was the case here. There was nothing she could do or say in this moment that would make things better.

Etienne looked at his nephew. 'Apparently, Madame Luce has not heard the news. Perhaps you'd be so good as to tell her about your plans.' Her stomach tightened. Etienne seemed so sure of himself, as if Julien's answer was obvious, a foregone conclusion.

Julien spoke. 'I think this is a matter better settled in private.' The last of her hope—her fight—faded. It meant Julien had already chosen. He was truly gone from her now in all ways. Her gamble, her trust in Julien to save her business, and in turn her independence, was lost. He'd sided against her. She felt as if her insides were ripping her apart, so complete was her sense of betrayal. She had a choice: she could stay here and be further humiliated as a woman who didn't even know what her own employee was doing, or she could gracefully exit.

'I see, gentlemen. Perhaps you'd prefer to complete all your discussions in private. I give you good day, and I look forward to your decisions.'

She managed to exit before tears threatened, before the dam of her reserve broke. She'd half expected—or was that half wanted?—Julien to come after her. But what would he say? Why would he suddenly have words when he'd had none in that room? He could not fix this. Nor did she think he *wanted* to fix this. He'd done nothing but shoot steely blue daggers at his *oncle*, but that had amounted to nothing in the end. Dear Lord, she'd almost believed him when he'd said he loved her. She'd been so close. So close to nearly being his fool, just as she'd been Redmond's all those years ago. She'd be thankful for this reprieve later, but right now it hurt like a knife stuck in her gut.

She did not allow herself to cry until she was in the safety of her carriage. She couldn't fight every front, the biases of the past with the injustices of her present. It was all the same—*they* were all the same. She managed to give the command for home before the sobs welled up. She let them come. Amid the noise of horses and the road, no one would hear her cry. The sobs racked her, loud and body-shaking, shattering the temple of her resolve. In some ways Julien's betrayal was worse than Redmond's. He'd known she'd been hurt before and in the same way. He'd not hesitated to poke at the wound, to re-create the betrayal and humiliation of the past. All for his own gain. For his damned vineyards. And she'd nearly fallen for it.

The truth was, she had no ally here, no true friend. How she missed Fleur and Antonia. But they had their own troubles. They could not come to her. *But you could go to them*, the temptation whispered. Leave. Go back to England. Sometimes retreat was the best option for self-preservation. She'd never felt so desolate in her life. She had wagered on love—on Julien's love—and she had lost. Perhaps, in her gut, that same gut where the metaphoric knife was still stabbing her, she'd known what would happen. She'd just needed to show up today at that meeting to see it in order to believe it.

A smart strategist knew when a game was unwinnable. She could not change those men's minds, not without Julien. They did not want her here. She could run the chateau from afar, a *laissez-faire* owner as Garrett had been. But that didn't help Julien.

Why should you help him?

He'd not stood up for her.

He is in an impossible situation, her heart whispered. *How can you ask a man to choose between his family and a woman he's just met? Some might say you were never meant to have this place, that you are the interloper, the one in the wrong.*

It was a thought she'd had since the night Julien had told her everything. That she and Garrett were the interlopers here, they were the aberration. She ought to return the chateau to its rightful owner and restore the historic line. That Julien stayed to work for another owner, knowing it was rightfully his, proved his love for the land like she'd never know it. It was the right thing to do even though it put her at an enormous disadvantage. She had money, though. Garrett had left her well provided for. She could find a place of her own in England and start over or participate in the family business. There was always room for her there even if there was no future.

Perhaps the chateau had served its purpose. She'd got over her grief; she'd learned that she could feel again. Perhaps that was all it was meant to do and now it was time to move on, to go back, healed, strong, and ready to write herself a new chapter in life. She thought of the words from Garrett's will, that this was to be a place of rest and recovery for as long as she desired it. There was no pressure to hold on to the place, to make it a family estate like Oakwood Manor. Perhaps she'd been too grandiose in her idea to run the vineyard. She'd recovered. She'd explored passion. It was time to go. Julien had made his choices and now she'd made hers. Once a decision was made, it was best to act on it immediately. She would start packing at once. For the first time since she and Julien had quarrelled, she felt better, stronger. This was the path forward. She was sure of it.

* * *

The heavy tread of boots sounded in the hall, followed by a low curse and the apologies of two footmen she'd just sent down with a trunk. Emma straightened from her folding. That would be Julien—she'd recognise that voice anywhere. Perhaps she wasn't the only one packing. She'd have preferred to have left without any goodbyes. She'd hoped he'd have the decency not to kick her when she was down.

'Emma, what is going on?' Julien burst into the room, sending the maids scattering. 'Yesterday I come home to find you hoisting a chandelier and today I come home to find you packing trunks.' He looked as if he'd ridden hard. His dark hair was wind-blown, much as it had been the first night he'd stood in the drawing room, dusty boots on an expensive carpet.

'I've decided to do some travelling. I am going to visit my family in England. I may stay awhile if I'm having a good time.'

'You mean you're leaving,' Julien paraphrased. 'One meeting with the growers and you're leaving? Are you going to let them drive you off so easily? What happened to fighting?'

She set aside the nightgown in her hand and faced him. 'It's not just one meeting, is it? My father taught me when there's a problem or even a success, there's not just one reason for it. I am not wanted here. You have made that plain. I am an interloper here, and an outsider. I have hurt your business with the consortium by laying claim to what was mine by law. I did not realise that until yesterday when you told me about the lost

funds. I am truly sorry for causing you financial hard-
ship. But it is not in me to pretend to be something that
I'm not. I cannot take a secondary role here, if I were
to stay, and I don't think I can. You warned me that
the days of a woman heading a Champagne house were
fading. The consortium showed me that today. They
have no confidence in me without you. Even if I could
make it on my own, I will not be given the chance.'

'Emma, stop,' Julien interrupted with a rough shake
of his head. 'That's what I came to tell you. You *do*
have me. I choose *you*.' Even as desolate as she was, as
empty as she was, the words stunned her. How could
she even think about believing them? They were the
perfect words, the words that made everything all right.
She simply couldn't believe them. They were illogical
against the backdrop of the afternoon.

'But your *oncle*? What about working for the family vineyard?' she started with the practical contradiction. He couldn't choose her. Julien confused her. Just
when she thought she understood him, he showed her
something different.

He gave another shake of his head. 'I told the consortium if they insisted on making me choose, I would
choose you. I told them you were brilliant, that you had
ideas for marketing the wines that were exciting, that
took advantage of this new world we live in.'

'Your *oncle* couldn't have been pleased. You would
have made him look like a fool.' She was still trying
to wrap her head around what had happened and what
she thought about it. She couldn't let herself believe;
she couldn't set herself up for loss again. There was

no reason to believe him, no precedent. When others had had to choose between her and themselves, they'd not thought twice about choosing themselves. Amelia, Redmond, Garret's family. Garrett had chosen her but it had not cost him anything.

'That's why I wanted to have the discussion in private. I wanted to find a way to help him save face.' He reached for her hands and she let him take them against her better judgement. Touching was dangerous. 'I could not go along with his plans any further, not when they were so malevolently aimed at you. It was unfair. His dream is not worth the cost of yours.'

Emma swallowed hard, her mind working against her heart, trying not to be swept away by the emotion of his words.

He'd chosen her.

This was new, but his motives weren't. Of course, the cynic in her argued, *He chose you because you hold the chateau.* 'And what of your dream, Julien?' she countered softly. She didn't want to argue any more, but she had to know.

'My dream is not the chateau. It is you. I can't say anyone was happy about the decision I made, except me. I want to be here with you, although it won't be easy. People are not happy with me or with you at the moment. They may take that unhappiness out on us in sales.'

'Only locals.' Her mind was coming alive with the impact of what this meant. Julien was staying. She could produce wines. 'Britain is a vastly unexplored market, no one there will care about the local politics of Cumières.' But then she slowed her mind. She was getting ahead of herself. 'I can't let you give up your family because of me. I will not be a wedge driven between you and your *oncle*.'

'He's done that on his own,' Julien offered, his eyes softening. She disengaged her hands and stepped back. This changed very little between them, in truth. It did not change the fact that she was living in his house. That her dreams would only be achieved at the loss of his. That any way forward would always be shrouded in doubt for them. Just like the betrayal in England had cost her more than a suitor, this betrayal had cost her that carefully rebuilt trust. She needed distance.

'Perhaps it would be best if I returned to England and ran things from there in the fashion Garrett did. Maybe out of sight and out of mind will help with rapprochement between you and the consortium.' At least she'd be leaving on better terms with him. At a distance, she'd be better protected, too, from the natural seduction of him. There would be no chance for Julien to woo the chateau from her, or for them to reignite the affair between them, which seemed a very real possibility from the look in his eyes. But reigniting the affair would also be done under a cloud of doubt about intentions, and that doubt would always be between them now.

'Leave? Three weeks before the gala? I can't possibly manage it without you.' There was genuine panic in Julien's voice. 'Besides, you just hung the chandelier.' He smiled and if the situation had been less fraught, she would have laughed. Instead, she had to stand firm.

'Perhaps this isn't the best time for a gala. Besides,

I doubt anyone would come with the way things are at present,' she conceded. She'd had so much fun planning it and she'd been looking forward to it. It was to have been a debut of sorts for her.

'I don't know about that. Your guest list was very impressive, as is the list of respondents. Nearly everyone you've invited is coming.' That list had been full of clients invited from all over Europe to come and taste the wines, especially the special one Garrett had put up seven years ago and the *couteau champenois*. They'd hoped to have a lot of orders come out of the gala.

'The growers won't come.'

'That's where I think you're wrong.' There was a spark of mischief in his eyes. 'I offered them a chance to show their wines as well if they attended. Now our guests can taste not just our wines, but all the wines of the region. I may even have suggested a tasting competition with judges and a prize in each category.'

'That's brilliant,' she said carefully, letting the idea roll over her in a slow wave. 'Why, you might make a decent marketer yet.'

He smiled warmly. 'I was taught by the best.' She made her decision. It couldn't hurt to stay another few weeks. It didn't mean she had to stay for ever. If the gala failed, then Julien could see first-hand what they were up against and he might agree that it was best she returned to England.

'All right then, I will stay until the gala, and then we'll decide from there.' Only time would tell which of them was right, and her heart desperately hoped it wouldn't be her, even as she realised it probably would be. She could not love a man she couldn't trust. How could she trust another when she couldn't even trust herself? Her world and her emotions at present were fragile like fine crystal and liable to shatter at any moment.

Chapter Twenty-One

'This is the infamous Baccarat?' Julien's tones cut sharply through her thoughts as she unpacked the crystal in the dining room. She'd been too lost in memories to hear him approach. She looked up, startled, nearly dropping a glass.

'Yes, nearly all of it. I just have this box to open.' She tracked him with her eyes as he made a slow perambulation around the table. She'd not seen him since the day of the growers' meeting when she'd tried to leave, the day they'd struck their bargain and she'd agreed to stay for the gala. He'd made himself scarce in the interim, perhaps understanding she needed time, space.

'Thank goodness,' Julien chuckled, stopping to pick up a goblet and holding it to the light. 'We're out of space on the dining room table. The collection is rather impressive.' It was indeed. Six glasses deep and rows that ran the length of the table.

'It's rather large,' she amended. 'Garrett insisted we buy everything in the set. I don't think there's a type of glassware not accounted for here. There are sherry glasses, brandy snifters, cordial glasses, water goblets and some I don't even know what they're for. I did not think it was *all* necessary but Garrett said I could give it to my daughter someday when she wed.' She gave a sad smile. 'But now, it shall be mine for ever.'

She watched Julien's long fingers still on a flute. 'Garrett wanted more children? At his age?' Julien's brow furrowed in a gesture she was far too familiar with.

'Yes, daughters if he could manage it.' She gave a shrug. She didn't want to talk about it: more hopes and dreams dashed. 'I'm afraid all of this unpacking has made me a bit maudlin. Happy memories mixed with the sad.'

'You wanted children, too?' Julien pressed, not taking her hint.

She nodded. 'Yes, but we do not always get what we want. I settle myself with being an aunt to my oldest brother's children.' She should not ask but suddenly she couldn't help herself. 'And you? Did you want children?'

He set down the flute. 'Once I did. I have not thought on it for a long time. There seemed to be no point.' His eyes lingered on her for an extended moment and she felt herself grow hot. No. She did not like the unspoken implication in his words that somehow he, who had not imagined children for years, could imagine them with her. The breach of trust was still too raw for her, the reconciliation still too new, and their peace too temporary. Perhaps that was when she'd first realised she would indeed be leaving no matter how the gala went. If she did not, her life would be filled with moments of temptation like this, glimpses into what could be, and she would not be able to resist them for ever. To stay would be to capitulate, to set herself up for disappointment after disappointment.

Julien smiled, breaking the moment. He picked up the flute and reached for a *coupe*. 'Do you know the difference between the two of these?'

She shook her head. 'There is no difference. They are both used for Champagne.'

Julien grinned. 'They are, but that's where you are wrong.' He gestured for a footman. 'Bring up a bottle of the forty-eight.' He winked at her. 'I'll explain while we wait. The flute is long and narrow. It allows the champagne to remain bubbly, fizzy, if you will, longer. It also allows the champagne to hold on to its scent, its aroma, longer. I think a serious taster would always choose to drink from a flute.' He set it down and held the coupe aloft. 'But a coupe is sexy.' His eyes were dark, his voice low. Emma braced herself. Julien *would* try.

'The coupe is wider, it holds more, but it trades quantity for quality. The wide bowl allows the fizz and the aromas to escape more quickly. The champagne doesn't retain its properties for as long.'

'How is that sexy?' Emma knew she shouldn't ask but she couldn't help it, she was drawn in by those eyes, by that voice.

He gave a wicked grin. 'Haven't you heard the story? A coupe is cut to be the size of Marie Antoinette's breasts. Her left breast, particularly.' There was a glint in his eye.

'No, that is not true,' she contested with a laugh, forgetting to be on her guard, forgetting that Julien was a master of seduction.

'You're probably right,' he chuckled. 'There are coupes that date prior to Marie Antoinette. But it makes a damn good story, and it's tempting, isn't it? To see if the glass fits?'

'Sort of like a naughty version of Cinderella's shoe?' She couldn't help the rejoinder.

'Well, yes, now that you mention it. Can you imagine the prince going about the kingdom with a coupe to fit over all the ladies' breasts? Quite the social visit that would have been.' Oh, he was wicked. She'd never look at a coupe the same way again.

The footman returned with the bottle and Julien poured. 'Try it in the flute first, and then let some sit in the coupe for a little while.' His eyes were hot on her, their message clear. He'd gladly take this sipping foray into a less public arena.

She shook her head. 'Julien, I can't,' she said softly, and he nodded as if he understood even as he regretted her answer.

He lifted his glass. 'There is no hurry, Emma. I will wait for you and in the waiting I will prove my worth. We have time, all the time we need.'

She raised her glass to his and she did not correct him. Time was her enemy. If she waited long enough she would fall for him again. This afternoon proved it. She would leave the night of the gala and she would not give him a chance to say goodbye because she could not risk being talked out of leaving again. For her, time had run out.

* * *

Time had been on his side right up until the night of the gala. Julien adjusted his cuffs for the umpteenth time as he waited for Emma to come downstairs. Everything was ready, even the weather. Outdoors in the gardens, a lovely June evening was under way: lanterns were lit, the fountains were burbling, the musicians were playing. The judges' dais had been set up and draped in white bunting. Beyond the gardens a sunset was turning the sky purple over the vineyards. There were even guests, with more arriving in the drive. He could hear the carriage wheels on the gravel. All that was needed was the evening's host and hostess.

There she was. Emma appeared at the top of the stairs, and his breath caught. For the occasion, she'd set aside wearing black and had opted for something more in line with half-mourning to complement the evening, a gown of soft grey silk. The gown was simplicity itself. It was not overdone with trimmings and bows, just a product of good tailoring, and it fit her to perfection. Jet earbobs hung discreetly at her ears and an ivory cameo on onyx hung with a black silk ribbon was at her neck, both pieces of jewellery a tribute to her mourning. It was tastefully done.

'I've never seen grey look so beautiful on someone before.' He bowed as she descended the stairs, his eyes noting how the dress flowed over each curve and plane of her. The last three weeks had been a special torture, working side by side with her, and yet not being able to touch her, to renew the spark that kindled so easily between them. She was not ready for that. She was still learning whether or not she could trust him. He bent over her hand, adorned in a long grey silk glove that reached her elbow and matched her gown.

'It's not just grey, Julien,' she teased. 'It's *gris de perle*.' Ah, the colour used to describe the mixing of black and white grapes.

'You've been reading the old wine manuals in the library,' he teased back. It felt good to tease with her again, to laugh. He wondered how far her goodwill extended. He was nervous tonight on several accounts; he wanted the event to go well, he wanted everyone to get sales offers in the hopes his goodwill with this event would smooth over his desertion of his *oncle*, he wanted his wines to show well at the tasting, but most of all, he wanted Emma to stay. He had only one trick up his sleeve left for that. If it should fail...well, he wouldn't think on that.

'Did anyone show up?' Emma whispered, taking his arm, and he realised she was as nervous as he. He wondered if it was for the same reasons.

'Yes, you cynic. The garden is filling up with guests. I am told Madame Clicquot has just arrived. She agreed to judge the blind tasting.'

'So, everyone has come to watch Rome burn?'

'Have faith, Emma. The consortium is interested in money and profit. If we can help enhance theirs, all will be forgiven rather quickly,' Julien assured her, and he hoped he was right. 'Tonight, we are going to greet our guests, we're going to laugh and dance and drink champagne as if all is right with the world.'

And for a while, all *was* right. Julien could not recall

a more perfect night, sipping ice cold champagne and dancing beneath the stars with the woman he loved. He'd not danced in ages and the feeling of Emma in his arms as they turned about the outdoor dance floor was intoxicating in a way that transcended the bubbles of champagne. She'd been surprised to find he was an accomplished dancer and he teased her mercilessly about it.

The blind tasting was scheduled at eleven and they eagerly lined up with the other guests to hear the results. The *couteau champenois* won a blue rosette, which he let his *oncle* claim on his own, Etienne basking in the applause. Some of the Archambeau wines took a few other second- and third-place ribbons, which also pleased his *oncle*. Then came the sparkling wines, the champagnes, and Julien felt his nerves ratchet up. Emma's grip on his arm tightened. Garrett's special vintage was in this category. Les Voyage des Noces, Garrett had wanted it called. The Honeymoon. Julien had taken special care with it, knowing how important it was to his friend.

There were several in the category, and it seemed to take for ever before the tasting was done. Madame Clicquot and the other two judges set aside their score sheets and Charles Tremblay, who'd offered to act as the facilitator of the tasting ceremonies, began to read the prizes. Julien's heart sank as the list went on. They'd not taken fourth or third, or second. He was beginning to think the great experiment had failed. 'This last wine has been described by the judges as bringing a new taste to champagne, it is crisp, sweet, and yet sharp. Like new love itself, as suggested by its name. Our winner is Les Voyage des Noces.'

'You did it,' Emma whispered beside him, and he understood that her nerves had been for *him*, that she'd cared because he cared, because he wanted it so badly for her, for them. He hugged her tight, not caring what anyone might think, or what *she* might think. In that moment he only wanted to share this victory with her. He felt her arms go about his neck, and she was hugging him and crying. 'Go on, go get that ribbon, you deserve it.' On stage, there were congratulations and hand shaking, and there was the expectation of a speech from him, which he made short work of, but when he made his way off the dais into the crowd, Emma was gone.

Julien told himself not to panic. She might have gone to deal with some detail of the party. A champagne supper to celebrate the victors was to be laid at midnight. He went to the kitchens but Petit had not seen her. He checked the retiring rooms but she was not there either. That was when real panic came to him. He stopped a footman on the stairs. 'Have you seen Madame Luce?'

'Yes, she just went out to the carriages in front.'

Julien began to run. He knew with a bone-deep surety she meant to leave, to slip away now that she'd honoured her end of the deal. She'd stayed until the gala.

But everything had gone so well. Why would she leave now? How would he find her amid the line of carriages? It was her dress that gave her away. The *gris de perle* caught the moonlight, her foot lifted to enter, shining in the dark at the last carriage in the row, one that was easily positioned to leave without alerting all the others. 'Emma!' he called, his voice laced with panic. If she got in and decided to make a dash for it, he had no hope of running her down in dancing shoes.

'Julien, please. Go back inside and celebrate your victory.' She was calm, as if she were just going into town on a short errand.

'Why are you doing this? There is no reason to leave, the evening is a success. Madame Clicquot has given you validation. No one dares gainsay us now.'

She put a gentle hand on his arm. 'It is you who received the validation. Your wines won. This is your world, Julien.' She was too calm. This was not a spontaneous decision and that chilled him. All night she'd been saying goodbye while he'd been hoping for more, for a second chance, for a new beginning.

'You were going to leave all along,' he accused in low tones.

She nodded. 'I cannot take you away from your family and I cannot pretend that this can only be a business relationship for me. If I stay, I will not be able to resist your charm, Julien, and that is a dangerous place to be when you're the woman who is keeping the man she cares for from his inheritance. I could never marry you and not wonder how much of your affections are for me and how much are for the estate. That shadow would always be there.'

'No, it wouldn't. I can make that shadow go away. When I told you that I chose you, I meant it. I chose you, not the estate or the vineyards, or the Archambeau legacy. That way lies poison. I see it eating my *oncle* alive. If you want to give this place up, sell it to someone else, that's fine. We can start somewhere new. Or…' He reached into his coat pocket. This was his last hope and it had to work. 'I will sign this agreement as part of our marriage contract.' He passed it to her and gave her a moment to read it, wanting her to see it with her own eyes.

She looked up, astonishment in her gaze. 'You are signing away your husbandly rights to the chateau?'

'Yes, I am giving up all claim to it through marriage. It must remain yours. I do not know of any other way to convince you of that.'

'You would give up your dream for me?' She put out a hand to the carriage side to steady herself.

'I've already told you, you're my dream. I am giving up nothing. I am gaining everything.' He reached a hand out to smooth back a strand of hair. 'You've brought me back to life, Emma. I was dead inside before you came. And now, I want to live and live and live but I can't do it without you. Will you stay as my wife?' A slow tear rolled down her face. He brushed it away with the pad of his thumb. 'Emma, what is it?'

She sniffed. 'I didn't think a person could find happiness twice in a lifetime.' She gave a shaky breath. 'But I have and I hardly know what to do with it. Do I dare believe in it?'

'If I can dare it, you can dare it. Will you say yes, Emma?' His world, his entire being hinged on this.

She nodded and he swept her into his arms for a kiss it seemed he'd waited a lifetime for. *This* was what love felt like. It was not hard or angry or ravenous like some of their other kisses, but it was consuming all the same.

'What do you propose we do now, Monsieur Archambeau?'

'We turn this gala into an engagement celebration. I want everyone to know right away.' She smiled up at him and he was acutely aware that he'd only survived the night because she loved him.

Epilogue

Late spring, 1858

'Papa! Papa! Pick me up! I want to go riding on your shoulders.' Sturdy three-year-old legs pelted towards Julien, arms outstretched. He turned from the vines with a wide grin at the sight of his son.

He assumed a teasingly stern stance. 'What do we say when we want something, Matthieu-Philippe?'

'*S'il vous plaît?* Please may I have a ride on your shoulders?' dark-haired Matthieu-Philippe amended eagerly, quicksilver eyes—like his mother's—dancing with the thrill of being outdoors and quite possibly out from under his nanny's strict, watchful eye.

Julien picked him up, giving him a twirl before settling him on his shoulders. He revelled in the solid, well-fed toddler weight of his son, in knowing this exuberant little boy was his. His to love, his to nurture, his to teach. The days of Matthieu-Philippe riding on his *père*'s shoulders would come to an end, sooner rather than later if the boy kept growing at this rate.

He would miss them; the gentle tug of pudgy fingers in his hair, the giggles when Julien would bounce him up and down. Julien would savour these days for as long as he could. But there was consolation in knowing that the days of walking beside him would begin.

Julien smiled at the thought. At last, he had a son to walk the land with him. A son named for both Julien's *grandpère* and *père*. A son who had his mother's eyes and energy, and his father's passion for the land. Matthieu-Philippe gave a tug. 'Père, how are the grapes this morning?'

'Why don't you see for yourself.' Julien bent low, letting the little boy study the vines.

'They're green. They've got buds!' the boy exclaimed, bouncing a bit on Julien's shoulders.

'They're growing,' Julien affirmed, his gaze drifting from the vines to the end of the row, caught by a movement. His smile widened at the sight of his wife. Someone else was growing, too. One could see the prominence of a six-months-pregnant belly when she stood in profile as she was now. Julien's heart swelled at the thought of another baby, another child to love in a few months. It would arrive just in time for the harvest. But if anyone could handle harvest season and a newborn all at once, it was Emma. His wife was indefatigable.

He loved her more now, six years after their wedding, than he had that beautiful summer afternoon in the vineyard when they'd said their vows before family and friends in an intimate service at home. Although, at the time, he'd not thought it possible to love her more. He'd been the happiest of bridegrooms. That happiness had only grown apace with their grapes. She'd become his partner in all things, or was it that he'd become hers? They'd added three new presses to their production line, they were bottling double the amount of wine they'd bottled six years ago, and sales were up.

She'd been right about the British market. It was definitely an unpicked plum. Emma's brother Gabriel had played an indispensable role in helping promote their champagne in England. Even now, they were experimenting with a *blanc de blanc* blend of sparkling wine designed with the British palate in mind. But more than her business sense, he treasured *her*. She was the heart of their home, keeping the house running, raising their son, running their business. Loving him. Even when he was stubborn and intractable, which he often was. They still quarrelled on occasion, but at the end of each day one thing remained constant: she was his heart.

Julien waved to her and she came to meet them, a picnic basket at her side. He balanced Matthieu-Philippe with one hand and took the basket from her with the other and a scold. 'You should not be lugging around something so heavy, *ma cherie*.'

She laughed at his concern. 'I won't start waddling until next month, I have some time to enjoy walking yet.'

He kissed her cheek. 'I love it when you waddle. I think it's adorable.' Julien nodded to her belly. 'How is our little *enfant* this fine day?'

Emma covered her belly with a hand. 'Stubborn like his father and just as insistent. He's been kicking since sunrise.' She stifled a yawn.

'Ah, that's why you were up early.' Julien led them

to a grassy area at the end of the row and set Matthieu-Philippe down. 'Help me with the blanket, *mon fils*,' he instructed. 'Mama is to rest. We will wait on her for luncheon. She is not to lift a finger.' Matthieu-Philippe giggled and thought it was a great game to unpack the picnic hamper. This was the life he'd dreamed of, Julien thought. To eat lunch on a blanket in one's own vineyard, his son and his wife beside him. Nothing could be finer.

Nothing could be finer than a vineyard picnic, even if one was six months pregnant with a mule kicking inside. Emma's eyes caught Julien's and she smiled. He was thinking the same. She could tell by the way he looked at her, his slate-blue eyes soft with a special tenderness he reserved just for her and their son. She was not sure she'd done anything to deserve finding such happiness twice in her lifetime. But she was thankful for it every day.

She had loved Garrett, fiercely, devotedly. She did not doubt that love now. She'd learned there were different kinds of love, that she could love Garrett and Julien, and that love would be different for each because they were different. That loving one did not demean the love she had for the other. Emma watched her handsome husband lay out the picnic and wondered if Garrett had known they might suit. That if anything happened to him, that Julien would be there in some capacity as a friend, perhaps to see her through? Had Garrett imagined something more for them? If so, she loved him all the more for it.

'What is it, *ma cherie*? You look contemplative.' Julien passed her a plate with a ham sandwich on it and a mug of lemonade. The only thing she didn't like about pregnancy was not being able to drink champagne.

'I'm just happy, that's all.' She smiled. 'Your *oncle* sent a note this morning. He'll be joining us for dinner. We can celebrate his birthday.' She knew it pleased Julien that the rift between him and his *oncle* had healed. It had not been easy and it had taken the birth of their son to really bring Etienne around, but it had happened. Etienne was her family now, too. She wanted that family to be whole.

Julien's eyes glinted mischievously. 'He'll be gloating about that new award his wine has won. He'll be insufferable.'

'He's earned it. I am happy for him. He can win all the awards he wants for the *champenois* as long as he leaves the champagne to us,' she laughed and then sobered. 'We'll have to be at our best though. I hear rumour there's a new widow looking to head her family's champagne house. Madame Pomeroy.'

Julien stretched out on the blanket. 'I'm not worried. I've got the best widow in town.'

She gave him a soft look. With Julien, she was home in all the ways that mattered. Gone were the days when she struggled against betrayal, struggled to find acceptance. She'd found it here with him. 'Here's to another good year, Julien Archambeau, and to my liaison with my Champagne Count. *Famille et terre tout les temps.*'

* * * * *

*If you enjoyed this story,
look out for the next book in
Bronwyn Scott's new
Enterprising Widows miniseries,
coming soon!*

*Whilst you're waiting, make sure to read her
Daring Rogues duology*

Miss Claiborne's Illicit Attraction
His Inherited Duchess

*And why not have a read of her
The Peveretts of Haverstock Hall miniseries?*

Lord Tresham's Tempting Rival
Saving Her Mysterious Soldier
The Bluestocking's Whirlwind Liaison

'Dr Peverett's Christmas Miracle' in
Under the Mistletoe

Get 3 FREE REWARDS!

We'll send you 2 FREE Books <u>plus</u> a FREE Mystery Gift.

FREE Value Over **$20**

Both the **Harlequin® Desire** and **Harlequin Presents®** series feature compelling novels filled with passion, sensuality and intriguing scandals.

YES! Please send me 2 FREE novels from the Harlequin Desire or Harlequin Presents series and my FREE gift (gift is worth about $10 retail). After receiving them, if I don't wish to receive any more books, I can return the shipping statement marked "cancel." If I don't cancel, I will receive 6 brand-new Harlequin Presents Larger-Print books every month and be billed just $6.30 each in the U.S. or $6.49 each in Canada, a savings of at least 10% off the cover price, or 3 Harlequin Desire books (2-in-1 story editions) every month and be billed just $7.83 each in the U.S. or $8.43 each in Canada, a savings of at least 12% off the cover price. It's quite a bargain! Shipping and handling is just 50¢ per book in the U.S. and $1.25 per book in Canada.* I understand that accepting the 2 free books and gift places me under no obligation to buy anything. I can always return a shipment and cancel at any time by calling the number below. The free books and gift are mine to keep no matter what I decide.

Choose one: ☐ **Harlequin Desire**
(225/326 BPA GRNA)

☐ **Harlequin Presents Larger-Print**
(176/376 BPA GRNA)

☐ **Or Try Both!**
(225/326 & 176/376 BPA GRQP)

Name (please print)

Address   Apt. #

City   State/Province   Zip/Postal Code

Email: Please check this box ☐ if you would like to receive newsletters and promotional emails from Harlequin Enterprises ULC and its affiliates. You can unsubscribe anytime.

Mail to the **Harlequin Reader Service:**
IN U.S.A.: P.O. Box 1341, Buffalo, NY 14240-8531
IN CANADA: P.O. Box 603, Fort Erie, Ontario L2A 5X3

Want to try 2 free books from another series? Call 1-800-873-8635 or visit www.ReaderService.com.

---

*Terms and prices subject to change without notice. Prices do not include sales taxes, which will be charged (if applicable) based on your state or country of residence. Canadian residents will be charged applicable taxes. Offer not valid in Quebec. This offer is limited to one order per household. Books received may not be as shown. Not valid for current subscribers to the Harlequin Presents or Harlequin Desire series. All orders subject to approval. Credit or debit balances in a customer's account(s) may be offset by any other outstanding balance owed by or to the customer. Please allow 4 to 6 weeks for delivery. Offer available while quantities last.

Your Privacy—Your information is being collected by Harlequin Enterprises ULC, operating as Harlequin Reader Service. For a complete summary of the information we collect, how we use this information and to whom it is disclosed, please visit our privacy notice located at corporate.harlequin.com/privacy-notice. From time to time we may also exchange your personal information with reputable third parties. If you wish to opt out of this sharing of your personal information, please visit readerservice.com/consumerschoice or call 1-800-873-8635. **Notice to California Residents**—Under California law, you have specific rights to control and access your data. For more information on these rights and how to exercise them, visit corporate.harlequin.com/california-privacy.

HDHP23